CJ West

The Cat Bagger's Apprentice

22 West Books, Rochester, MA
www.22wb.com

© Copyright 2013, CJ West

All rights reserved.
No part of this book may be reproduced, stored in a retrieval system, or transmitted by any means, electronic, mechanical, photocopying, recording, or otherwise, without written permission from the publisher.

Requests for permission to make copies of any part of the work should be mailed to the following address: Permissions, 22 West Books, 352 Mendell Road, Rochester, MA 02770.

The following is a work of fiction. The characters and events are of the author's creation and used fictitiously. This book in no way represents real people living or dead.

Cover design by CJ West

ISBN 10: 0-9767788-7-4
ISBN 13: 978-0-9767788-7-5

Acknowledgements

Special thanks to Tina Sa, who reads my work before it is ready for anyone else. She never seems to run out of energy. Thanks to my beta readers Dawnna Hale, Jennie Hunt, Gwyn Martin, Mary Michela, Cindy-Lee Samuel, and Nancy Violette.

Other Books by CJ West

<u>Marking Time Series</u>
The End of Marking Time

<u>Randy Black Series</u>
The Winemaker's Son
Black Heart
Gretchen Greene

<u>Standalone</u>
Dinner At Deadman's
Addicted To Love
Taking Stock

In loving memory of Terri Streetman Krause who left us April 27, 2012.

Terri was a great friend, always willing to lend a helping hand. Her love and kindness touched thousands of people online and off.

Chapter One

Wendell Cummings ordered me forward, but I wasn't about to step inside the partitions and leave him free in the hall. If he was going to lock me in front of the viewing window, he was going to be trapped in here, too. I balked, and the feeble old gent took a step toward the crack in the floor, the remote buried in his palm where he thought I couldn't see it.

"What's wrong, Jordan? Afraid?"

"I'm not afraid of you, Wendell. Never have been."

"That's your biggest mistake. And it will be your undoing." Trembling hands betrayed his fear, not of me, but what was going to happen to me. It was too late for either of us to turn back. Our conversation appeared casual, but I knew the armed men who had shepherded me inside wouldn't let either of us leave until I stated my case and a decision was made.

Wendell shuddered when he stepped over the partition buried in the floor. A dull guillotine to the crotch was a gruesome image for any man, even if he held the switch. Other men held similar switches. Men neither of us could control.

"We're just going to talk," Wendell said.

"It's pointless talking to you. You're washed up, old man."

He toed the near partition, not wanting to cross out of the box, trying not to look down, as if I didn't know what was beneath the two inch gap in the floor. I'd exposed so much of what he tried to do to me, he should have admitted defeat and given up on the head games. He could have just told me who was behind the window and asked me to step up, but he didn't want the jury to lose respect for him. If they had any left.

He considered grabbing my arm and yanking me across, but he wasn't strong enough.

"Step over here, Jordan. This is the way it has to be."

"I'm not diving into your aquarium."

He blew the air out of his cheeks in an attempt to act surprised. I'd seen Joel trapped, and I wasn't going to let him do the same to me. His act might have convinced the folks behind the glass. Maybe they hadn't seen Joel in here, or maybe he thought it would excuse what he did next.

The click startled me.

I saw his thumb on the red button and I dropped to the floor and lay still, my arms and legs askew where they'd fallen.

Wendell grabbed my calf and pulled me across the tiles, sliding me six feet down the hall until I was centered between the two partitions hidden in the floor. Dead ahead of the window.

He huffed hard as he looked forward and back, considering which end of the hall he wanted to be on while I faced judgment, but I wasn't about to let him slip out and leave me stuck alone.

I hooked my foot behind his ankle and provoked an instantaneous reaction. He hit another button and two Plexiglas partitions shot up out of the floor, connecting the floor, ceiling, and both walls, trapping us in front of the window together.

He stood back, awed by my superhuman power. He'd never seen anyone move so soon after being immobilized and by the way he looked at the glass, I could tell he wanted protection. He didn't find the courage to ask, and no one came to help. Just Wendell and me trapped behind the glass, facing the window without any clue from beyond what would happen next.

By now you know how this works. I'm not going to pretend you are behind the glass. We both know you're reading the book. And you know you won't find out who's behind the glass until the end. Fair enough.

You may be wondering how I know what's going on. Well, Michael O'Connor was a special case. The poor sap had been in a coma four years while the rest of us were teaching each other to beat the reeducation counselors' tricks. I'm a lot smarter than Michael, too. I finished college at fifteen and went to work plying technical skills that made me rich, even in a world of abusive taxation and government intrusion. So, I know the drill better than Wendell ever expected. That's what made him crazy the last eight days and why, even as scared as he is to be trapped in here with me, he's glad this case is finally over.

I pulled myself to my feet, acting groggy and disoriented. Wendell barely kept his mouth from falling open. If moving my foot was a surprise, standing amazed him. Not only that, but there was nowhere to run in the six-by-six Plexiglass box that cut the hallway in three. I'm not huge, but I'm twenty-two and sturdy, a huge threat to a nerdy, middle-aged schoolteacher. He couldn't go anywhere in that box where I couldn't reach him, and he couldn't hide his fear.

The droop in his expression spread to his fingers and I knew I had him. I turned my eyes to the window and nodded then waited for him to explain what came next.

He took the bait and turned, his eyes falling somewhere behind the glass, to the people we couldn't see. I waited until he was just about to speak then made my move. He was too slow to react when I swiped at him. My palm smacked the back of his hand and the remote bobbed in the air between our faces.

The poor old man's expression flashed shock, betrayal, a change of circumstances he couldn't imagine, but there between us floated the only control he held over me. When I snatched it out of the air, Wendell Cummings was powerless.

Chapter Two

I tossed the remote to the floor and it rattled in the corner where the Plexiglass met the cement blocks. It would have been safer in the pocket of my jeans, but I wanted him to see it there on the tiles and not be able to reach it. To feel trapped the way I felt trapped in that apartment. To feel controlled. Manipulated. Abused. He had it coming.

"There'll be no more zapping," I said.

"I'm not the only one with a red button."

"You think Charlotte will shock me for you?"

His eyes flashed angry. He didn't say he knew how far I'd gone with Charlotte, because he didn't want the people behind the glass to know how badly his control had broken down. "There are others," he said.

"Should I call my friends?" The mention of Winchester and Koch set off a panic inside him. His cheeks flushed and fear filled his eyes as he checked both ends of the hall.

Wendell had so much technology and money on his side, his charges had no hope of escape. Monitored every minute, most relearners broke down and submitted to his will. How could they not when Wendell had godlike control? My influence over Wendell was an anomaly to the people behind the glass. As we stood wedged in together, he was truly afraid. That should have been enough for the judgment to go in my favor. I'd faced the system and come out on top. Not many relearners could say that.

"You're making a mess of this for both of us," he said.

I was a special case. I had money. Goons of my own. When I called for help, my guys came running. Wendell had never dealt with a rebel like me. I wouldn't back down. Wouldn't conform.

He didn't know what to do for the week I was in his care, though now he'd gotten me locked up behind the glass, the path was clear.

"It's late. I'm done sparring with you," I said. "Tell me what this is about, so I can get back to bed."

"Your reeducation is over. It's time for you to tell your story to your jury. I'm afraid you won't be getting much sleep tonight."

"What are you talking about?"

"Your jury is behind this window." He pointed grandly to the window you are supposed to be behind. "We have taught you all we could. It is time for your jury to decide if it was enough."

"You haven't taught me anything."

"You're not helping your case, Jordan. Tell your story to the folks behind the window. Tell them why you deserve another chance."

The little weasel wanted me to lie. We had a deal and he wasn't even going to mention it. How dare he? My muscles tightened and he pushed back until his shoulders touched the Plexiglass, knowing I wanted to plow him in the face. He glanced longingly at the remote behind me in the corner, then flashed his eyes back to the glass in a mute cry for help. I waited a few breaths. No one came to rescue him and finally his eyes met mine.

"Taught me? You think you taught me? You locked me up and annoyed me. Had people follow me. Recorded my every waking moment on video. What am I supposed to learn from that? Was there some lesson I missed about the depths of our government's evil?"

I poked his chest and a tremor shook through him. He wanted to scream, but a man of his status wasn't allowed to let his emotions loose. I had no such restraints. I bucked him at every turn and the poor old guy had no idea what to do.

"Tell your story. It's the only way out of here," he said.

"Why can't I just pick up the remote and set myself free?"

"That won't work until you're finished."

Another lie. More plausible than much of what Wendell had told me, but another lie all the same.

I turned and took a step toward the remote and I heard a squeak from the old man. He couldn't tell me to stop. Couldn't tell me what would happen if I let myself out of the box, but he couldn't contain his fear either. He watched, trembling. Not courageous enough to fight me for the switch. Not clever enough to say something to change my mind. Just a panicked old man, defeated and tired at the end of a very long battle he was completely unprepared to join.

I turned and folded my hands, trying to pretend the little squeak convinced me to stop, as if it was a menacing warning in a single note. Truth was, I didn't want the old guy to faint. I needed him conscious, because eventually he'd have something to say about what had happened while I was locked up.

I tried to smile. "Why did you bring me here this late?"

"It's time for you to tell your story."

"What story? What are you talking about?" I didn't have to fake exasperation.

"Tell them what you've learned. Tell them how, if we let you back out on the street, you'll walk the straight and narrow. That you've learned what you were doing was wrong. That you won't do it anymore."

"I've never done anything wrong."

His eyes went wild. The people behind the glass couldn't see his expression as closely as I could, but if they had, they would have been impressed by his self control.

Wendell, Charlotte, and I had a prolonged tug-of-war over what I'd done and whether I warranted punishment. The teacher was at his end. He couldn't stand me anymore, and if he could have reached the red button, he would have pressed it again.

"Don't be stupid, Jordan. This is your last chance. Tell them what you've learned. Tell them or you will fail."

Wendell had never told me what failing meant. What punishment I'd meet if I didn't follow his rules and learn his lessons. The program would have been much more effective if the student knew he was being tested and that failing meant a trip to the wrong end of the hallway.

Michael O'Connor sure had no idea what he was in for, and Wendell was making exactly the same mistake with me.

"You haven't taught me anything, Wendell. Not a thing."

"I can't help you if you won't try."

"This was never about helping me."

Wendell slumped against the glass and sagged until his butt hit the floor, his knees pushing against my shins, forcing me to step aside. I'd finally broken him. All that's left is to tell you what happened.

Chapter Three

In 2013 it was nearly impossible to maintain one of those big brick mansions tucked in the hills above Route 9 in Brookline, because the tax man punished anyone who made a decent income. Some people found it obscene that I lived there at twenty-two years old and that's where my troubles began.

To understand why someone was mad enough to turn me in, you have to understand the changes we'd been through. The Supreme Court ruled that felons couldn't be held in jail more than forty-eight hours—even if they were tried and found guilty. The cops let out two million rapists and murderers and it was up to people like Wendell Cummings to teach them how to behave.

It was a big job to discipline hardened criminals without walls, but there were few rules for these new prisons to follow and very little oversight for Wendell and his team. The things they did to me shouldn't happen to anyone, but law-abiding citizens were so scared, they looked the other way while felons—they called them relearners—were tormented. Wendell got a bottomless pit of funding and leeway to psychologically torture anyone convicted of a crime. Most relearners who graduated went on to live productive lives. Those results are a far cry from the eighty-percent recidivism common under the old system.

If you're ready to declare Wendell a hero, hold on. The feds did some things that really took a bite out of crime. First, they got rid of cash and replaced it with electronic credits. Computer programs ruthlessly tracked those credits and locked down the flow of money from person to person. That stomped out burglary and other petty crimes. It didn't do you any good to steal something if you couldn't sell it. That forced guys like Michael O'Connor to go straight because they couldn't make a living.

The second change was even more brilliant. The feds gave everyone a living wage. You made forty thousand credits whether you did anything or not. No taxes. No work requirements. Nothing. It was brilliant because it took away the reason for most crime: poverty.

Capitalism was out of fashion. Fairness was in.

Most people were happy, but there were some unintended consequences. Serious consequences.

Like Major League Baseball. Want to go to a game? Enjoy your drive to Canada. Like The National Football League? Get your passport ready.

Confused?

All the money had to come from somewhere. Forty-thousand-dollar government checks sounded great. And if you could handle watching a thirty-inch Sony television and eating frozen food five nights a week, it was fine. You didn't have to lift a finger. No questions asked. Anyone who signed up got forty thousand credits deposited automatically in their account.

For some of us, forty-thousand wasn't enough. Overachievers with a passion for work had real problems. Athletes and movie stars had to move out of the states because the tax man took eighty percent of anything over that first forty-thousand. What good was it to make a million bucks if the government got eight hundred thousand? Hollywood splintered across the globe. Some companies moved their executives to Europe, Canada, China. Smarter ones opened headquarters in Aruba and the Cayman Islands.

The people left behind were bitter when their forty-thousand started buying less and less.

When I first saw dozens of thirty-something white guys playing cards on Friday afternoons I was stunned, but after thinking about what was happening in the business world, it made perfect sense. Companies hated paying the high taxes, but they had to do something to keep workers energized. If you could get forty-thousand for doing nothing, you expected a lot more if you had to work. Most companies paid workers over the scale, but they couldn't afford to make work lucrative while paying the huge tax burden. They offered free lunch, dry cleaning, soda, anything that wasn't taxed. It didn't take long for companies to realize the forty-hour workweek was history.

People worked for gratification. Everyone had an office and an important title and they enjoyed their time off conspicuously. That's why the guys played poker outside even though the wind spoiled a lot of hands by blowing cards over. They wanted everyone to know their company thought they were important. They made a contribution and still had time to hang out with their friends.

That group of guys on the corner glared at me when I walked by. They knew I bought fresh steaks and organic vegetables. And they knew where I lived.

It was all okay until a month ago when one of my construction clients rolled into the neighborhood with a load of lumber. Nothing gets built anymore and there are tons of people with too much time on their hands. So, when the truck drove up Fisher Ave and turned onto Buckminster, it didn't take long for a crowd to gather. I'd bought the four brick behemoths cheaply a year earlier without attracting too much attention, but the crowd was outraged when the carpenters started framing ramps connecting all four houses together.

The wooden half pipes and ramps made it obvious I owned all four mansions on my block. The guys were jealous of my food, my parties, the women hovering around. I guess seeing me skateboard from one house to another was the last straw.

I can't help that I'm smarter than those guys.

Can you blame me for having fun?

Chapter Four

My trouble with the law started about the time I mastered using the ramps to travel back and forth between houses. I got up that Monday morning, had breakfast, and climbed to the second floor for a quick glide to work.

The bedroom window retracted into the ceiling, opening a clear shot down the half pipe to the house next door. Halfway over the lawn, the board hit maximum speed. I tapped the tail to get control before reaching the hump over the stairs that used to lead to my neighbor's back deck. My early jumps from the stair hump all the way into the back door had been a disaster. Once, I came in too high and nearly decapitated myself on the upper trim. Another time I landed on the sliding door track and wiped out face first all over the kitchen floor.

Chilling out was the answer. I dropped a little speed, hit the remote, and sent the sliding door rolling open. A short hop over the hump gave me time to make a second jump over the door tracks then drag the tail on the tiles on my way into the foyer. All under complete control.

I'd removed the pictures from the hall after a few rough landings. With my fingers smoothly gliding along the plaster for balance, I flipped my board to the foot of the stairs and walked into the living room I'd converted into an office.

"Music. Volume twenty-five."

"Natalie Martin. Missing You."

The music cranked, but the stately brick walls and large yard kept the neighbors from complaining. Natalie had that deep luxurious voice that got richer the louder you played her songs. Country and pop weren't my thing. Maybe I listened for the voice. Or maybe because she was so beautiful.

Natalie serenaded me while I clicked on my monitor and checked email.

No new business, which wasn't a surprise. I made big deals with big clients. My product solved a problem every big company had, but it was one of those things you couldn't advertise. It was moral, but not strictly legal. So I had to wait for word of mouth to bring my next assignment.

No matter. I lowered the music with the button built into my desk, grabbed my game controller, and started a virtual killing spree on the big monitor in front of me.

My soldier hustled over the rubble and settled into one of my favorite ambush points, nestled in beside an abandoned hot water tank with a good view through a busted out window over a field of bomb-leveled buildings.

Far in front of my solider, another man scrambled over the rubble and stopped at the foot of a ruined wall. My sighting dot settled on his back and I nailed him.

"Shit."

The words came over my headset milliseconds after the shot. My name appeared on my virtual friend's screen and he knew he was in for a long session.

"You sissy. All you do is hide."

The instant replay would show him where I was. He'd come for me, but he'd pop back to life in a random spot and it would take him a while to hustle to my location. The other guys heard him whine. They knew some of the spots I used and tried not to step out in my usual killing fields, but I nailed two more of them before I decided to move someplace safer.

If not for multi-player video games, society might have melted down after "The Ruling". Young guys had a lot of time on their hands and needed an outlet for their aggression. Killing each other from afar was a safe way to spend a whole day entertained without spending a lot of money.

I could have stayed hunkered down in the rubble all day, but a pop-up alarm took over a quarter of my screen to show me a car coming down my driveway. It was time to get to work.

Two guys hustled into view across the rubble then disappeared behind the pop up. I was steamed because closing that window distracted me so long I didn't get a shot. I was also annoyed because it was a deathmatch. Those guys should have been killing each other, but they were running side by side, working together against me because they couldn't get me alone. I would have thought that was the beginning of this program, if I wasn't so sure Wendell didn't have access to me then.

The man at the door was about to set me on the path to meet Wendell Cummings. Only a psychic could have known then what was coming. But when I opened the door and saw the faces in the car across the street, I should have been more wary. People were jealous of anyone successful in 2013 and many times their jealousy turned to malice.

"Afternoon, Mr. Charest."

We shook hands and he stepped through the foyer and into my office. He nodded approvingly at the three large monitors arrayed on my desk, probably thinking I used them for hours of programming and analysis. If he knew how much time I spent in deathmatches, he might have balked at my ten thousand credit fee, but he stepped around and sat in my guest chair, eager to conduct our business.

Mr. Charest straightened to receive the three velvet boxes from my top drawer, each monogrammed with the initials of an executive. He laid them side by side and seemed to understand that each box held a set of identities meant for one of his people. He looked to me for guidance, not wanting to show his ignorance, and certainly not wanting to make a mistake in such a sensitive matter.

I motioned for him to pull one open.

When he saw what was inside, he shifted to the box marked "S.M." and smiled when he saw my handiwork.

"Sandra's slide on over her nails. She can apply makeup to them if she plans to wear them for any length of time, but I suggest wearing them for the transaction, peeling them off, and storing them away."

"What are the initials inside for?"

"Ahh," I said. "This is important. Each print is a separate identity. It's very important they don't mix them up. They should get in the habit of using the print for a transaction and putting it back in place."

Charest grimaced at the thumb-sized latex sleeves. He could have been having second thoughts about the whole scheme or just worried his executives would accidentally expose him. No matter how nervous he was, there was no denying the rewards of beating the tax man. Charest couldn't afford to reward his team without me. If he didn't, his people would flee to a competitor who could pay them what they were worth. My fee was safe. My only worry was Charest losing his nerve.

"You need to remember a few things," I said. "For this to be convincing, they need to use all of the accounts on a regular basis. Each account needs regular transactions. Ideally they'd make a schedule for each and stick to it."

"What do you mean?"

"Real people frequent the same places. They have patterns that show up in the government's reports. Your team should get used to grocery shopping, buying gas, whatever they regularly do, but doing it in different places with different identities."

"Like they're five different people."

"Exactly. If they can do that, no one will ever suspect what's happening."

Charest frowned nervously. The guy was stuck. It wasn't his fault either. Everyone had a scheme to beat the obscene taxes. Mine happened to be one of the best. And safest. He was lucky he came to me, but I couldn't be sure the reverse was true. Charest was a big wig. The kind of guy who'd turn on his mother to save his skin.

"How are they supposed to keep track of the balances in all these accounts?"

At least he was trying to think it through. Ready to help his team avoid detection for a while. I figured I had a year before I needed to go underground, but boy was I wrong.

"Have them plug this thing into their computers." I picked one of the miniature flash drives from its nook in the velvet case and showed it to him.

"When it's plugged in, they'll see all their Govbank accounts at once. It will help them make sense of which accounts they're using and when."

He walked to the door, the velvet boxes trembling in his hands.

"Put those away. No need to draw attention," I said.

He pushed the velvet boxes deep in his pockets, shook my hand, and hesitated in the doorway.

"Don't worry," I said. "I've done this dozens of times."

The eyes across the street watched Charest hike to his Escalade.

Chapter Five

The next morning I lay prone on the deck of the water tower. I was Zeus firing down from the heavens, killing any combatant that lingered too long in the open. The tower looked over the entire battlefield, so I could see anyone who wasn't in or behind one of the remaining buildings. It was a difficult climb that left me exposed the entire time on the ladder, but once I reached the top, I was nearly invincible with the solid platform protecting me from my enemies below. I telegraphed my intentions, choosing the name Zeus when I planned to attack from above, but my fellow competitors weren't smart enough to see me enter the game as Zeus and head to the ladder to pick me off on the way up. They didn't connect my multiple identities with my style of play or my mode of making a living.

Living among such simpletons it's no wonder I owned four mansions.

Down in the rubble, two oblivious saps squared off in a machine gun battle. One ducked behind a blown out car, the other in the collapsed corner of a building. They took turns popping up and spraying rounds at each other.

I zeroed in on the guy behind the car and blasted him. When I started to zoom over to the guy in the corner, the upper right quadrant of my screen popped to a view of three blue and white police cars rolling in line down my driveway. One click restored my view of the guy in the rubble, but before I could settle the sight on him, he hustled away.

That was the end of my game for a few days.

The cars parked and eight cops jumped out. This wasn't a team assigned to question me. These guys were serious about hauling me in.

To my left, Oleg Shuplyak's Voyeur depicted a couple bathing at the beach. If you stood back, Sigmund Freud's profile appeared in the picture. The officers gathering outside my front door would see only the surface. They'd never see through to my secrets because they weren't that smart. I didn't panic and run for the back door. I calmly sat at my desk and watched them surround the house.

I could have opened the safe and flushed my next few deliveries. They'd never search the sewers, so my latex finger creations would have been lost for eternity there, but I wasn't afraid of the guys in blue. I didn't expect much from them and usually that's what they delivered.

I switched the game back to full screen and a few guys scampered around the remains of buildings. I fired seven shots and missed seven times.

The banging on the heavy front door jarred me from my seat.

The pudgy face of the group smirked at me. "Lieutenant Paige," he said, "Brookline P.D."

"What can I do for you, Lieutenant?"

"We have a warrant to search the premises."

I gestured and he handed it over.

I wasn't a lawyer, but I knew the address had to be correct and they had to list what they were looking for if they planned to take it from my house. They had 200 Buckminster Road correct down to the letter and they listed "Fraudulent Fingerprints" as one of the items they were searching for.

"You want to explain this to me?" I asked. "The alliteration is catchy, but do you really expect to dust this whole place looking for fingerprints that aren't really fingerprints?"

"Nobody likes a wiseass," the lieutenant said. He was probably insulted because he didn't know what alliteration meant.

He tried to push past and I blocked him in the doorway.

"Want to explain what a fraudulent fingerprint is?"

"This will go a lot easier if you stop playing games. We know you've been defrauding the government of millions in tax revenue. We have several sets of your handiwork down at the station."

With that he pushed past me into the living room. I followed, and the others streamed in, fanning out around the lower floor of the house.

I should have called a lawyer, but I wasn't afraid of reeducation. The toothless judicial system was why I got into the fingerprint business in the first place. If some sociologist weenie wanted to have a battle of wits and try to reform me, I was ready to take him on.

The cops scurried around, hardly touching anything until I sat behind my desk. At first, I thought they were going to force me up and rifle through my drawers, but they focused on the Voyeur hanging to my left.

They knew what they were looking for, and somehow they even knew where I kept them. In a few seconds, one of Paige's lackeys found the release hidden beneath the wallpaper. The button sent the painting motoring up out of the way.

"Combination?" Paige asked.

That safe was bolted to two-by-fours on four sides. The mechanism was way too sophisticated for the beat cops that prowled my house. The latex impressions inside that safe were my ticket to reeducation, but no way were these idiot cops going to get them without reinforcements.

I grimaced and shook my head, refusing to give up the combination. He didn't persist with the onslaught of admonitions I expected. My gaze fell on the opposite wall, avoiding Paige and the barrage of questions that should have been headed my way.

The next officer in the room came armed with a Sawzall, instead of questions. He marched in and stood to the side of the shiny black safe where I could see the silver dial beckoning for the five numbers that would give them passage to years of research.

The officer plugged the tool in, looked at me, then at Paige.

"Go ahead," Paige said.

The tool whined to life. I was sure it was a bluff until dust started flying. The blades sliced through plaster and strapping, slowing to chew through the stud centered underneath the safe then vibrated around the corner to the next.

I flew from my seat without realizing, enraged by the growing pile of sawdust and plaster crumbs that resembled mounds of dirty snow. Two officers blocked my way, and then I realized they'd been assembled to block my exit. Paige never planned on me giving him the combination. He knew exactly where my work was stored. He knew I wouldn't give up the combination, and he came with the tools to take the identities I'd created. No amount of protesting was going to slow him down, but I couldn't help rushing around the desk.

"You can't do that," I screamed over the moaning saw.

An officer stepped up from the doorway and grabbed my arm.

When another officer grabbed me from the other side, Paige moved in.

"This is the end of your scam," Paige said.

I watched helplessly as they carved the supports from around my safe then hauled it out, leaving a gaping hole in the wall.

Before he cuffed me, Paige presented three more search warrants.

Every letter was in order.

They knew about the laser press I used to create the latex impressions. The velvet boxes. The computer I used to hack into Govbank. Even the tiny devices I gave clients to manage their multiple identities.

Someone had talked. Until that moment I'd never been a violent guy, but right then I felt a rage like no other.

Smart as I am, I couldn't find a way out. This thing was going to court in a rush and only one outcome made sense. Years of long nights hacking and programming, studying fingerprints, and messing with patterns to make new ones unique—all of it wasted. Ripped away in ten minutes by an electric saw and a cop with an attitude.

They led me to the back of a cruiser and that was the last time I saw my houses on Buckminster Road.

Chapter Six

The driver wove down Sumner, Tappan, and Cypress rather than pick up Route 9. The mile-long jaunt through moneyed neighborhoods wound around to the public library. We turned down an alley to the back of the police station and went in through a large overhead door. The cops stashed their guns in metal boxes hanging on the wall when we were locked inside.

Four guys struggled to lower my safe from the back of a police van to a wheeled dolly while I sat caged in the backseat. Once they were done, three cops led me into the station. The dolly rolled behind us, a reminder that in a matter of hours they'd open the door to my secrets and seal my fate.

Laser scanners had replaced ink and paper in the booking room. Lieutenant Paige enjoyed having me alone back there. They weren't arresting a lot of citizens then. I might have been the only one in the station, so he had to get his fun where he could.

He scratched at my thumb, his grin proving how smart he thought he was. "Guess this will be the real you," he said, not finding a latex impression stuck on.

I shook my head, my best condescending smirk on my face, the ends of my long blond hair slapping my neck. Cops have a thing for long-haired guys. Maybe because they're not allowed to wear their own hair long. Maybe because long hair is one of the first signs of rebellion.

"Look at that," he said, his eyes on the monitor. "Seems you've been lucky for a few years. Guess that ends now."

"We'll see."

Paige grabbed me by the arm and led me to a small room with a telephone. "This isn't the Matrix, kid. All the computer skill in the world isn't going to get you out of this room. Better call a good lawyer."

"This is great service. I thought you'd sit me in a room for a few hours."

"You've got a lot to learn. Better make that call."

He locked me in with a wooden table and chair, both bolted to the floor. I made the call for help and waited to see what two hundred an hour bought.

Forty minutes later, Colin Nixon walked through the door and introduced himself in an inexpensive, but well-tailored suit. Seemed taxes took a bite out of lawyers the same as the rest of us.

"Let's go, Jordan," he said, leading me to a meeting room down the hall that was only slightly more comfortable. I didn't complain because my butt barely had time to get sore on the wooden chair.

"We've got some problems," he said when I sat down.

"Go on."

"Seven arrests for computer hacking give a lot of credibility to the charges. They've got photos of you withdrawing funds using several different identities."

"Can they really prove that in a photograph?"

"Based on what I saw, I think the judge will agree with the prosecution."

"You've examined the evidence and you're ready to give up? I called you less than an hour ago. For a guy who works by the hour, you're in a mighty rush to get this over with."

"Your other trials probably lasted weeks. Months even. Things are different now. The court has forty-eight hours to sentence you to reeducation or set you free."

"Let me get this straight, years ago it took months to win a case. Now the government has gotten so good they can try a case in two days so well you can't win?"

"How many citizens did you see in the station today?"

"None."

"Exactly. All these cops, they're working on your case. They've been working your case for a while."

"How can they do that?"

"You only get one chance now. You lose and you're a relearner forever. Used to be, the same people kept coming back, tying up the cops time after time. No more. No clutter means you get a whole lot of attention."

"The judge will know I haven't been in trouble for a long time."

"True. But he'll also know about Golddigger."

"That was a years ago."

"You caused ten million dollars damage with that virus. Judges don't like vandalism, definitely not on that scale. The cops don't bring any case that's not a slam-dunk. The judges all know that. With your record, it's going to come down to one thing."

"What's that?"

"What they find in your safe."

I didn't tell Nixon about the twenty thumb impressions I planned to deliver the next day. I sat and listened while he told me the cops had an expert working the safe. That they'd videotaped the entire process from the moment they walked in my door. The video wouldn't stop rolling until the safe popped open. My only hope was that the safe would hold out forty-eight hours. Then, with no evidence, they'd be forced to release me.

The knock sounded two hours later. The safe had succumbed, and it was time for me to meet the judge.

Chapter Seven

Nixon motioned for me to sit on a wooden bench that held a line of men waiting to be tried. Four men sat between me and the double wooden doors, each accompanied by a lawyer in a dark suit. My watch read 2:00 P.M. Impossible they'd get to me before the end of the day. No judge could conduct four trials in three hours. I relaxed in my seat until the bailiff came out and waved the next defendant in.

Nixon sensed my unease as we moved one position closer to the doors.

"You know what's going to happen," he said.

"Will they release me if they don't hear my case in forty-eight hours?" I sounded more desperate than I'd intended.

"The judge will see you in thirty minutes."

"Are you serious?"

"You've seen the evidence. Could we argue your case and win?"

"Not a chance."

"That's why these guys," he tilted his head down the bench, "are here. They're facing irrefutable proof and there are only a few choices the judge can make. It won't take him long to decide."

The reality began to set in. There was no maneuver Nixon could use to help me avoid justice. The facts were on video, and they were about to speak loud and clear. Legal wrangling had been replaced by intense preparation and ultra-swift justice. Without a jury as a wildcard, courtroom BS was out of fashion.

The bailiff waved in the next case much too soon.

In twenty-three minutes, Nixon escorted me down the aisle of wooden benches that had long ago seated an audience. Trials weren't a spectacle anymore. Maybe the public was barred. Or maybe just discouraged. But the only people in the courtroom were the judge, a clerk, the prosecutors, and an important guy I was about to meet for the first time.

Wendell Cummings sat on a bench against the wall by himself. I hadn't seen him come in, but he didn't look settled enough to have been there the entire forty minutes I'd been outside. There was a private door beside the bench that could have given reeducators access to claim their pupils without being seen by the rest of us in the courthouse. He sized me up as I took my position behind the table and turned my attention to the judge and the men at the prosecution table.

"Mr. Voss, you've been charged with fraud, tax evasion, and conspiracy to evade taxes. The people believe you've defrauded the government of millions in revenue. How do you plead?"

Nixon stood. "Guilty, Your Honor."

The judge barely paused. "Do the people have any guidance to offer on Mr. Voss' sentence?"

"There never was a question of guilt in this case, Your Honor. Mr. Voss has been convicted three times previously of computer crimes and is considered a master of his craft. Breaking into Govbank's identity database and adding fictitious citizens took tremendous effort and skill. Although Mr. Voss is only twenty-two years old, he holds a Ph.D. in computer science and the intelligence to defeat any basic reeducation program."

"What are you suggesting, Mr. Miller?"

"We suggest Mr. Voss begin reeducation at level 3."

All of a sudden, Nixon found some energy. "Objection. That's unfair to anyone. The prosecution wants my client to fail. Starting at level 3 is inhumane."

Nixon leaned on the desk, and Wendell, who'd been calm to that point, sat erect and stared at me as though I were some sort of freak. Either he didn't like the insinuation that I could outwit him, or level 3 reeducation was pretty nasty stuff. All I could tell from his posture was that he was upset by the proceedings. Once the prosecutor suggested level 3 reeducation, I no longer seemed like a bargain to Mr. Cummings.

"Your Honor," Miller pleaded, "I have the utmost faith in our reeducation system, but this man is too determined and too intelligent to be handled like a petty criminal. We must take measures to keep him in check."

At that, Wendell glared across the room, his attention now squarely on Miller. Nixon seemed pleased with himself. Maybe because he read the judge's reaction. I couldn't be sure.

"He doesn't look dangerous to me," the judge said, "rebellious maybe." His Honor glanced around the room, taking us all in, measuring an idea that could satisfy us all at once. "How about this? Mr. Voss, if you can penetrate Govbank's systems, your consultation would certainly be valuable to our technical team. Why don't you work off your debt by helping shore up our systems and making sure this sort of thing doesn't happen again?"

Nixon's head bounced like a puppy dog. Apparently it was the best deal he'd been offered in a while.

"The government can't pay me enough to be a drone. No thank you, Your Honor."

Wendell gasped so loud we heard him at the defense table.

The prosecutor's pen bounced off the table and rattled on the tile floor.

Nixon braced for an explosion of anger, but the judge kept his composure.

As I waited for a good scolding, I realized the government could pay me what it wanted. All those taxes went right back to them. The judge probably understood how much the ridiculous taxes hurt companies and why they needed a scam like mine to stay competitive. That's why it was so important to stop someone else from doing the same thing. And why it was so convenient the taxes didn't hurt government employees.

The whole thing was unfair, but not nearly as unfair as what Wendell Cummings would try to put me through.

"Reeducation is not a vacation, Mr. Voss." The judge said evenly. He didn't implore me to accept his offer, and he didn't impose a punitive sentence to assuage his ego. "You are hereby remanded to reeducation under the direction of Wendell Cummings. This is not a sentence to be taken lightly, Mr. Voss. You will begin at level 1."

"Your Honor," Miller whined.

"You'll begin at level 1, Mr. Voss. You will live in the apartment assigned to you, and you will complete the program in its entirety. Follow Mr. Cummings' directions carefully. Otherwise you'll be facing a far more serious penalty."

The gavel banged.

The men behind the prosecution table had won, but they eyed me with awe. Most citizens had heard about the horrors of reeducation and were desperate to avoid the high-stakes psychological games, but what could that little middle-aged guy really do to me? He couldn't lock me up against my will. I had to follow his reeducation program if I wanted to be free again, but I could match wits with Wendell Cummings while beating four people at chess.

My biggest worry was that the cops had confiscated five identities and six hundred thousand credits. In 2013 that much cash was hard to come by.

I shook hands with Nixon who regarded me like the village idiot for choosing reeducation over government service. Then I walked over to Wendell Cummings and put out my hands expecting him to cuff me for the trip to my new place.

"I can't cuff you in reeducation," he said.

That was Wendell's first mistake. He lost control of me before we even walked out of the courtroom.

Chapter Eight

Wendell escorted me down a long flight of granite stairs and held the door, while I climbed into the back of the cruiser at the curb. I scooted across the bench seat and waved him in beside me, but he was too smart to take my invitation. He had a soft spot for relearners, but he didn't want to be locked back there with me even if I wasn't convicted of a violent crime.

"Don't you have a car, Wendell?"

"It's being repaired," he said from the front seat.

The officer behind the wheel let out the hint of a smirk. He knew Wendell was afraid to be alone with me so soon after my trial. There might have been some contempt in the cop's expression for this new age prisoner coddling, even though he was young and probably hadn't seen many of his collars released from prison when "The Ruling" came down.

"How'd you get here then?" I asked.

Wendell said something to the driver, but I couldn't hear over the traffic noise and radio static.

"You said we're going to be together for the next few weeks. If you can't cuff me, you're going to have to get used to sitting next to me."

The officer squinted a silent warning in the rearview mirror.

We'd known each other less than twenty minutes and already Wendell was afraid. A fifty-seven-year-old scrawny dweeb should be afraid of a young male convict. He couldn't restrain me and certainly couldn't catch me if I ran. All Wendell had were his wits against mine. He might as well have gone lion hunting with a box of rubber bands.

The cruiser pulled up at the Red Line Diner. Wendell stepped out, but didn't open my door until the officer came all the way around and blocked my path down the sidewalk in the other direction.

Not even twenty-four hours after my arrest, the legal system had chewed me up, spit me out, and handed me over to Wendell to be fixed. The air didn't taste any sweeter, but the long concrete sidewalk offered a path to freedom from Wendell and whatever mind games he had planned for me.

"Don't even think of it." The cop saw me looking and didn't want to chase me. No wonder. His shiny black shoes and dress pants weren't exactly runner's attire. My jeans weren't much better suited to a sprint, but I rode my skateboard every day and could have outrun those two guys and eaten my lunch at the same time.

I remembered a quote from my friend Frank who said, "Nothing is as it seems in reeducation."

Did they drive me to a maze with cops around every corner waiting to arrest me and drag me back to a level 2 reeducation program? Was this sidewalk as much a prison as a place of commerce? No shoppers walked the concrete and not a single car moved anywhere in sight.

"Let's have some dinner," Wendell said.

I was starving, so I followed him inside and sat across from him on a cracked vinyl cushion at a chipped table in the middle of the diner.

"I don't know much about you yet, Jordan, but I want you to know that whatever happens and however hard and crazy this program becomes, your success is my goal. I want you to graduate and go back to a happy life with a good job and a nice family."

Wendell seemed apologetic. He had me captivated until I noticed a man at the bar and a woman several booths down peeking in our direction. The cop was gone, so maybe in this little prison the customers were in charge of keeping order.

I jumped up from my seat and took a quick step away from the table.

"Where are you going?" Wendell hollered.

Six people flinched all around me. My watchers had conveniently identified themselves. I feigned pain in my hamstring, rubbing, looking around, and slowly sitting back down. The man at the bar and the woman in the booth were working with a man seated on each side of the front door and a couple seated two tables down from us in the other direction. The waitress had flinched, too, but I couldn't be sure she was in on it. She could have simply been on alert because she worked the restaurant and felt an obligation to help maintain order.

"Just a cramp," I said.

Wendell didn't have a clue how far ahead I was thinking.

"I don't know what you're going to teach me. I received my Ph.D. in computer science at fifteen." His lesson plan was irrelevant. We were going to have a battle of wits, and I wanted him to know how badly he was outgunned. The court could order me to stick around for two or three weeks, but they couldn't stop me from having fun at the expense of my handlers.

"We'll get to that in time." He looked over at the waitress and her footsteps sounded immediately, coming to his aid because most of the remedial crap he taught didn't apply in my case. He was in trouble and needed food to distract me from picking him apart.

He ordered a burger with the works and an iced tea. I ordered the same burger, rare with a Coke.

"If you weren't hacking computers, didn't work with computers at all, what would you do?"

"Die," I said. "Actually, I'm so hungry I might die."

"I'm serious. If you had to choose another career, what would it be?"

"Why work? I'd go on the dole like everyone else."

"You're too smart to sit around all day."

"Who says I'd sit around? I'd do yoga. I'd skateboard. There are thousands of things I like to do besides work on computers."

"You need to contribute something."

"I'm not going to drive a truck or wait tables when I can sit home and take down forty grand. Who'd be stupid enough to do that?"

Wendell didn't show his anger. He tried steering the conversation in different ways, but since I wasn't afraid of him and didn't take everything he said as gospel, his words had little effect. His frustration grew with every failed attempt to steer me toward the straight and narrow.

He was glad when the chunky waitress delivered our food. I thanked her in my friendliest voice then looked at my burger and sighed deeply.

"What's wrong?" Wendell asked.

"They cooked the crap out of this." I pushed it to the center of the table and he took a halfhearted look at the brown meat peeking out between the buns. "Can I see yours?"

He pushed his a few inches ahead. I leaned forward and snatched it in my hand. His mouth dropped when I took the biggest bite I could manage. He didn't say anything, just watched while I chewed. I attacked the burger with much more hunger than I felt and waited to see what he'd do with mine. I knew he planned to knock me out while we talked, but not where he planned to hide the drugs. It wasn't the burger because he daintily cut mine in half and started eating.

"For starters, we're going to teach you better manners."

"You can try," I said with my mouth full for emphasis.

He eyed me suspiciously. He must have known he was in trouble then. That I was too much for him to handle, but he tried to act comfortable while he sipped his iced tea and ate my burger.

A ten-year-old kid wandered down the aisle alone. I raised a hand and stopped him when he got to our table. "Thirsty, kid?" I asked, holding out my full Coke. "I'm not going to drink this."

The waitress practically leaped a chair to intervene. Wendell's glass slapped down on the table hard as he reached to stop the kid from taking my Coke. I let go and watched it fall. The glass shattered on the floor, soda splashing the kid's sneakers and cascading in every direction.

The waitress grabbed the kid by the hands and yanked him a foot off the ground to keep the soda from touching his skin. Instantly I knew she was in on it and that there were extremely powerful drugs in my Coke.

Wendell jumped from his chair to help. I snatched his iced tea and took a huge gulp before he could react.

The kid scowled at the two grownups who had cost him a free soda.

Wendell shook his head at me and grimaced that an obnoxious punk with bad manners had just gotten extremely lucky. The long hair sold my reckless image. The Ph.D. should have made him wary, but he was worn out from years spent on hopeless relearners who would never go straight.

But if the fight was beaten out of him, and I'd just made him look foolish, why did he look so smug with his toes in the soda puddle?

A gloved finger pressed down intently on the bare skin above my collar. I spun and swatted the arm away, frightened that someone had gotten that close. I needed to be on guard every second in reeducation. But I was doing that, wasn't I? Still, I hadn't heard a single footstep.

"A smart one, aren't you?" the man asked in a deep, cool voice.

"Thanks, Forty-three." Wendell sounded relieved.

What kind of person was named Forty-three?

My head felt woozy. It couldn't have been the tea. Wendell drank half the glass and he was fine. He might have known I was thirsty, but he couldn't have known I planned to make a grab for his iced tea far enough in advance to drug me. Not possible, but my vision blurred and waved.

I turned to the guy behind me. "Who are you?"

He ignored me. Not one of the two by the door. Someone else. A specialist. A heavy hitter. He'd played this game before, because I was good and he was a step ahead of me.

I blacked out so fast I didn't even remember falling.

Chapter Nine

Dreamily tugging something sticky on my neck yanked a dozen short hairs so sharply my eyes watered. White-hot pain woke me from a drug-induced stupor, my fingertips gooey with adhesive. I gently flicked a hard plastic corner then traced the outline of a large square bandage adhered to the base of my neck. The source of my pain lay underneath.

The bandage hadn't been there the day before. The last thing I remembered was the finger on my neck in the diner then blacking out and falling forward. Even if I had fallen backward, the soreness in my neck was much deeper than the bruise from a two foot fall. It flared the way a deep cut burns if you move before it has healed.

Sitting up, my stomach barrel rolled and threatened to give back Wendell's burger. The drugs explained my nausea and my frustration. I knew they were going to try to drug me, but still couldn't stop them. Once they knocked me out, they could have done anything. I had no memory of the bandage or the deep wound beneath. All I knew was that the light at my window was fading and I'd lost most of another day, while Wendell and his team put their plans into motion. There was no law against them keeping me sedated while they worked. Technically it could have been days or even a week I was under, but that was unlikely even with the roadblocks I'd erected for Wendell and his team.

I'd done my homework on reeducation. At this point, the game was on. Anything I saw and anyone I spoke to was probably part of my reeducation team. If I was going to succeed, I needed to clear my head.

The tiny bedroom was a huge downgrade from four brick mansions in Brookline. Cheap linoleum covered the hall floor and white paint coated the walls, trim, and ceiling. The relearners before me probably did a lot of damage. Painting the whole place one color made repairs quick and easy.

The kitchen packed a microwave, range, and fridge in close proximity. No dishwasher and barely any counter space. The small table seated two in much less comfort than I was accustomed to. Backing the kitchen was a beige couch facing a black television on a polished black stand. Otherwise the place was mostly empty.

The food in the kitchen could have been drugged before I got there and my stomach somersaulted at the idea of another round of drugs, so I moved over to the wall by the window, sat in the lotus position, and closed my eyes to get in tune with my new surroundings.

The air handler blew softly. Footsteps vibrated through the wall. Either from the hall or the next apartment. A truck rumbled outside the window.

A knock came louder than all these things combined. I ignored the bullying demand for entry, listening instead for more subtle signs of life. The air handler and traffic sounds died away, taking their cue from the man at the door that my attention should be focused there. Impossible that reeducation could be orchestrated with such precision, but for a fleeting moment I believed it.

My feelings reached out beyond my body through the limits of the room. I couldn't see while my eyes remained closed. I felt the sounds conspiring with the man at the door to fade into the background. He knocked again. The only sensation I felt was tightness on my right ankle, an unyielding object pressed deep into my opposite calf.

"Open up."

I opened my eyes and peeked down without moving my head. Ankle bracelets had mythical powers in the new world of reeducation. Sometime during the night a thick black band had been clamped down on my leg. The green light shone to let me know I'd followed the rules so far.

"What are you doing in there?"

Wendell had seen me. He might not have technology to see me from the hall, but he didn't start knocking until I was awake. He quickly became irritated because he knew I was resisting. The only way he could be sure I was ignoring him and not still sleeping off the drugs was if he could see inside my apartment. That was a handicap I might not have been able to overcome. I had to neutralize that advantage if I wanted to emerge from reeducation unscathed.

He banged the door so hard I felt the vibration travel through the wall and into my back.

"Jordan! Jordan! Open this door!"

I closed my eyes again in case he had a video screen out there. Anyone watching would know I was intentionally ignoring him. If he didn't know already, someone on his team would tell him eventually.

Deep slow breaths helped me focus, slowly cut through the medicinal haze, and helped me hear the door handle furiously rattling. Metal teeth slid into place. The knob turned and the door burst open. Had I the presence of mind to chain the door when I stumbled from bed, Wendell would have been stopped, but that first visit he barged into my living room uninvited.

"What are you doing?" he barked.

I kept my eyes closed and steadied my breathing. "Why knock if you have a key?"

"It's the decent thing to do. So is answering the door when someone comes to visit."

"I didn't invite you." I could feel him fuming even with my eyes closed.

"Get up," he said. "We've got work to do."

"I need to recover from the drugs you poisoned me with."

"I didn't administer any drugs. You collapsed in the diner and hit your head."

I didn't bother arguing the lie. I knew how to fall. All skateboarders did. "Who's Forty-three? Is he a secret agent or something?"

He didn't deny knowing Forty-three. He ignored the question and moved over to my television. He set something down on the carpet and I heard a fastener snap open. Curious as I was, I kept my eyes closed. I couldn't focus on my breathing anymore, so I listened intently to the sounds of Wendell's work.

"A name like Forty-three gives no hint of his ethnic background. No clue where he came from. It's a name you could forget in ten minutes. He must be pretty slick to warrant a name like that."

I opened my eyes this time.

Wendell kept his eyes on the black box, now attached to the top of the polished black stand. When he turned to me, he acted as though he hadn't heard a thing I'd said. Instead of answering my question, he showed me a small remote control and pressed the "on" button.

"Each day you'll have a lesson to complete."

"You didn't answer my question," I said.

He kept on talking about how important the lessons were. How they would determine whether I succeeded or failed reeducation. That I mustn't leave the apartment before passing my daily automated test.

When I couldn't take the spiel anymore, I slipped the ankle bracelet off and shook it at him. "What's the point of putting this thing on me while I was unconscious? Did you really think I wouldn't notice?"

"Put that back on," he said.

I threw it at him.

He scampered to his left, fumbling it in his hands. Once he had control, he tossed it back. "You must wear this every second. Never take it off. Not even when you shower." He looked afraid.

I flung the bracelet down the hall, and it slid to the furthest wall of the bedroom. Wendell chased after it faster than I thought he could move and ran back to me with the bracelet clutched in his fingers like a prize. He brutally forced it over my ankle. He would have continued playing fetch for at least a few more throws, but that seemed cruel.

"You must never be more than three feet from this bracelet. Never."

Exertion flushed his face red. What would he have done if I tossed it out the window? "Why not?" I asked flatly.

"When you have that on, you signal the world you are following the rules. Take it off and you are a criminal."

"Who is going to know if I take it off?"

Wendell wanted to tell me what I already knew, but that would have meant confessing his lies. If he had leveled with me, maybe I would have gone along with what he wanted. But he lied to me from the very beginning and never stopped. That's what's wrong with this world. No one can tell the truth about what things really mean, what we really need, and how we should be expected to behave. Wendell wanted to trick me into following society's rules instead of simply explaining why they were important. That's why he failed. And that's why we are here tonight, locked in this Plexiglass cell, talking to you through a darkened window. If there were more honesty in the world, there would be no need for this charade.

That night Wendell left me in my tiny apartment without explaining what he wanted from me. I wasn't a child. I wasn't going to follow his lessons simply because he told me to.

The second he left, I walked over to chain the door behind him. I found the hardware mounted to the door, but the chain had been removed. I had no way to know who was watching me or when they'd come barging in.

I couldn't live like that and I didn't for very long.

Chapter Ten

The little hologram popped up when I swung the door open. "Where do you think you're going?" asked the four-inch projection of Wendell Cummings. The fuzzy electronic image stood in mid air, twelve inches in front of the black box, and spoke with Wendell's voice.

"Out of here," I said.

"That's not allowed."

"You can't cuff me. And you can't force me to stay in this apartment. Imprisonment is cruel and unusual punishment. Haven't you heard?"

"You're not in prison. You're in reeducation. There are rules, Jordan. You must complete your lesson before going outside."

"I'm not doing a lesson today. The sun is shining and I'm going out."

"The sun has already set. It's dark. Not the time of night to wander this neighborhood. Get accustomed to your new apartment and relax."

I shut the door and stepped back inside. If I'd been talking to a computer program, I would have walked out, but somewhere there was a human behind that voice, and I couldn't risk leaving with an operator watching me.

I turned the television on for background noise, but no matter which channel it was tuned to, the lousy thing played an introduction to reeducation lessons.

I turned out the lights. The room was dark, but not dark enough for what I had in mind. I pulled the plug from the television and the glowing numbers went dark. That didn't do anything to the black box, but the hologram had disappeared and it wasn't emitting any light, so I left it alone.

The cord to the microwave was plugged inside a cabinet above the stovetop. I yanked it out and bucked the range forward until I could pull its cord from the wall. Even with all the lights out and the electronics all off, the glow from the window was enough for me to see my way around.

My place had four windows. One in the bedroom. One in the bathroom. And one on each side of the combination living room and kitchen. The bathroom window was the easiest. Three towels stuffed underneath the bathroom door blocked all the light coming out into the hall. The cracks on the other three sides were so tight that almost no light escaped. The hall fell dark except for a faint glow at each end.

The mattress and box spring fit easily over the large windows in the bedroom and living room. That made travel up and down the hall impossible without using the walls to guide the way.

I waited on the couch ten minutes to see if someone would come running and put a stop to my shenanigans, but the door never opened and little electronic Wendell didn't pop up to scold me. You might think I killed him by unplugging the television, but Wendell's program wasn't that simplistic. He expected relearners to resist, and he was prepared to a point. Unfortunately for him, I took things well beyond that point.

Any corrections officer worth his pension would have put a halt to my scheme in short order, but Wendell let me draw a curtain around myself so his technology couldn't see me anymore. You may be thinking that I'm not much of a risk to society and that they weren't worried about what I was going to do, but I assure you that judge wanted me dealt with as harshly as a mass murderer.

I should have opened the door to see if there was a motion sensor outside. If I were in charge of reeducation, I would have put motion sensors inside every room and outside every possible exit. I didn't think of it then, but it didn't matter, Wendell wasn't that sophisticated.

The only things allowing him to track me were the cameras all around me and the bracelet on my ankle, and I was about to shed them both.

The comforter from the bed stuffed pretty well into the window frame above the kitchen sink, but it kept falling out, letting in the light from the floods aimed at the parking lot. I stretched a towel across the window frame, and nailed it into place using butter knives for nails and a hardcover copy of *Gone With the Wind* as a hammer. The first towel made a pouch for the comforter and threw the room into darkness except for a faint glow where the comforter sagged at the top. The second towel held the comforter higher and blocked the remaining light, but it had to be secured in the dark. I kept pounding my wrist, trying to hit those last two knives. When I was done, the place was as black as the inside of a bank vault.

I felt my way down the hall to the empty bed frame and sat in a tangle of blankets while I slipped my ankle bracelet off. To anyone monitoring me, it looked like I shut off all the lights and went to sleep. The ankle bracelet on the bed frame was proof enough that I was following the rules.

The next part made me nervous.

I'd never seen the rest of the building, but I knew the stairwells and common areas would be monitored carefully. I had to learn enough about the layout to find my way back to my own room without lingering outside where the cameras could capture me.

I waited ten seconds with my hand on the doorknob, expecting holographic Wendell to scold me, or for the real Wendell or one of his flunkies to knock from the other side of the door. They didn't come. Nothing moved while I stood in the dark.

I opened the door and bolted, hesitating only to drop a quarter on the floor in front of my door.

I plunged down two sets of rubber-treaded stairs, catapulting myself from the metal handrail as I made each corner. At the bottom I burst out into the night and veered onto the grass instead of following the path. Anyone watching the building would have focused on the stairwells, sidewalks, and paths. It was less likely they'd notice me running across the grass and it turns out they didn't.

Chapter Eleven

My phone could have plotted my exact location and guided me to find what I needed, but they'd taken it away and dumped me on an unfamiliar street. A taxi could have had me back in Brookline in ten minutes, but it would have been too simple for them to find me there, and running would only get me to level 2. I needed to stay in Wendell's program. To outlast and outsmart him.

The tarnished brass number beside the center set of doors read 1900. The long brick building looked like an apartment house, a little upscale from a housing project, but not much. A few lights glowed, mostly on upper floors. A few of the residents were relearners in programs like mine, but the rest were con men hired by Wendell to scare us straight. None of them could be trusted. Criminals or con men, they all had an angle.

The cameras on the outside of the building would have been too small to see in the dark, so I didn't bother looking. The wide lawn offered enough shadow between the dim lights outside the building and the bright street lights on the main street that ran in front. I stayed on the grass until I reached the tall picket fence that funneled me along the edge of the property to the sidewalk.

The cab parked half a block down was tempting, but it was a trap. The off duty light was lit and there was condensation on the inside of the windshield. The scraggly-haired guy with the thick beard was stationed there to pick up wandering relearners and keep tabs on them for Wendell. It was a great idea, but without my ankle bracelet to alert him I was coming, the guy let me walk right past. What a waste of money to post a guy outside my place and for him to be so lax as to let me walk right by. That's our government in action, though. Isn't it?

The sign at the next corner marked my new road as Centre Street. I paused beside a black Audi with my eyes lowered to memorize my new address. Tires rushed toward me. Headlights flashed overhead. Behind them, a black SUV passed by, then turned sharply, tires screeching.

I hit the deck prone with my head tucked against the rear tire of the Audi, my body invisible to traffic. The curb blocked me from crawling underneath the car, so I pressed my head against the cement and watched the black tires prowl past.

The men in the SUV were more like cowboys than cops, riding the city in search of stray relearners, the tinted windows hiding their angry faces. Relearners called these reeducation cops "black bats" because they rode around in big silent SUVs, dressed in black from head to foot and enjoyed using their black batons more brutally than officers of the law should. Tracking devices allowed them to home in on a relearner wherever he went, which was as amazing as a bat's ability to fly at night.

Cops were never this efficient. I'd been gone three minutes at most and they already had me lying flat on the sidewalk with concrete pressed against my chest, afraid to get up. The SUV didn't happen by. They knew I skipped out and that I was in the area.

But my ankle bracelet was on the bed. They couldn't have known I left my apartment unless I'd been caught on camera. Even if they knew I'd skipped out, the only way they could track me was by sight, and I wasn't leaving the ground until they'd gone.

The tires stopped. The SUV's engine didn't make a sound. I had no idea they'd pulled up on the other side of the Audi until I saw the tires fifteen feet away. When the doors opened, I was sure they'd tracked my exact position somehow. Heels hit the pavement. Coming for me.

I couldn't breathe. The weight of my head pressed my cheekbone to the sidewalk, and as I scooted forward, my knees banged the cement.

Doors slammed beyond my view. Heels swirled to a run.

I pressed up on my hands, ready to run, but the boots ran away from me, darting for the opposite sidewalk. Surprised and feeling safer, I pulled myself up and peered over the Audi's trunk in time to see the men swarm around the cars on the opposite side of the street. A young blond guy ran a few yards, but was surrounded by four black-uniformed men. Two others stood apart from the SUV with light automatics. Were they expecting an attack? Who would attack the reeducation cops?

The cops at my house hadn't displayed such force. They came in and took what they wanted, but these guys deployed like a Special Forces assault team, and when the blond guy stopped running, they swooped in and whacked him with batons. No questions. No instructions. They attacked and didn't stop thrashing until he was motionless on the ground.

Maybe I should have run, but a mixture of curiosity and fear kept me there. This had to be a case of mistaken identity. Those batons were meant for me. Luckily another guy with long blond hair happened to be in my vicinity and these cops, so accustomed to technology doing their work, accepted him for me because he showed his blond hair in the wrong place at the wrong time.

He didn't squirm when they carried him to the back seat. He hung limp from six arms, the men with automatics now at the back, covering their teammates as they loaded and boarded the SUV and sprinted silently away.

When they were out of sight, I followed and turned at the next corner.

For the first block, I felt lucky. Glad the black bats had screwed up. I kept on. The further I moved from the apartment, the less likely they'd find me after discovering their mistake.

Near the next corner I wondered if I'd underestimated Wendell. Reeducation was a psychological game. We all knew the black bats liked to use their batons, and they could get away with it since the only penalty anymore was reeducation, even for them. But what if Wendell thought mental torment would be more effective than whacking me with a baton. What if the capture was staged for my benefit? The whole thing an act?

Chapter Twelve

I walked four blocks before I saw another cab and practically dove into the street to stop it. The driver pulled right over, almost as glad to see me as I was for the ride.

"Where to?"

"Is there a bus station nearby?"

"Every hundred feet."

"I mean a terminal."

"South Station is thirty minutes depending on traffic."

"How about a T station?"

The driver swung around and took me right back to my apartment and two blocks east to the train station. I hadn't seen a single sign to know the station was so close, but the commuter rail to Boston gave me another way to disappear if things got scary.

He stopped beside the empty platform and scanned my thumb to accept my fare. He looked at me sideways for a second, and I held my breath, thinking Wendell had cleaned out my account, but the transaction went through and I climbed out of the cab.

Three cabs waited in a line at the curb. I hopped the first and felt free for the first time since being arrested. Wendell might have guessed I'd come here, but he couldn't control the line of cabs. The guy behind the wheel was a regular guy, driving a cab to make a buck. He took me to the nearest electronics store and I had him stop two blocks short in front of a corner bar.

The thumb scanner would alert Wendell within fifteen minutes that I'd hired a cab. If his team was paying attention this late at night, they'd know I was on the outside even though my ankle bracelet was on the floor where my mattress was supposed to be. The thumb scanners, ankle bracelets, and cameras were impossible to beat for very long. I had to hope the guy at the monitor would assume I was going into the bar and give me a break. If he followed procedure and called the cab driver to track me down, he would have found out where I was headed and called a carload of black bats to greet me when I came out.

The people in the parking lot stopped to watch me sprint into the big box electronics store. Speed shopping isn't a recipe for success when you're buying high-tech gadgets, but I knew exactly what I needed and getting something and getting out was a lot more important than getting exactly the right gear.

Ten minutes later, I slipped across the shopping center to a hardware store then dodged into the shadows two blocks from the bar. I couldn't see if there was a black SUV outside the bar or not, and I didn't want to get close enough to find out. Those guys liked their batons a little too much.

Fortunately, I didn't need to walk down to the sidewalk to hail a cab. Once I had a phone I didn't need cabs at all. I called a guy who really owed me. He picked me up and had me back at 1900 Centre Street by ten o'clock.

Wendell's cab driver watched the building from the same spot. The swarm I expected outside my apartment wasn't there. No one in the lobby either.

The quarter sat outside my door at the top of the stairs. You might think leaving a quarter is as risky as Hansel and Gretel leaving breadcrumbs, but quarters were useless once America started running on credits. That quarter was no different from a shiny rock. I stuck it back in my pocket and opened the door.

I ducked when I walked into the dark room, expecting someone to be standing inside ready to take a swing at me. But when I shut the door, I was alone in a place so dark I couldn't see a thing.

Booting the computer would have given me enough light to see, but doing it in the living room would have spoiled my plan. The hall closet gave me the privacy I needed, though my legs cramped while I configured my new machine and its special accessories.

The fun began in the hall. I slipped my cell phone onto the floor and clicked a key to light the display. My computer paid for itself then. Of the fourteen cameras in my apartment, the cell phone light showed up on three. No encryption. No security. Nothing. If I wanted to find reeducation sites and broadcast the in-room feeds on the Internet for the world to see, there was nothing stopping me. And when I graduated from reeducation, that might have been a profitable endeavor if not for the consequences.

My work began then. I moved the phone then went back to the closet and checked the camera image. It took a while to pinpoint the tiny device in the ceiling because I couldn't see it and had to keep going back to the closet to see how close I was. It would have been a lot faster to walk around with the screen in my hand, but I didn't want Wendell to know how I'd defeated his feeble attempt at security.

Back and forth I went. Over and over until I'd found all fourteen.

The walking didn't seem like much, but I was exhausted when I finished. It might have been the drugs still working their way out of my system, or the nerves of being under continuous surveillance. Either way, I was ready to crash with no bed to crash on.

Getting the mattress and box spring back in place wasn't too tough. And I had the lights on when I made the bed. Taking the knives out of the wall in the kitchen was a little trickier. The drywall crumbled, leaving two inch holes around the window.

As I pulled my ankle bracelet back on, I thought about how neatly it appeared to anyone tracking me that I'd been sleeping in the same place for hours. I wondered how mad Wendell would be when he saw the holes in the wall. He might be upset about the damage, but I would have bet he wouldn't even notice the holes when he came up to scream at me.

Just before I dozed off, I remembered one last surprise. I hopped out of bed and got it ready.

Chapter Thirteen

Bang. Bang. Bang.

Flimsy mattress springs poked into my back. Pain flared in my neck, shot down my spine, and settled between my shoulder blades. I rolled over halfway then flopped back down. The plush pillow top that blanketed my mattress at home felt like sleeping in a cloud. Sleeping in this rat trap felt like torture. The rattling, banging noise at the door awakened me into Wendell Cummings' nightmare no matter how hard I tried to ignore it.

"Jordan!" The muffled voice wasn't loud enough to force me up.

Bang. Bang. Bang.

No one ever disturbed me at home.

I never scheduled a client before nine, and I wasn't about to jump out of bed to start reeducation. I could cook my own food and do the program when I was ready. My sore eyelids were evidence enough it was too early to get out of bed.

Wendell used his key. The knob turned, but the door slammed to a stop a few inches in.

"What's going on here?" Doctor Dweeb was angry. "Jordan. Jordan. What is this?"

A good chuckle improved my mood. I pushed myself up and pulled on the pants and shirt I'd worn the day before. The cold linoleum on my feet didn't bother me because I needed to see Wendell's face when he came up against my security system.

A slam from the outside sent a crack ripping through the door casing.

A second kick followed. The third ripped a long strip of trim off the wall and left it dangling away from its parent. The wavy strip of exposed wood stood out starkly against the white background, allowing the door to open a foot, but the stubborn strip of pine refused to let it swing further.

Wendell lowered his shoulder and barreled his weight against the door. The sliver cracked free and the door flew open. The three chains I'd installed whipped away under the force of Wendell's narrow shoulder, but the strip of wood bounced off the wall on the far side of the door and rebounded just as fast. The sharp edge slashed across Wendell's arm on the return.

He stopped and gripped the scratch as grimly as if his arm had been sliced off with a katana.

"What's wrong with you, Doctor Dweeb?"

Rage lit his eyes. To an observer who didn't know about my late night trip or what I'd done to his cameras, it was a valid question. He might have wanted to curse me for his new nickname, but he was even more disturbed about what I'd done to his newfangled prison cell.

He took half a step forward and his knee buckled. He canted right, clutching and rubbing his knee, then limped to the couch and sat on the rounded arm.

I looked down at my bare feet then gestured around the tiny apartment.

"You are my responsibility, Jordan. I had to make sure you were okay."

"So you busted in?"

It dawned on him then that I'd locked him out, something no other relearner had ever thought to do. Criminals had been obsessed with finding ways to escape since the days of dungeons and castle towers, but this apartment wasn't much like prison. He was baffled that I'd make myself at home. He looked back at the chains and the strip of trim he'd ripped off the door casing, puzzled that I'd try to lock him out.

"Why wouldn't I be okay in my own apartment?" I asked.

He rubbed his knee and walked over to the door. "You're going to pay to have this fixed."

"I didn't break it."

The Cat Bagger's Apprentice

He threw his chin in my direction then turned toward the kitchen. I wanted to ask how many kicks it took him to break in, but he had discovered my handiwork with the insulating foam and was stifling his anger until he could respond without completely losing control.

The foam blobs over the cameras were too accurate to be accidental.

He crossed the room hastily, the pain in his knee forgotten for the moment. Straight to another camera and another thick dab of insulating foam covering the miniature lens. His face flushed red. His jaw clenched, stuffing down curses he wanted to spew at me.

I took his spot on the couch and rested my ankles on the coffee table, my back to him.

He rifled the bathroom, then the bedroom. When he opened the hall closet and paused, my breath caught. I didn't turn. Didn't give him any indication that he was looking right at what he sought. But he wasn't thinking clearly enough to check inside the single towel in the closet. The laptop wrapped inside had guided me to his cameras. If he'd picked it up he would have known how I'd fooled him.

Instead he stormed back down the hall and searched the kitchen cabinets. When he found the foam, he opened the window and tossed it outside.

"You shouldn't litter," I said.

He wheeled toward me, his eyes insane with hate.

"Aren't we here to learn right from wrong?" I asked.

He took a step toward me and his face swelled, repressing every cussword he knew. He knew he was beaten even then, but he loved his program too much to admit failure. The pioneer of reeducation had never dealt with someone like me.

"I'm going to teach you, Jordan. Trust me on that."

"Someone in this room is going to learn a few things."

He straightened. Indignant at my challenge. This was his turf, and he'd probably never had his authority questioned so openly here.

Instead of answering me, he walked to the television and clicked it on. "You will finish your lesson each day before going outside."

"I don't need to go outside."

My matter-of-fact tone brought him up short, and he looked at me cockeyed.

"I don't," I said.

"You still need to finish your lesson."

"You know I have a Ph.D., right? What could you possibly teach me?"

"Not to steal from the government."

"How about I agree that's wrong, and we move on?"

"It's not that simple. You need to prove that you've learned."

"Or what? You keep me locked in this room?"

He closed in on me and made a noise that sounded like a growl.

"You can't really punish me. You can't cuff me. You can't throw me in a cell. All you can do is ask me to watch videos. Reeducation is a gutless waste of time. Just like you, Doctor Dweeb."

"You're a smart guy aren't you?"

"Very."

"Do you know what the recidivism rate was for violent criminals in two thousand one?"

I had a guess, but I refused to help him make his point.

"Eighty percent. Know what it is now?"

He came up until his shins met the coffee table and glared across at me. The geeky old guy couldn't pull off the tough guy persona, but what he said had power. "Less than one percent."

The number shocked me. He was forbidden from telling me what would happen if I failed, so he told me that I needed to be afraid without telling me why. Pride radiated right out of the little guy.

"Finish the damn lesson," he said.

He turned to go.

"Send someone to fix my door, will you?"

He slammed the door, but the jagged piece of trim wedged in the opening, and it shimmied open wide enough for me to watch Wendell walk away.

Chapter Fourteen

I got up and locked the door, still barefoot. The jagged piece of trim would have made a good weapon or a decent lock if I'd screwed it to both the door and the frame. Instead, I unchained it and tossed it aside, doing my best not to get splinters.

A holographic version of Wendell projected a few inches above and ahead of the black box. The little guy implored me to start my lesson and told me how easy it was to use the remote control to get started.

He practically begged me to come back when I went to fetch my camera. When I sat on the couch in front of him and clicked the remote, he cheered right up.

After a few minutes of instruction that I couldn't skip no matter what button I pressed, the game opened with a view of an old house and me as a kid. Wendell used impressive graphics for my avatar. Ten-year-old me looked authentic with long hair, jeans, and a black T-shirt. The controls for running, jumping, and kicking were clunky, but I did what any gamer would do in a new game. I hacked around and discovered the best ways to move around the virtual world.

A green line led to a school playground. Before school, at least fifty kids milled around a huge square of blacktop lined in white and yellow. Different colors for different courts and different games.

A short kid walked by and dropped a square bit of something on the ground. I bent down and the graphic resolved to a cell phone. Inside Wendell's world, the challenge was unambiguous. Return the phone to the kid because it was his. I didn't particularly care for Wendell or his feeble-minded reforms. It wasn't a big surprise the game didn't know how to cope with what I did next.

I chased the kid down, and when he turned, I drop-kicked him in the chest. The teacher was only fifteen feet away, facing our direction. She couldn't have possibly missed the attack. In real life, I would have been suspended, maybe expelled. All that happened in the simulation was the kid bounced backward three feet. He didn't fall. Didn't even lose his balance. I punched him for good measure and went back to get his phone.

It was still there in a white circle that might have marked the center of a soccer field had it not been asphalt underneath. I jumped and landed squarely on the phone, but didn't crack the plastic. I tried a front flip, but the rudimentary controls weren't designed to allow that degree of flair. I jumped and jumped until I got bored. The phone remained intact.

I ran around and punched a few other kids until the teacher lined us up and brought us inside. I tried to leave the line, but the rectangular portal that led to the classroom sucked my avatar in along with the rest of the kids in line. So much for free will.

My avatar sat at the back of the class without my guidance.

The kid I'd drop-kicked on the playground sat hunched over the desk next to mine. The other kids picked on him and his head hung lower and lower. A text window popped up and gave me the choice to intervene or to talk to the kid who was getting picked on. I chose to talk.

"Don't be such a wimp. Fight back or these guys will own you forever."

The kid flashed me a look.

The teacher pointed a finger. "Jordan, don't interrupt," she said.

She started lecturing again, and the kids went back to throwing things at the kid next to me. Pencils and erasers flew sporadically when the teacher wasn't looking. Waiting for the drama to play out bored me to tears, so I got up out of my chair and tried an elbow smash on the back of the wimpy kid's head. Wendell must not have been a fan of pro wrestling because my maneuver came out as a punch.

I hit him a few more times and he sat there and took it.

The Cat Bagger's Apprentice

Finally, the other kids started pelting him. I tried to join in, but the things I picked up stuck to my hands.

Then the kid came at me with a pair of scissors. I drilled him in the face, but then my limbs went still. The game steered to a pre-determined outcome. Wendell's program completely lost my respect at that point. I could have—and would have—beaten the crap out of that kid, but the game wouldn't let me. It wanted that kid to hack me up with the scissors and that's what happened. He jumped on top and repeatedly stabbed me until my avatar collapsed. The simulation ended with my blood all over the floor.

Holographic Wendell scolded me, saying I needed to learn how to treat others, or I would never graduate from reeducation. He didn't tell me that the simulation got harder every time you failed, but I wasn't worried. I spent half my time playing video games at home. I could beat any game Wendell designed.

Failing served a purpose.

I stopped my camera recording and went to the closet for my laptop.

I tossed the towel on the floor and walked to my bed with the computer in my hands. The moment I started it running, someone banged on my door.

I felt like I'd been shot. Like I'd stupidly wandered out into the middle of the battlefield and been gunned down. My mistake couldn't be undone.

It didn't matter how Wendell had someone at my door so quickly. He might have stationed someone in an apartment across the hall 24/7. What mattered is that Wendell had outplayed me. Maybe some of his anger had been an act. Maybe the guy was smarter than I gave him credit for.

I'd been too cocky. I'd screwed up and it was time to pay.

Chapter Fifteen

The guy outside didn't kick the door in. After what happened to Wendell, he expected some kind of trick, so he didn't even try his key. He banged and hollered, but waited outside while I started looking for the camera Wendell had planted.

The computer whined, and while I waited for the system to come to life, I pictured a group of men nearby watching me pull the computer from the closet then congratulating each other for solving the mystery of their disabled cameras. It wasn't coincidence the man outside appeared seconds after I took the computer out of the closet. Wendell and his team had been watching, and now they knew what I'd been hiding.

Having the computer proved I'd left my room without my tracking bracelet. That was offense enough to be hauled back to relearner court and sentenced to level 2. I was headed for a stern reprimand at the very least.

As the video software started and the new rogue image came to view, I realized the guy would try to take the computer with him. My only chance was to make sure he couldn't find it. First I had to find the new camera so his friends couldn't tell him where the computer was hidden.

The camera view showed a closed door. I moved over to the end of the bed until my view matched the camera's. A wave past the bed post blacked out the view for a second. Then I moved my hand slowly up the post until the view went black. There, taped to the opposite side of the post, was a solid wire strip with a bulb on the end. It looked like a miniature toothpick with a black olive stuck on the end at about one-fiftieth the size.

The Cat Bagger's Apprentice

I didn't remember Wendell coming this far inside the apartment, but he had picked his location well. I would never have found it unaided. The far side of the bedpost was too close to the wall for me to squeeze by and the view looked right down the hall, across the length of the apartment.

I didn't snap it. I covered it in a wad of toilet paper to make it go dark and stuffed it in my pocket. I hid the computer in the oven and answered the door.

"Maintenance," the guy in jean overalls said. He had barbed wire tattoos well down his arms. What were the odds this guy was more of an actor than a carpenter?

"Amazing service," I said.

"You break it, we fix it."

I waved him in and stood back to see how good of a carpenter he was. He took two steps in and set down a large plastic toolbox. In the hall, he had an extension cord and a tall piece of white trim that matched the measurements of my door frame precisely.

Wendell's preparation was impressive. No maintenance company in the world would have had a repairman to the apartment within twenty minutes of the accident. And this guy already had everything he needed. It was almost as if he knew the door casing was going to break and had prepared himself to fix it even before Wendell smashed my door. Impossible?

Was Wendell somehow watching me even now? Did he have a better set of cameras in my place? Encrypted cameras I couldn't hack so easily? If he did, he was way ahead of me, but I convinced myself all the head spinning was psyching me out. Wendell was a boob.

The carpenter pulled out a cat's paw and hammer and started gouging nails out of the old trim board.

The multi-layered thinking gave me an idea. The clear tape from the bedpost would adhere Wendell's camera to the toolbox, and then I could follow the carpenter to Wendell's office. He had to have one nearby. Knowing where it was could be a first step to taking control.

I sat on the coffee table and pulled the tiny camera from my pocket.

The carpenter worked quickly. He yanked on the cat's paw and flipped nails out toward his toolbox with flair. If he was an actor, he'd been a carpenter first. Not surprising Wendell would go to that length.

I pulled the toilet paper off the lens and reached over to the box. I'd almost attached it when I realized my mistake. I covered the camera quickly, pocketed it again and excused myself to the bathroom.

If that camera had come live, Wendell's people would have seen it and realized my trick. But the cameras under the insulating foam had been dormant much longer. No one was watching them after they'd been black for twelve hours.

The insulating foam popped off in a few big chunks. I couldn't go back to the kitchen for a butter knife, so I gouged the drywall around the miniature camera with the butt end of my toothbrush. After a minute of rushed and clumsy digging, I drew the metal sliver out of the ceiling and brushed it off with the lone hand towel.

Back in the living room, the carpenter dabbed paint on the cut end of the trim and fanned it dry with his hand.

"Nice job," I said, standing close so I could reach the toolbox.

When he held the trim board in place and started tacking it up, I dropped to one knee and quickly taped the camera to the side of his toolbox.

"Those tools get counted when I get back to the shop," he said without turning around.

"I'm no thief."

"How'd you get here?"

The rapping hammer forced me to wait until he drove a nail home.

"It's a long story."

If he wore an earpiece it didn't show. It made sense that he'd be on his own while he was with me. But if Wendell and his team saw me attach the camera, they'd let him know as soon as he left my place.

The curiosity kept me standing by, wishing I could help him finish and get him on his way.

"I can't let you keep these," he said and began unscrewing the chains I'd fastened to the door.

Wendell wanted unfettered access.

"This is my apartment. Isn't it?"

"You're a temporary guest of the state."

"And I don't have a right to be safe?"

The guy turned around and I took a good look at him for the first time. His belly jutted out of the overalls and the plaid shirt was all wrong for the neighborhood. He was a cartoon carpenter. Probably was a manager in the city before "The Ruling" came down.

"You couldn't be safer."

"How many criminals live in this place?"

"There are no criminals here. Just relearners."

"Are you a carpenter or a counselor?"

He double-clutched his answer. We both knew he'd blown it, but I pretended not to notice.

"We all have to pitch in. Keep an eye. You know?"

"I get it."

I offered him the garbage can for the cracked pieces of wood, but he refused, bundling them instead with a cord from his toolbox and hauling them out the door on his way.

I rushed to the oven the second the door closed.

Chapter Sixteen

Of all the cameras tiled on my screen only two had light and only one was moving. I maximized that one and watched the stairs disappear behind the carpenter.

"All set," he said out loud even though he was alone.

The camera on the toolbox didn't show the carpenter, only the view behind him. I hadn't heard a phone ring so I assumed he'd called Wendell to check in.

"The trim is fixed. The chains removed."

More stairs disappeared. The carpet leveled and a key fitted inside a lock. A door opened and closed. The apartment on the first floor.

He walked past six microwaves like mine. A few ovens. Two fridges.

He stopped and a phone flipped open.

"I couldn't tell," he said.

I couldn't hear the other end of the conversation. I wondered why he was talking in the hall before he dialed the phone, then I realized the halls and rooms were bugged, so he could talk to his teammates when he was in the apartments or common areas, but couldn't hear them. The room with the extra appliances was out of bounds. Only the counselors went in there, so there were no cameras or microphones. He needed the phone to communicate while he was in there.

"Yes. It's there. Can you see it?"

He waited some more then said, "On my way," and hurried through another door.

Travelling backward was disorienting. He crossed a hall and went into another apartment, moving faster now that he was done talking. Wooden trim and cabinets were stacked against the walls. He kept on in the same direction, so he had to be walking the length of the building to the far end. Wendell had made a hallway out of connecting apartments so his team could move around without being seen.

The camera stopped on a view of a stairwell that looked exactly like mine, looking all the way across the ground level.

"Is he as crazy as they say?" a man's voice asked.

"The kid's smart and polished. I was with him twenty minutes and he figured out I'm on the team," the handyman said.

"That's the last thing we need."

The toolbox camera bobbed when the big guy shrugged.

"The old guy is falling apart. One more case going off the rails and we're screwed." The voice paused. "I'm not going down with him. Not again. He starts losing it, I'm going over his head. Maybe if I burn this guy, they'll put me in charge."

"Why you?"

"You know I'm next in line."

"After Charlotte, sure."

"Yeah right. She'll follow him to the grave. Trust me. If this kid is as smart as you say, the old man will fall flat, and I'll be running this circus in a month. Be nice to me or you'll really be fixing doors for a living."

The handyman grunted and the camera started moving again.

The last door opened to a tiled floor and white halls. The place was brighter than the rest of the building.

"Nice going, Joel."

The camera nose-dived then settled at knee height where my view was completely blacked out. What rotten luck for the handyman to face the camera toward a wall.

"What's he doing?" Joel was the man from my apartment.

"Staring at his computer."

My view cleared and I saw Wendell sitting in front of a bank of monitors with his back to the camera. Joel stepped up behind him, and I realized it had been his jeans blocking my view. He'd set the toolbox on a chair and luckily, set me facing the room from the corner.

"Should we prompt him to try the lesson again?" Joel asked.

"He failed his lesson on purpose," Wendell said.

He was right. I'd run the simulation as long as possible because I knew what I'd find in the video and I wanted to get it all.

"What's he doing? Surfing?"

"I can't see," Wendell said. "But I don't have any traffic coming from his room."

I shook my head and at that same moment Joel said, "Shit, what was that?"

I froze and kept watching my screen.

"He can hear us."

Damn they were good. I was watching them watch me and they were so good at it they knew what I was doing without seeing my screen. They saw my reaction to their conversation, and they knew I could hear them. I stifled my urge to look for their camera. If I had, they would have scoured their own room and found mine. Instead, I scratched my head and stared at the computer, pretending to work on the most difficult computer hack imaginable.

"What's he doing?" a woman's voice asked.

"Joel was just up there fixing the door. Now he's on his computer. Doing what, we don't know."

She stepped forward and flipped her long red hair. The curls hung way down her back and the camera was perfectly positioned to capture her long legs and tight backside. I don't usually go for redheads, but the voice, the hair, and the body captivated me through the ether. To be honest, I was captivated by Charlotte long before she arrived in that room.

"Shouldn't we have more cameras up there?" she asked.

"He deactivates them as fast as we install them," Wendell said.

The Cat Bagger's Apprentice

I scratched my head for their benefit, then went for my cell phone and dialed. The guy on the other end had been expecting my call.

"The day's finally come has it?" the man asked.

"Yes."

The conversation downstairs crackled with intensity.

"How'd he get a phone?" Charlotte asked.

"Who's he talking to?" Joel asked.

It was nearly impossible not to look at the screen when Wendell and his team talked. If I kept looking back, they'd realize what was going on, but I couldn't help wondering how long it would take them to start eavesdropping on my call. Wendell worked feverishly at the keyboard. Another scenario was even more frightening. My computer was off the shelf and I'd done nothing to harden it. A decent hacker could have connected to my machine and found the camera on the toolbox within a few minutes. At that moment I was way ahead of Wendell Cummings and I didn't want to lose my lead.

"Has it begun?" the man on the phone asked.

"Yes."

"Do you know where you are?"

"Nineteen hundred Centre Street. West Roxbury."

He reminded me of the outrageous fee they charged for the four-man team. Credits were easy to manufacture at that point, so I didn't give the fee a second thought.

Bodies scrambled on my screen, but I couldn't follow the action in my peripheral vision.

The man asked if I could hold out until morning, and I told him it was no problem. When we hung up, Wendell said, "What the heck is he working on that's so important? You think he's still hacking? Even in custody?"

"Where did he get the computer?" Charlotte asked.

"He shouldn't have that up there," Joel said.

Wendell stared at my image on the screen and I watched the back of his head from the camera on the chair. I decided they'd seen enough. I found the camera Joel had taped to the bottom lip of the microwave.

"What's he doing?"

I pulled off the tape and wrapped the tiny camera in a paper towel. In a few days that camera might prove useful. From then on I didn't break any more.

"He keeps finding our cameras," Joel said. "We're down to one view."

I scratched my head again then checked my computer. The only remote camera broadcasting was the one in Wendell's control room. If they had a view into my apartment it must have been hard wired.

"Little bastard." Wendell lowered his head like a bull preparing to charge, but I knew the old guy didn't have much fight left in him. He should have punished me for leaving my room. And for chaining the door, gouging the walls, and destroying his cameras. But he couldn't, and that left me in a weird position. I was in prison without oversight. I could do basically what I wanted. Though, eventually the consequences would come calling.

"We should get that away from him," Charlotte said.

She was hot, but not very nice. Too invested in her work to ever return my interest. Maybe if she'd met me in my four mansions, she would have thought differently, but as long as I wore an ankle bracelet, winning her affection would be an uphill battle.

"Can we kill two birds?" Wendell asked.

"What do you have in mind?"

"Where are we with his family?" Wendell wanted to know.

"Nowhere. He doesn't seem to have one." Charlotte seemed embarrassed by her failure to find my family, but when you can hack the government's genetics database, your family can be whomever you want them to be. I chose the appearance of being dropped here by aliens.

"I haven't told him about you. Want me to go up and introduce you?"

"I can handle it," she said.

"Take him out for a while, and we'll get the place wired up properly."

I shut down the computer to keep Wendell from hacking in and seeing my camera in his control room. Charlotte was on her way up, and as soon as we left the room, a team would slip in for another round of electronic hide and seek. My bigger problem was hiding the computer well enough so they couldn't take it before we got back.

Chapter Seventeen

Her knock came gentle and soft. I forced myself to wait on the couch until she tried again. Her second knock was too loud to ignore.

I opened the door to sultry eyes and a little shrug that drew me instantly to a sexy bare shoulder. She was delectable. Sensuous hair gathered to one side, a daintiness to her pale skin. "Hello, Charlotte," I said.

"Hi, I'm—"

"I know who you are." I blocked the door and took her in from crimson locks to snug jeans and back.

"Mind if I come in?"

"I do."

She leaned in toward me before my words registered, assuming I'd let her in. She didn't realize I wasn't moving until we almost bumped heads. "We can't very well talk in the doorway."

"Suit yourself." I shut the door and took two steps back with my heart pounding. Charlotte Finch had appeared on my computer screen years earlier and captivated me since that first day. My hands desperately wanted to touch her now that we were just feet apart, but it wasn't time. I waited while she stood dumbfounded outside my door, wondering what to do next.

She chose to knock a third time rather than retreat downstairs.

I opened the door six inches and poked my head out. "Can I do something for you?"

"We need to talk."

"What's on your mind?"

"Why won't you let me in?"

"Every time I let one of you in, I end up with another camera in my place. You want to strip your clothes off and leave your bag outside, you're welcome to visit as long as you like."

"You'd like that, wouldn't you?"

"What guy wouldn't?"

She looked down at her patterned top as if she was considering pulling it over her head and dropping it on the floor. Charlotte was really committed to her job, but I had no illusions of getting her clothes off so easily.

"Why don't I buy you dinner?" she asked.

"Same problem. I leave, one of your buddies comes in and wires my place all over again."

"How can I help you if you don't trust me?"

"This isn't about you helping me. You're here because you want something. That's why you didn't leave when I shut the door."

"Reeducation isn't a joke, and I'm not going to let you quit. I'm here to help you learn what you were doing is wrong. If you don't, you'll be in serious trouble."

Every counselor hinted at serious trouble, but they wouldn't tell me what was in store if I didn't fall in line. Reeducation might have been more successful if they came out and told us what was going to happen, but one percent recidivism was success you couldn't argue with.

"Fine. I'll make you a deal," I said. "You convince me I'm wrong and I'll go to dinner with you."

She accepted my challenge and came inside on the condition that she stand on the kitchen floor where she couldn't reach anything that could hide a camera. She put her hands on her hips in protest of my distrust. They accentuated her curves so nicely that, win or lose, I couldn't refuse her dinner invitation.

"Can we agree you're a tax cheat?"

"I'm a patriot."

"You're breaking the law. That's not right."

"If I earn ten dollars, is it right for the government to take eight? If this continues, two years from now no one will work and the country will fall flat on its face."

"If our country is going to succeed, everyone needs to pay their fair share."

She scowled at me. I wondered what Wendell paid her to believe this insane socialist crap. "Fair?" I asked. "Imagine the guy who makes a million bucks. Is it fair for him to pay eight hundred grand in taxes? He gives the government four times what he takes home."

"You and your clients are greedy."

"Greedy?"

"You heard me."

"Why is it greedy to keep what you worked for, but not greedy to take your living from someone else? Isn't that greed? And sloth?"

"You are breaking the law."

"A flawed law that's destroying this country. If I didn't help companies pay their top performers, no one would work. Why would they bother?"

"You help people steal from the government." Her halfhearted tone wasn't nearly convincing.

"You don't even believe that." I laughed as I stood and waved toward the door. "You can go now."

She seemed genuinely confused as I came closer.

"What?"

"You didn't convince me of anything. Game over. You lose."

She turned, and in two quick steps, whipped open my fridge.

"Hey," I said. "We had a deal." I closed the distance between us in two running strides. Instead of running from my heavy footsteps, she bent at the waist and peered into my empty refrigerator.

I came up from behind and wrapped my arms around hers, pinning them to her sides. "I'm not going to let you bug my food."

"Like I need a camera to know what you're thinking."

She let me hold her there. The longer she pressed her backside against my thighs, the harder it was for me to resist. Her wispy hair fluttered in my face and my heart stuttered.

"You don't have a thing to eat here. Why not come with me?"

"I gave you a chance. You failed." I pulled her toward the front door, not planning to let her leave my apartment alone, but giving her the impression I would wrestle her out and slam the door behind her. She didn't seem surprised that I released her inside the threshold.

"What's it going to take to get you out? Pizza? Chinese? Steaks?"

I turned my head toward the bedroom then back to meet her eyes.

Her coy smile stoked my appetite. She shook her head and straightened with a hint of a wiggle. "Something else you want?"

"If you bug the place I'll clear it out again."

"That's not what I'm after."

I believed her.

"I want to know about your family," she said. "That's my job. To make sure family issues don't get in the way of your treatment."

"I'm not sick."

"What's it going to take to get you to open up a little?"

"There is something I want to know." I let her curiosity build then told her I wanted to know about Forty-three. She should have refused immediately. But she chose not to follow protocol. Maybe she liked me, but more likely, Wendell had pushed her to do whatever it took to get the cameras back in my place.

Chapter Eighteen

The valet opened my door. I stepped onto a wide carpet that stretched to a revolving door, framed inside a two-story wall of sparkling glass. Charlotte's strawberry hair waved over the roof of her sedan, and she smiled at me as she came around.

"My tax dollars at work," I said.

"They are going to feed you."

We walked shoulder to shoulder down the carpet, our hands narrowly missing each other as they swung in stride. She nearly matched my height after changing into four-inch black heels in the car. When we joined the throng decked out in sport jackets and cocktail dresses in the lobby, it was clear why she'd changed. My jeans and dingy polo shirt were decidedly low brow in comparison. If I'd come in on my own, they probably would have shown me the door, but the maitre d' recognized Charlotte and waved us in without checking for a reservation.

We trailed through low partitions topped with green plants then climbed a winding staircase to a private balcony. Other relearners must have been intimidated here. I felt the tightness in my throat, but refused to let it take hold.

"You're pulling out all the stops," I said. "You must be at a loss."

"What are you in the mood for?"

I folded my menu and let my gaze descend from blue eyes and freckles to her plucky little breasts. When I raised my eyebrows, she turned sour.

"They don't serve those here."

"Shame."

She fended off my innuendos until the waiter took our orders and disappeared down the stairs. I'd done my research on Charlotte long before I wound up in Wendell's program. Every relearner wanted her, and that's partially why she excelled at her job. She charmed men to get their attention. Once she had a guy hooked, she guided him into deeper waters, teaching him about his own past and helping him overcome hurdles erected during his childhood. I had no such problems.

"You don't have anything to be afraid of," she said. "Parents love their children. It's universal."

"How can you say that? You of all people."

She recoiled and her eyes flashed left and right for an escape. Her duty pressed her to dig into my history, but she didn't dare continue.

I let her stew a moment then said, "I've seen the MacPherson tapes."

Her back straightened involuntarily. She glared at me, disbelieving I knew the truth about her very first reeducation encounter. She hoped the name was little more than a rumor to me. Normally Charlotte was an enigma to her clients, while she knew everything about their past. Having the tables turned unnerved her, but she was more than capable and quickly moved to change the subject.

"Your parents will be glad to discover you're not a ghost," she said.

"I'm sure they have no idea what you're talking about. They don't care about your silly identity database."

"You seem to know a lot about it."

"I make my living tinkering with that database," I said.

"So you wiped out your own history?" She didn't appreciate my shrug. "Your fingerprints don't lead anywhere, but what about your DNA? Even if you messed around in the database, your DNA will lead to your true identity. And your family."

I held my hand over the table, inviting her to prick my finger.

My offer was too good to be true. DNA records allowed her to grab a guy by his roots. To go back home and get his mom and dad to help bend a criminal to her will. Hacking the database stole her power and turned it around. When I offered to let her prick my finger, she should have known the data would prove useless, but she assumed it was a bluff. Otherwise, she was powerless and she couldn't entertain that possibility.

"If I can create new identities, who says I can't change my parents' files? Or simply erase them altogether?"

I turned my eyes to the stairs, inviting her to give up and go home.

Her expression iced over. The question came, but she wouldn't let it pass her lips.

"I like to see a woman committed to her work. You give me a little. I'll give you a little."

She sat up straighter, mortified that I wanted a sexual favor in such a fancy place. Underneath, there was a hint that she'd do anything to avoid failure, and I was struck with a powerful, sexy, dirty feeling in my gut.

"Tell me about Forty-three. Who has a name like that?"

"The Agency is big on secrecy."

"You're in the Agency and you have a name. Charlotte is your name?"

"Forty-three is the boss."

"He runs the Agency?"

"No one knows who runs the Agency."

"How do you get anything done?"

"I want to know about your parents."

"You haven't told me anything. Tell me how high Forty-three is and why he's so special, and I'll tell you about my parents."

She balked. For a second I thought she was bugged because they hadn't been able to wire my room, but it seemed her honor was the only thing in the way. She softened and said, "Forty-three oversees our program and one other. He has a number and not a name because he makes important decisions about relearners. It's critical that no one can find him."

"Does that make him high up the chain?"

"I don't know. I can only see two levels up. Wendell and Forty-three."

"And those are the only execs you know?"

There was more. She changed the subject to the dangers of unchecked crime. That the system had to be protected and that the work was extremely important. It was a big show and I told her so.

"What about your parents?"

"My father is an economist."

"Does he have a name?"

"His name isn't important. He teaches at a major university. He's authored six books on the U.S. Economy. He advised a fed chairman or two before we switched over to credits."

"Do you resent what happened to him?"

"You think I'm punishing the government because he lost his job?"

"Maybe."

"We're not that close, and even if we were, he's doing fine without an official government capacity. His work has nothing to do with why I help people beat the tax man."

She furrowed her brow and squinted as she met my eyes, as if she could look deep in my soul. For the first time, she saw my power as a threat. If I could hack the most sensitive government database, I could cause economic chaos. Complete anarchy if I randomly assigned credits. If I had reason to take revenge on the government, my power made me a threat to the entire country, not just Forty-three. Her eyes hinted that danger was attractive. Intelligent women are incredibly sexy to me. If she'd told me how deeply she was thinking about my machinations in that database, we might have gotten together right then.

She let the silence linger. An old psychology trick, but I let her get away with it. "My mother is a medical researcher," I said. "She's something of an engineer and works on cardio-vascular technology."

"Artificial hearts?"

"Her most successful invention is a device that filters blood."

"Like dialysis?"

"Similar."

"Where do she and your father live?"

"They're still in the States."

"You're not making this easy," she said.

"Tell me about the other exec you know. The one you wanted to tell me about a few minutes ago. If you do I'll let you take a blood sample."

"We already have your DNA."

"You had my DNA when you cut me open, but once you ran your test, you disposed of it. When the results came back inconclusive, you wished you had another sample."

She wanted to know how I knew so much about the Agency, but she couldn't ask. She didn't want to show how nervous she was. And she didn't want to let on how far behind Wendell and his team were.

I held out my hand and she took the kit from her purse. She swabbed and stuck my finger. My question had to wait until two waiters brought our dinners and set them out before us.

"Who is he?"

"His name is Sixteen. I don't know what he does, but he's sent me a few text messages."

"Just because he has your phone number doesn't make him part of the Agency."

"Wendell was scared when I told him about the first message. Sixteen is pretty important. I doubt he's in charge of the whole Agency, but he might be Forty-three's boss. Wendell knows who he is, but wouldn't tell me anything about him."

"Do you want to meet him?"

She smirked at me the way she would a fourth grader who'd just told her he was going to Mars. "You'll never find Sixteen or Forty-three. I can't find anything about them, and I can get into the database anytime I want."

"I know a whole lot more about that database than you do. Trust me, I'll find them and introduce you."

Chapter Nineteen

"I guess we're not going back to your place."

"Afraid not."

Charlotte kept the heat high in her car. I dreaded leaving the front seat, but it wasn't the evening chill that held me back. It was losing her and going to the rickety apartment alone. She gestured to the door twice before I finally pulled the handle.

"It's against the rules, isn't it?" I asked.

"I can't even tell you where I live. Don't take it personally."

I slid out and made the long walk up the stairs. My best chance with Charlotte might have slipped past. She'd been in my apartment with the cameras removed. She needed to get me out of there, so she had no choice but to cooperate and I'd squandered my chance.

I still had some leverage, but it was going to be really tough to get her in a position that vulnerable again. We'd have another talk after she ran my DNA, but what she found wouldn't be that much of a shock. As I reached the top of the stairs, I wondered how badly she wanted my background and whether I was deluding myself about being with her. Every relearner wanted Charlotte. Why would I be the lucky one?

The knob twisted. The lights flipped on. The place looked clean. More empty than clean, but apparently the way I'd left it. Something was out of place. A new smell or a piece of furniture in a new position. My mind told me someone had been in the apartment, but I couldn't see what had changed.

It was no mystery that Wendell's team had been inside. That was the other bird of my dinner conversation with Charlotte. She got her blood sample. Wendell planted his bugs. And I got a chance to make my case to a woman who saw me as a broken cog to be fixed.

The oven door lurched open, but my computer wasn't inside.

"Bastard," I stifled my curse, knowing I was on camera. The whole team would be downstairs enjoying my aggravation.

I opened the kitchen cabinets one after another. Searching every available space for my computer, getting more certain with each failure that Wendell had stolen it. Without it, I was forced to live with his cameras monitoring my every move. Even worse, I lost my greatest advantage, seeing inside the operation downstairs. I wondered if I could slip away and get a new computer. Very possibly not. Even if I did, it would be impossible to hide a new laptop with new cameras popping up in my room every day.

The longer the search went on, the lower my hopes dwindled. The refrigerator held the same few scattered items. The microwave was empty. Not sure why I looked in there other than the obvious fact that the laptop would fit.

Remaining calm for the cameras, I got on my knees to look under the couch, found nothing, then walked toward the bedroom.

Halfway down the hall, the closet held the one single towel. The thickness gave me pause. I'd left the computer in the oven and here it was back in the closet where I'd originally hidden it.

Even before I picked it up, I knew Wendell was sending me a message. The uneven feel confirmed just how angry he was about his disappearing cameras. The mass inside the towel clanked as I unwrapped the first fold. And there it was. A broken pile of cracked glass, green circuit boards and tiny resistors, sprinkled with black plastic.

The devastation suggested a sledge hammer.

The camera lens among the remains told me my camera had received the same treatment. The hinged door to the accessory compartment had been crushed and twisted flat. It took two minutes with a butter knife to pry the door open and find the memory card missing.

That memory card held the entire footage of my first video lesson. My counselors were all pictured, but I hadn't taken the time to view them before leaving. It was asinine for me to leave the memory card behind when it was tiny enough to hide in my wallet, but I'd never expected Wendell Cummings to go that far.

He'd seen me find his cameras and assumed I'd know about the subliminal images. If Wendell was smart, he'd take the subliminal images out of my lessons. Then I'd have to be wary of every person I met. I wasn't sure if he was thinking that far ahead, and I didn't care. I was angry about the computer, and Wendell Cummings was going to pay.

I carried the towel to the garbage can in the kitchen and dumped the computer bits. Acting as relaxed as possible, I walked to the bathroom and started a bath with steaming hot water.

While the tub filled, I went to the television stand and probed around for the release that set the black box free. I tried inside the shelf. Underneath. Down the side. Even on the lower surface near the floor, though it made no sense for a mechanical device.

I pressed every surface on the black box itself to no avail.

Finally, I fished the laptop battery out of the trash. I stripped the cord from a lamp with a kitchen knife and tightly wrapped it around one of the hinge pins from the bathroom door to create a magnet. I slowly waved the makeshift magnet behind the black box and when it hovered over the right spot, something inside the television stand clicked and the black box lifted two inches off the surface. The connectors between the box and television married under the center of the box, and when I pulled the box free, the male connector retracted into the tabletop and disappeared into the glossy finish. Impressive craftsmanship. It must have cost a fortune.

I wished I could have seen Wendell's face when I walked into the bathroom with his precious black box, shut off the water, and tossed it in. The box sank and bubbled.

Climbing into bed felt good knowing the person watching the monitors was freaking out. I shut out my light and burrowed under the worn comforter, ready for whatever retaliation headed my way.

Chapter Twenty

In my dreams, Wendell pulled his hair out ten different ways. My dead laptop couldn't link me to the show downstairs, but my imagination painted hysterical pictures of Wendell breaking chairs and windows, even chasing me with a semi and crashing into every car in the neighborhood.

I opened my eyes without moving, like an old west gunfighter who wakes up to find his camp infiltrated by a sheriff's posse. Retribution waited for me nearby, but my dark room betrayed no hint of where it might be. No birds sang outside. Nothing moved inside my apartment. I was alone, probably because I hadn't stirred yet. Those new cameras had been watching me all night. The moment I got out of bed, Wendell would set his plan into motion.

Lying there all day didn't make sense, so I got up and padded to the bathroom. The tub was empty. Dry. The black box removed while I slept. I relieved myself and went out to the mouth of the kitchen. A new black box waited for me. No sign of anger or even displeasure accompanied the box Wendell had installed overnight. Trading the box for my laptop was an even monetary exchange, but I was supposed to be the pupil. Subservient. Pliable. There had to be a punishment for destroying the box.

The dozen eggs in my fridge looked inviting. A tampered egg had to show a crack unless Wendell had developed a drug that could be absorbed through the shell and survive cooking. I doubted he was that smart as I scrambled three of them. Any idiot with a key could have drugged my orange juice. I took the risk and poured myself a tall glass while my coffee brewed.

The key zipped into the lock, the knob turned, and Wendell walked in. He looped around the table to the coffee maker with no more than a glance in my direction and poured himself a cup then sat down as if he lived there.

"You think you're smart, don't you?"

"Have you seen my file?"

"That stunt is going to cost you one thousand credits."

"Which stunt are you referring to?"

"Giving my black box swimming lessons. I charge the government one thousand credits for those. You're going to reimburse them."

Losing a thousand credits didn't faze me, but I glared across the table to let the little dweeb know there would be a price to pay for destroying my laptop and stealing credits out of my account. I wasn't a child. He couldn't keep destroying my gear, walking in on me, and robbing my bank account without me standing up for myself.

After my last bite of eggs, I turned my back on Wendell and walked to the living room window.

"Your free money days are over," he said.

Bigger problems for Wendell arrived in a black van with tinted windows. "Things are going to change for you, little man," I said and headed for the door.

"This isn't a joke. You're headed for serious consequences."

My sneakers rumbling down the stairs drowned out whatever he said next. He chased me out the door and continued yelling. He stopped when he saw the cargo van with the small satellite dish on top.

I turned back from the lawn. "Your consequences are already here."

"You arrogant bastard," he said. Doctor Dweeb was fighting mad. "You're going to bring big trouble to both of us."

"Think you can film me day and night. Think you can walk in and out of my apartment. You're going to pay for my peace of mind."

"The government isn't—"

"Not the government. You. I'm holding you responsible. Personally."

The Cat Bagger's Apprentice

The little guy stopped cold. Hands on his hips. Flabbergasted look on his face. He couldn't imagine how I could show him so little respect. He controlled everything in my new world, but he refused to take a hard line. He didn't want to punish me. He wanted his headshrinkers to fix me without leaving a mark. I had no such qualms about violence, and as he stood there and watched, he began to know it was true.

The side door rolled back and two hulking men in black tactical suits stepped down onto the curb. A man inside the van passed them each a large hard-sided case. I rushed over to meet them, leaving Wendell alone on the path.

"Good morning, Mr. Voss. Ready to start the clock?"

I looked at my watch and agreed it was time.

The two men introduced themselves as Winchester and Koch. I recognized the pistols on their belts and the spare magazines strapped to their chests. They had a dozen other pouches with gadgets I didn't recognize. Whether Winchester and Koch used the stuff or not, the gear was intimidating.

Wendell wasn't sure where to be. He gaped at the men I'd hired. Their short haircuts. Their solid posture and rigid muscles. His team used psychological tricks to perfection, but they wouldn't match well against the firepower Winchester and Koch lugged in those black cases.

The men escorted me across the grass about fifteen feet from Wendell on the walkway. "They can't come in here," he said meekly.

They bracketed me on the way upstairs.

Koch took the rear when we went inside, closing the doors behind us. The two men coordinating seamlessly without words was an awesome comfort. When we were inside the apartment, the two of them stood facing the door with me safely behind.

Wendell pounded less than a minute later. He could have used his key, but he knew better.

Winchester opened the door and let him in one step.

"Far enough."

"What do you want, Dr. Dweeb?" I asked from the edge of the kitchen.

"We have work to do."

"Not today," I said.

Winchester put his hand on Wendell's chest and pushed him back onto the threshold.

"You can't do this. This is a government program. You live here under my rules or you're gone." Being gone should have been frightening, but the words rang hollow.

"I'm done talking to you," I said. "If you want to continue my program, send Charlotte up."

"You don't make the rules here, Mr. Voss."

"In this room, I do. From now on this is my private space. Get the hell out. If I want you back, I'll let you know."

Wendell was stupefied by my bravado.

Winchester didn't wait for him to recover. He shoved his meaty hand into Wendell's chest and sent him stumbling backward into the hall. When he slammed the door, even I was in awe.

Chapter Twenty-one

The case clicked open one second after the door closed. Koch kneeled, pulled out a black cube, and flipped a switch. The indicator light went red then green. "We're clear," he said.

Winchester opened his case and immediately covered the black box with a black vinyl hood. "Camera," he said. "We haven't figured out how to jam the transmissions." He took a wand from the case and went on a search and destroy mission for the tiny cameras the reeducation team had placed in my room while I shared dinner with Charlotte the night before.

Winchester quickly pinpointed the cameras with his wand and deftly pulled thirty-six of them from my walls.

Koch removed a laptop from his case and set it on the kitchen table for me to use while they worked. I wanted to see Wendell's reaction downstairs, but couldn't connect to the camera on the toolbox. Koch saw my frustration. "Something wrong?"

I motioned him over and typed on my screen.

`Can they hear us?`

He held his fingers a fraction of an inch apart. Slim chance.

I typed. `I have a camera in their HQ. Can't connect.`

"Wi-Fi is jammed in this room. You'll get service from our van."

He took over the keyboard, and in a minute the camera feed popped up. Wendell paced in and out of view on my screen. Joel sat turned away from the camera. The cab driver faced Joel. Charlotte sat with her legs dangling off the counter top, her back to the monitors, her entire body in view on my screen.

"We have to send her up," the cab driver said.

"He's not running my program," Wendell said. "I don't care if he has enough money to hire a thousand thugs."

"The only way we're getting anywhere is if I go up," Charlotte said.

She was committed to her boss, but maybe she liked me, too.

Joel stood. "The protocol is clear on this. He's refusing to complete his lessons. We need to bounce him to level two or we need to flush him."

Wendell snapped at him. "Whose program is this?"

"Jordan thinks it's his." Joel challenged his boss, and I could almost feel the energy radiating off the others.

"What do you think?" Wendell asked Joel.

"I don't think we should put the whole team and the public at risk. This sorry ass stole millions of bucks. I think we flush him and we flush him now."

I was intent on the outcome of the confrontation, but a tap on my shoulder pulled my attention from the monitor. Winchester held out a thumb scanner. "Our fee is thirty thousand for the first week."

My fingerprint impression moved thirty thousand credits from my account to theirs and lit the spark of a smile in Winchester's eyes.

Koch said, "We have a go, blue team."

I gestured to him, wondering if I was part of the blue team. He smiled and pointed to a tiny device in his right ear then waved a two-button controller he kept in his pocket. "These are scrambled. Team members can communicate with each other up to two miles from the van."

Winchester wore a similar radio, so tiny I hadn't noticed.

With the confusion of the conversation in the room, on the screen, and in his ear, I understood why Koch spoke so few words.

Koch unhooked my refrigerator and wheeled it out the front door onto the landing. He did the same with the oven then carried the microwave as easily as a cereal box. "We don't know what's inside those skins," he said when I eyed him strangely. "They could release drugs into your food as it cooks or spray a contact agent on the bottles and wrappers you keep inside."

"You pay for security, we'll make you safe," Winchester said.

The movers on the blue team were strong and combat ready. Their job to carry new appliances up the stairs and stock them with groceries wasn't glamorous, but they attacked their mission with precision, silence, and efficiency.

Their first trip to the living room convinced me I'd hired the right guys. They set an eighty-inch plasma television against the outer wall and connected a game console. The same console and games I played at home.

When the new appliances were all in place, the men lugged a series of batteries and space heaters and arranged them in a neat line at the end of the hall. I could stay safe inside my apartment as long as I wanted, and while I was here, I was insulated from Wendell's mind games. Eventually I'd reach the end of Wendell's patience, and he'd start listening to Joel. Until then, I had everything I needed.

The blue team leader, a big guy named Smith, offered to get me anything I needed to be comfortable in the apartment. I ordered a plush mattress and a leather couch for gaming. When they charged me three thousand credits, I had an idea.

The security team cost me sixty thousand for two weeks. Wendell had smashed my computer and camera. My new phone had disappeared. It wasn't the cost of all that stuff, but the violation that irked me. Wendell had crossed the line, and it was time for him to feel the pinch.

His accounts held ninety-five thousand credits. I bounced sixty-five thousand around a few times and landed them in a few accounts the cops hadn't discovered yet. The remaining thirty-five went to some people Wendell despised. The National Rifle Association. The Tea Party. Westboro Baptist Church. I made sure the credits were filtered clean so he couldn't ask for them back, but I offered his name and address so the charities could send a thank you. No doubt they would for such large donations.

I tried playing a deathmatch while I waited for something to happen downstairs, but I couldn't play and watch my captors at the same time. Once

I got killed a few times, I gave up and turned my full attention to the teachers downstairs. A little after noon the call came. Wendell pulled the tufts of hair on each side of his head and paced feverishly. At one point he looked right into the camera with more anger than I thought the little guy capable of. If I didn't have the security team in place, he might have stormed upstairs and attacked me.

"What's wrong?" Charlotte asked.

Joel and the cab driver had seen plenty of psychological games. Most of them crafted by Wendell. I couldn't tell if they saw the justice in what I'd done or if they simply didn't care. But the two men waited calmly for orders while Wendell suffered in the little prison I built inside his personal life.

Only one person exerted that much pressure on Wendell, and I knew just how things had gone down. Wendell's wife had gone to a fancy lunch, showing off her status by over ordering for the entire table. When the bill came, her credit was refused, and she was embarrassed in front of her friends. She mercilessly screamed at her husband over the phone, and when he tried to fix the problem, the news got worse. He was broke and nothing was going to fix his credit problem today. He'd have to live paycheck to paycheck, like those people he pretended to help.

He wanted to strangle me. Luckily, the little dweeb had no way to get within reach.

Chapter Twenty-Two

Wendell had connections in Govbank. He could make a thousand credits disappear from my account with a single call, but he couldn't get credits restored in his own account. The opportunity for abuse was too tempting, so he had to report fraud on his account like anyone else who'd been hacked. The person on the other end of his call got an earful, but no matter how much he yelled, procedures had to be followed and that took time. He paced and screamed at the empty monitors between calls. Eventually his stress plateaued and it was time to let him suffer while I used the distraction to my advantage.

The first order of business was to let my lessons teach me about my reeducation team. I settled on the old couch with my camera pointed at the screen and turned the television and the black box on at once.

The camera recorded my avatar entering the schoolyard. The same little boy dropped his phone, and I immediately picked it up. He moved away so fast my avatar could barely keep up. Wendell had upped the difficulty after I destroyed the first black box. The boy stopped near a basketball hoop, and I ran circles around him. He didn't lash out or start trouble. In a few seconds, he started wandering the blacktop with his head down.

Another thing changed. Other kids started dropping things, too. I scooped it all up and ran circles around the klutzy kids. They didn't challenge me to get their stuff back. They took their losses silently, waiting for the bell then heading for the classroom.

"Give the stuff to the teacher," Koch said.

"Ever seen so many elementary school kids with cell phones?"

Koch shook off my joke. Thirty thousand credits seemed steep, but apparently Koch had done this a few times. When I indicated the camera beside me on the couch, he knew exactly what I was doing.

The lesson led from the playground to the classroom no matter how many kids I punched and tripped along the way. Once inside, I didn't wait for chaos to ensue. My avatar attacked with punches that had no effect. When the other kid mounted his counterattack, my character was doomed.

I stopped the recording while miniature Wendell scolded me for failing my lesson. This time I didn't give Wendell a chance to steal my memory card before I checked out the video. A small slot on the side of the computer received the memory card and soon the video played back in slow motion.

"There's one," Koch said from over my shoulder.

"Pretty good at this, aren't you?" I asked, and stopped the video on the single frame that had been spliced into the game.

"It's important to know who we're up against."

Red flowing hair surrounded a smiling face. We didn't save Charlotte's picture. None of us had trouble recognizing her. The carpenter appeared without his toolbox and overalls. The bearded cab driver appeared behind the wheel of his cab, an arm extended welcomingly. Two men rounded out the subliminal images. A thin white guy in a suit who looked completely unremarkable. Brown hair. Plain features. An average but not muscular build. At the end of the video, an Indian man faced us with a critical eye. His dark blue shirt resembled a uniform without official badges or patches.

A soft knock drew Winchester to the door.

"Hang on a sec," I said with my hand up.

Instead of answering the door, Winchester came to see the photos. Very likely the face on the other side of the door was pictured on my screen.

"Looks like he wants you to trust all of them except maybe this last guy. Experience says you'll probably meet them in the order they were spliced into the video," Winchester said.

I shut the laptop. Winchester covered the black box and answered the door. Charlotte took two tentative steps forward. Winchester pulled her further in and out of the way then Koch rushed out behind her with his gun extended, covering the hall.

He said, "Clear," then came back in.

"Leave your coat and your purse on the couch," Winchester ordered.

She peeled off her coat revealing a form-fitting black sweater above her snug blue jeans. Koch patted her ankles for a weapon and worked his way up, but not far enough to be positive she was unarmed. She took her keys and left her purse on top of her coat.

Koch put out his hand before letting her pass. She feigned ignorance and Koch stopped her. "The red button is designed for him, but it won't do anything to us. It's useless here." He pulled the keys from her grasp then showed me the button on her keys and a matching button built into the side of her smartphone.

She backed away in awe of Koch's knowledge. She was so glad to get away from my bodyguards that she followed me to the bedroom where a listening device in her coat or purse couldn't pick up our conversation.

I moved the pillow and leaned back against the headboard. She refused my invitation to sit farther down the bed and measured me from the middle of the room instead.

"Thanks for coming. It's always a pleasure to see you." My eyes wandered the length of her figure. The tight-fitting clothes had been chosen to keep my attention. Obvious as Wendell's attempt to manipulate me was, I couldn't fight my attraction to Charlotte whether she wore tight sexy jeans or a Disney poncho.

"What's with the goons out front?" she asked.

"I'm tired of being on Candid Camera."

"Smart. Your father taught you well."

I didn't answer.

"When's the last time you went out west to see him?"

"I didn't say he was out west." Most of the country was west of Massachusetts, so it wasn't a bad ploy, just not one I was going to fall for.

She turned her head away and took a step toward the foot of the bed.

"DNA wasn't helpful. Was it?"

"We're still processing."

If they'd gotten a match, it would have come back quickly. My tweaks to the database had worked. I'd run my own sample to be sure. "Don't waste your time."

"You want me off your case?"

"I'm not a fan of being manipulated, but I like having you around. Let's give up this reeducation thing and get to know each other."

"We can't do that."

"Of course we can. Keep me here two more weeks. Pronounce me cured and we all go back to our lives."

"That won't help you."

"Look around. Do you think you can help me?"

She turned toward the closed door. The armed men beyond put me in control no matter what the court had ordered. Wendell was so swamped with his personal problems, he sent Charlotte up to be my prisoner with no supervision or backup. She hid her vulnerability well, but we both knew she shouldn't have been alone in that room with me.

"How long do you think Wendell will let me keep you?"

"That was nasty what you did to him."

"What did I do?"

"Emptied his account. His wife is furious."

"I'm a helpless prisoner. How could I do that?"

"It's not funny." She opened the door to leave, but didn't step over the threshold.

I couldn't see around the corner, but her pleading eyes told me Winchester or Koch was out there blocking the hall.

She closed the door quietly and turned back to me. "He's been under a lot of pressure. You're going to give him heart failure."

"Tell him to get off my back and pass me out of this course. You get paid. I go home. We can all be friends."

"Three weeks ago he would have let you. But not now."

"What's changed?"

"It doesn't matter. You need to complete the program or eventually you're going to wind up," she hesitated for a long time looking for words, "back in court."

"You mean rapidly dissolving in a pool of acid."

She gasped and fell back against the door. The acid bath was the most closely guarded secret in reeducation after the Plexiglass box. She couldn't hide her shock and couldn't help flashing a look at the window, measuring her chances of getting out by hurling herself through the glass.

"If I wanted to hurt you, I would have cuffed you when you came in."

The mention of cuffs didn't relax her a bit.

"Wendell himself said recidivism is one percent. Hardened criminals are disappearing at an alarming rate. You think we wouldn't figure out what you're doing to them?"

"Are you here to destroy reeducation?"

"Hardly. Those guys are outside to keep me breathing. That's all."

"Why didn't you follow your program? That would have been a lot easier." She relaxed slightly, but stayed within reach of the door.

"I heard a rumor that Wendell's on the brink."

She swallowed hard and I knew she was as scared as Wendell.

"He killed his own son in the program," I said. "After that he hasn't been able to terminate anyone. Your team helped some people, but you also let some hardened criminals walk. A few are getting into real trouble. That's the word on the street."

"Who told you that?"

I pointed toward the kitchen.

"That doesn't have anything to do with you."

"I don't want to end up in acid so Wendell can prove he can terminate a relearner when he has to."

"So why are you acting like an ass? You should've..." She trailed off. I'd pushed her hard. Being in that room with me, knowing what I knew, she was afraid to speak her mind.

I stood up from the bed and took a small step toward her. "I want to help." I moved a step closer, resisting the urge to wrap my arms around her or soothe her with a hand on her arm. "Tell me what I can do to take the pressure off and get out of here with my skin."

She looked through me, terrified she wouldn't get out. "You should do your lessons."

"We both know that's not going to cut it."

I stepped around, opened the door, and led her out. Her pace quickened down the hall, and I heard her sigh when Winchester and Koch stepped aside and let her into the living room. "You want to take a minute to decompress before going back to the office?" I asked.

She rubbed her arms, warming herself. She noticed the new couch and the plasma TV, but didn't comment.

"I've got some strawberry rhubarb pie." Mention of the pie wiped away any questions she had about my fancy television.

"Strawberry rhubarb?"

"It's my favorite," I said. "The woman next to my parents used to grow rhubarb every year. She was always giving it away. You like it?"

"Love it." She'd loosened up after leaving the confines of the bedroom, but she didn't stay any longer than she had to. She took a longing look at the kitchen table, then a harsher look at me.

I could tell she was trying to figure out whether I knew strawberry rhubarb was her favorite. I'd done my homework well, and I wasn't about to tell her where my insights came from.

She waved me off, choosing the safety of the hall over her favorite dessert.

"Take it," I said, pulling the pie from the fridge.

When she left with the pie, I turned on the view of the control room downstairs. If she ate a slice, I had her trust and eventually I'd get what I wanted.

Chapter Twenty-three

"I've never been down here so much," Joel said through my computer speaker. He stood out of frame, talking to Wendell who sat with dark computer screens behind him.

"That can't be helped," Wendell barked. He tapped his fingers in a repeating cascade on the countertop. How much of his anxiety stemmed from his financial crisis and how much from his lack of control over me wasn't clear. But Joel's tweaking aggravated him for sure.

"We shouldn't be letting him hole up like this."

"Why don't you go tell his goons to get lost?" Wendell snapped.

Joel was right. It was Wendell's job to clear the way for the team to work, but he wasn't up to the challenge. I couldn't blame him for backing down from Winchester and Koch, though. I hired them to intimidate the reeducation team, and I certainly got my money's worth.

"Why is she the only one who gets to go up?" Joel asked. "He likes me. It's you that annoys him."

"He asked for her by name," Wendell said.

"With that hair and those tight little buns, she could move in if she wanted. If you want to go up and have a gun pointed in your face, be my guest." I didn't recognize the man's voice, but he crossed in front of the camera and asked for an update on the situation. I assumed he'd just walked in.

"Nothing yet, Nathan," Wendell said.

I found his face in the images from my lesson and labeled it. In the background, I heard Charlotte walk in to a rousing greeting from the three men. They chided her about getting gifts from me, but it only took a moment for her to send Joel and Nathan into the other room with the pie. For a group of psychological manipulators, they weren't very smart. They'd drugged my Coke in the diner. Why wouldn't I put something in the pie to retaliate? If I had, I could have gone down there and taken over as soon as they'd all had a piece.

When the two guys left the room with the pie, Wendell asked if she had any luck placing a new camera. "It's futile," she said. "They took my purse the moment I walked in."

"You were up there a while. Any ideas?"

"Maybe."

Her trepidation came right through the camera. Wendell spotted it immediately. "You don't like this one, do you?"

"He's a little spooky."

"We knew he was a genius. Know anyone else who received a Ph.D. at fifteen?"

"It's more than that. He doesn't show up in our DNA database. He finds our cameras minutes after we install them. He's more in control of his program than we are. It's not supposed to be like this. We're not going to accomplish anything if we don't turn it around," she said.

"You want to punt?" Wendell didn't wait for the answer he was afraid of. "Early on I would have agreed, but now is not the time to give up."

"He hired armed thugs. No one is going to blame us for flushing him."

The words hit hard. In the car after dinner I'd considered going in for a kiss. She seemed to be warming up to me. Then she came to my place in spite of the armed guards and stayed while she was defenseless. Ten minutes later, she told her boss it'd be best to throw me out with the trash. It was one thing when a woman refused a second date, but when she condemned you to die, that hurt.

"Think about how this will look after our last three cases," Wendell said. "We need to show we're worth our fees or we're in real trouble."

The gossip painted Wendell as an egotistical, liberal bastard who would push his team to extremes to save even the most ruthless relearner. He didn't care how much he spent or whose life he risked, but down in that room I saw a completely different guy. He dealt with Charlotte as an equal, and the program he created for me was far from extreme. Either the gossip was disinformation coming out of the Agency to scare relearners straight, or something about Wendell had changed.

"We should call—"

"We're not calling," Wendell cut her off. "As of now we have zero we can use. We've got to come up with something before we open our records to anyone."

"Maybe we can put him to work helping us the way we did with..." Charlotte trailed off nervously.

"You can say his name, Charlotte."

"Jordan practically volunteered to help the same way *Michael* did." The name caught in her throat, and she watched Wendell for a sign it was okay to continue. "Those guys he's got upstairs have heard about our problems. Jordan thinks if he helps us, we'll release him."

"Couldn't hurt." Wendell scratched his chin, ruminating on the details without speaking them aloud.

"It's the Farnsworth rouse all over again," she said. "He thinks he's helping us, doing the right thing. Only this time he really is helping us. At the very least we'll get something we can use for our report when he goes outside."

Wendell asked how fast they could put something together, and the two of them moved off camera.

Chapter Twenty-four

"How was the pie?" I asked.

"Good." She flashed a broad smile that wasn't worth much because she'd proven herself a virtuoso in the art of telling lies big and small.

Winchester folded her coat and took her purse while Koch checked her ankles for weapons. His position gave him license to explore, but he chose to eyeball the tight jeans and sweater rather than give her a more intimate pat down. Her clothes couldn't have concealed much more than the slim folder in her hand.

We started down the hall, but Winchester stopped us. He came around the couch and ordered Charlotte to spread her arms to her sides then waved the wand two inches from her, starting at her high-heeled boots and rolling upward with her curves. The red light went solid near her throat and Winchester removed a tiny camera woven into the collar of her sweater. It was so small that we never would have found it without the wand.

"That guy never gives up," Winchester said.

When he let her go and we'd taken a few steps down the hall, I said, "Bold of you to eat the pie considering what you've done to me so far."

The thought seemed to hit her for the first time. She recovered quickly, "Attacking a reeducation counselor is a zero tolerance crime. If you drugged us, you'd be toast."

"Always euphemisms. You guys never talk about the end, do you?"

She walked inside the bedroom and resumed her post by the wall. I reclined against the headboard, eager for her proposition.

"How is this all going to end?" I asked.

"Depends on how much you help us."

"You've got orders in that folder?"

"You volunteered, Jordan. Unless I misunderstood."

"I want to stay alive. If helping you means you'll set me free, then that's exactly what I'm going to do."

Charlotte glanced around the room. The place was clean of microphones and cameras. Her loyalty was to the program, but there was a hint of guilt in her unease. She wanted to tell the truth, but that would have been counterproductive.

"So far you are a spectacular failure."

I asked why she didn't simply fail me out of the program, but she wouldn't answer.

"I can't make any promises," she said. "It's not up to me. But if you help us, my report will be favorable and that usually means you'll be released."

"Usually?"

"It's not my decision. I can't set you free."

"Relax." Charlotte and Wendell were supposed to determine how I behaved under pressure. Stress was the only true way to discover how someone would act when no one was looking. Judging by the red blotch on her neck, Charlotte was under far more pressure than I was. Wendell had almost reached his breaking point when his available credits hit zero and his wife wouldn't stop harping on him until their credit was restored.

I needed them to hold it together a few days longer. If they didn't, I would have been gutted by the sharp end of the stick.

I patted the bed beside me. "Show me what you brought."

The first sheet in her folder was a color photo of a young guy in a hooded sweatshirt. Not a mug shot, but it looked posed. According to Charlotte, it was taken during reeducation.

"What did this guy do?"

"He's a drug dealer."

"Still? He's on the dole, isn't he?"

"It's not about the money for this guy. He thinks everyone should be snorting cocaine or shooting heroin."

She showed me a map with his apartment and a few regular haunts highlighted. The park and the bars he frequented were all in a ten-block radius that lay a short walk from my apartment. The tiny area so close by troubled me, but I didn't let on. It could have been his territory or maybe the guy couldn't drive. Either way he'd be easy to locate. What to do after finding him was the bigger problem.

"So he's still dealing drugs, and that's a big problem for you?"

"The cops are closing in. If they catch him, we're going to have to go up for review. They could shut us down."

"What do you want me to do?"

"Scare him. Do anything you can to stop him from dealing."

Not an easy assignment. If reeducation couldn't reform this guy, how was I supposed to stop him from dealing drugs while I was being monitored every step of the way? Wendell and his crew had complete control of their subjects. All they had given me was a face and a map.

I took the folder from Charlotte and put it behind us on the bed, bracing myself with my left hand behind her back. I squeezed above her knee with my right and my body responded like a sports car when its accelerator has been punched.

"This isn't going to be easy," I said. "And if I fix this, it means you keep your job."

She grabbed my hand the second it started climbing toward her thigh, taking it off her knee completely and dropping it on my lap. She pivoted toward the edge of the bed, not getting up, but signaling she wasn't getting cozy no matter how important this job was.

"It's very important work you do," I said.

Wendell wouldn't employ a number two who wasn't maniacal about helping people. She carried a hint of superiority in her eye, because she believed she had something valuable to teach me. It was a cause more than a job for her. That's the only reason anyone worked anymore.

I leaned in and whispered. "You're very brave to be locked in here without the red button. Your parents must be proud."

The shock disarmed her. She turned to meet me and I covered her lips with mine. She rose in protest, but I was above her, blocking her back toward the bed, pushing her with my dead weight until her knees buckled and she collapsed backward.

I let her breathe and pinned her arms to the bed, my weight pressing down. "We can't do this," she said urgently.

I kissed her again. "No cameras." And again. "No one needs to know."

"Stop."

"You know you need this." I raised my head from hers, contradicting my insistent words. "You never date. You only meet dweeby intellectuals and lowlife criminals. I'm neither."

She stopped fighting for a second, and I traced my right hand up her arm and found her tight little breast.

I kissed her again and she returned my passion for a moment before recovering and pushing me away.

She crawled off the bed and stood, smoothing her sweater with an intense look in her eyes that could have been hatred or passion. Maybe a mix of both.

"I'll be here when you change your mind."

She pointed to the crumpled folder. "Your mind should be on that."

"If I take care of this, I'll be expecting another visit."

"Don't hold your breath." She opened the door and showed herself out.

Chapter Twenty-five

"What happened up there?" Joel demanded.

"She's coming out now. We'll ask when she gets here," Wendell said.

Joel hated being sidelined. If he couldn't be upstairs, he wanted to see what was happening. He complained that they couldn't eavesdrop on my web browsing and telephone calls. That they didn't have a single camera in my place except the one in the black box—and that one stayed covered most of the time.

"She'll be here in a minute," Farnsworth said.

Winchester tapped me on the shoulder. "It is strange." When I gestured for him to explain he said, "Usually they make a move when we get involved. We've brought their program to a halt and they're sitting on their hands."

"They are burning a lot of credits on me. I've been here four days and all I've done is run the simulation twice." I chuckled out loud. "And I kicked the crap out of those school kids."

"They won't wait much longer," Winchester said. "They'll need to submit their first report soon if they want to get paid."

Winchester knew even more about the reeducation system than Koch. The four men protecting me were experts in technology, weapons, and the inner-workings of the new criminal justice system. Winchester told me they'd never run up against Wendell Cummings before, but his role as the father of reeducation was legendary. If anyone had a trick sneaky enough to outsmart Winchester and Koch, Wendell was the guy.

"What do you expect him to do?"

"The first thing they usually do is send in the goon squad."

"Like you guys, but in black Suburbans?"

"They're nothing like us. They're leftover dopes from the old SWAT teams who can't win a fight unless it's six to one."

"And that's exactly how many guys ride around in those whisper wagons," Koch added. The big SUVs ran on electric power around the city, moving with barely a sound until their tires screeched. A huge contradiction to their immense proportions.

"They're mean bastards who enjoy beating people. Show him your scar, Koch."

Koch bent down and spread his fingers along a six-inch scar he received from a baton. He said they were scared of him so they beat him until he couldn't fight back. Koch got level 2 reeducation. The goon with the baton walked away to beat someone else.

"You're safe as long as you're in here," Koch said.

I didn't get a chance to tell him I was leaving, because Charlotte appeared on screen and we all stopped to watch her join the conversation downstairs.

"No luck bugging the place?" Nathan asked.

Joel jumped to answer. "They've got a wand that detects the signal. We wove the camera into her sweater. It was completely invisible and the big guy up there found it in less than a minute."

"So we're basically screwed," Nathan said.

"Let Charlotte tell us what happened." Wendell's fidgeting made him look much more nervous than his voice sounded.

"Jordan wants to help. He took the folder, and I think he'll get started right away." She didn't mention being pinned to the bed, probably because Wendell couldn't handle the stress. That didn't surprise me, but I was impressed that she didn't seem flustered. Maybe other relearners had tried the same thing, but then she had her little red button to stop them cold. Dealing with me was a whole new level of vulnerability. Wendell would have been proud if he knew, but he treated Charlotte like a daughter. He would have lost control had he known I pinned her down and kissed her against her will, even if she wasn't exactly fighting to get away.

"What is he going to do in a day or two to stop Mandla from selling drugs?" The insubordination in Joel's tone reverberated all the way upstairs.

"This will get him outside. At the very least, we'll get something for our seven day. Otherwise the thing will be complete fiction," Wendell said. His tone hardened when he spoke to Joel.

"We should have flushed him two days ago. This assignment of Charlotte's is a waste of time." Joel crossed his arms and stepped from view.

Wendell pointed a finger across the grainy screen and jumped up more angrily than we'd seen him act all week.

The discussion degenerated into a shouting match. Winchester and Koch enjoyed it for a minute, but then looked at me gravely. "You know flushed means dipped in the acid, right?" Winchester asked. I nodded, and he said, "That guy is no friend of yours. Watch yourself around him. Don't give him anything he can send up the chain without Wendell knowing."

They asked about my assignment, and I showed them the photo and the map. They offered to send someone to beat the crap out of this Mandla guy. Break his legs so he couldn't sell drugs for months. The point of the exercise was for me to prove myself worthy. Hiring thugs didn't prove anything about my character. It was time for me to get my hands dirty.

Koch brought me a holster and a .45 from one of the cases and helped me clip the gun on my belt. He reminded me to keep my jacket over it and to stay out of any place with a metal detector. Walking into a secured building would bring the black bats faster than my team could swoop in and pick me up.

"Forget her. She's evil," Winchester said. "Keep your eye on the ball."

The comment came out of nowhere, but Winchester was right on the money. I couldn't pretend I wasn't hot for Charlotte. She had a master's degree in psychology, and she knew exactly how to help a guy become a complete citizen, but none of that mattered to me. Her coy attitude and her sexy little body were irresistible. I knew she was playing me and still I couldn't help myself.

The Cat Bagger's Apprentice

"These people are sick," Koch said. "Whatever she told you, it's a trick. It's always a trick."

Winchester looked plaintive. "You don't have much choice. If you don't start playing ball, they're going to send fifty guys in here to drag you out. Once you leave, you're on their turf. Watch yourself every second."

After hearing Joel, I knew I was on the edge. The only people between me and the acid were Wendell and Charlotte. Destroying their cameras, hiding away in my room, and attacking Charlotte the way I did, I asked for trouble. Winchester and Koch told me I was lucky. That if Wendell wasn't so far off his game, I'd be dead already.

The only way out for me was to go outside and let Wendell get video for his report.

Koch patted the gun through my jacket. "This won't stop a carload of black bats. If you see a whisper wagon, disappear."

Winchester nodded toward my feet, and I lifted the leg of my jeans so he could see my ankle bracelet. He nodded his approval, and the two of them slipped outside to make sure no one ambushed me when I went out to find the guy in the photo. They'd track my ankle bracelet and stay close by, but they had to stay out of sight so I appeared to be doing this on my own.

Chapter Twenty-six

Charlotte stepped away from the others clustered around the monitors to look at a text that had just come in. She set the toolbox on the floor and sat down in the corner.

You okay? I heard there was trouble. The message came from Sixteen. A man she'd never seen and only knew as a shadowy figure atop the Agency. He may have been Forty-three's boss. It made sense that the lower the number, the closer to the top the person was.

Did Joel call you?

Never mind how I know. Are you okay? I'm hearing that this guy isn't cooperating.

I'm fine.

We knew Jordan would be a tough nut. He's very smart. But we don't want another embarrassment. Your numbers can't drop any lower.

We who?

Forty-three and I.

We'll take care of him.

Take care of yourself, too.

Sure.

We care about you, Charlotte. I care about you.

You don't know me.

I know you better than you can imagine and I want you to succeed. Don't be afraid to ask for help.

Okay.

One more thing?

Sure.

Keep an eye on Wendell for me. I hear he's having a really tough time since Michael.

He is.

Help keep things together. If you feel like he's not going to make it on this one, let me help. Don't let him go down alone.

She didn't answer the last message, but she didn't have to. She was already doing everything she could to help Wendell get through and that wasn't going to change.

Chapter Twenty-Seven

The New England chill hit me on the concrete landing. The streetlights lit islands of pavement along Centre Street, and in the murk, Winchester held a short rifle low against the hood of a dark van. My footsteps on the path drew Koch from behind a sedan fifty yards down on the opposite side of the street. He popped his head up and watched while I turned on the sidewalk and walked north, swiveling his head north and south to watch for an arriving intercept.

Koch's intensity troubled me. Their rush outside to clear the way ahead had seemed like a formality earlier, but their staggered position prepared them to shoot an approaching car from both sides, denying a carload of attackers any cover.

I slipped my hand to my waist and felt the pistol clipped to my belt. I'd fired a few times on the shooting range, but didn't have the skills for a firefight, so the gun didn't give me as much comfort as it would a trained marksman. Winchester and Koch had fetched assault rifles because they expected trouble and that put me on edge. Any moment, a black Suburban could stop and send half a dozen uniformed men rushing to pummel me.

Nothing we saw on the spy camera hinted that Wendell wanted me dead, but when I saw the cab parked in the usual spot near the fence, I headed over. I knew who was inside and that he'd trick me into doing Wendell's bidding, but I wanted off the street no matter how bad a strategy letting the cabbie dictate my moves might have been.

The "off duty" light was lit, and the bearded driver gnawed a thick sub sandwich. I tapped the glass anyway. "Got a minute for a quick ride?"

He thumbed toward the back, and I climbed in.

The thick partition between us calmed my nerves. Wendell could have outfitted the cab with poisonous gas or any number of weapons in back, but it didn't fit. Wendell wanted everyone to pass reeducation. That's why he had problems with guys like the drug dealer I was tracking. If the cabbie decided to take matters into his own hands, he'd have to find a weapon he could use through the narrow opening passengers used to press their thumbs to the scanner. Highly unlikely he'd try that sort of an attack with me seated behind him.

I relaxed into the seat and waited while the cabby finished chewing.

"Where are you headed?" he asked.

"Nowhere special. Just needed some fresh air." His face was the third image spliced into my black box lesson. If I hadn't known that, his reluctance to talk with his mouth full and his perfect diction would have been clues that he was too polished to work as a cab driver, especially in a world where good jobs went unfilled for lack of interest.

The cabbie knew about the mission to find Mandla and stop him from selling drugs. If I'd asked straight out, he probably would have told me where to find him, but I wanted to keep the appearance that I was struggling to find this rogue relearner on my own.

"Hungry?"

When I said I was, he told me about a great little pizza place called Katie's on Lagrange and Centre. My answer was a formality. He had the car in drive and started rolling south before I agreed to go.

Koch slipped between cars as we passed, ready to cross the street in our wake. The cabbie saw him, but tried to hide his interest by facing forward.

I shimmied over to the center and came eye to eye with the driver when he checked the rearview for Koch. He shifted to the outer mirror, constantly switching from the mirror to the road and back to try and spot him.

"Something wrong?" I turned behind us and saw Koch join Winchester at the van. They didn't follow us right away, and I didn't do anything more to distract the cabbie.

He didn't bother answering, just drove along and made a U-turn half a block beyond Lagrange. The trip took less than five minutes, a straight shot four blocks down Centre Street. Even though it was obvious I could walk home, I asked the best way back to my apartment. He said he was usually on Centre Street and that he'd try to stick around and give me a lift when I was ready. We both knew he'd follow me, probably by a tracking monitor hidden in the cab.

I didn't mind at all. Worried as I was about the black bats showing up, I needed a place to run. With my ankle bracelet on and Wendell's team following me, I was in strict compliance with my program. That made the back seat of the cab a safety zone, like gools when we played tag as kids.

The cabbie parked at a meter a hundred feet short of Katie's, behind the only car parked on that side of the street. The distant spot gave him a clear view of the door, so I couldn't slip out behind him. That meant he'd be there when I finished. It also alerted me that Centre Street was deserted. The only people I'd seen for four blocks were connected to my program. I searched the far curbs for the dark van, but couldn't spot my protectors, probably because there were no vehicles for them to blend in with.

On the opposite side of the street, a solitary figure waited outside the liquor store in a wash of neon colors advertising American beers. He was too far away to make out his features, but he was the only other person on the sidewalk. By his height and slim build, I guessed he was Nathan Farnsworth. Nathan had a brother in the reeducation game who had a reputation for being a decent guy. Nathan was ruthless to relearners and staff alike. More than likely Nathan was either step two in the process of finding the dealer or stationed there to catch me if I tried to run. The pizza joint was step one, so I grabbed the metal door handle and swung inside.

The scanner by the door picked up my ankle bracelet and let out three high tones. It paused a moment then sounded two more, one high and one low. The "all clear" signal would have mattered more if the place had a few customers to react. The densely stubbled guy behind the counter had summed me up before he heard the tones. He was close to Wendell's building and had lots of relearners in. Probably why his restaurant was so empty. Citizens avoided relearners whenever possible, so it wouldn't have been a stretch to learn that the guy behind the counter was part of my program, too. Apparently, he needed the revenue.

The one customer in the place was the least supportive member of my reeducation team. "Small world," he said as I passed his table.

I ordered a chicken parmesan sub and waited at the counter while I thought about what to say when I sat down.

The cook laid the chicken on my bun bare-handed. I wondered what he'd been doing before making it, and what kind of germs he'd transferred onto my sandwich, but I had bigger problems than his dirty hands. His speedy work left me little time to prepare to meet an unfriendly guide.

The counselor made a show of crossing his heavy work boots on top of the empty chair at his table. Dust dropped off and coated the seat. He sipped from a straw then crossed his arms facing the glass door with his back to me. Most of Wendell's people operated like Charlotte and the cabbie, nudging me in the right direction no matter what I did. They wanted me to complete my mission. But as I approached the square table, I knew to choose my words carefully.

The carpenter couldn't hide his disdain. His private heart wanted me flushed. Disposed of. I couldn't trust anything he said, but he was the first guide on my quest, and the way to freedom ran through his square table.

I stood looking at him several seconds before he acknowledged me.

He lowered his feet and pointed to the chair. "Go ahead," he said. "You came this far."

Chapter Twenty-eight

Joel watched me eat the first three bites of my sub with his arms crossed, lips tight. Neither of us said anything until he pushed his chair back two inches. The scraping vibration of wood against tile signaled trouble. I was back in the simulation classroom again with the kids about to attack, but the stakes were much higher in the outside world. The conversation was being recorded, and since I hadn't been out of my apartment in days, whoever was tasked with judging me would surely see these moments.

"Got any advice? I could use the help," I said.

"You want my help? After what you did?" Joel snarled to provoke me.

Any film that made it to my jury would be heavily edited. If I incriminated myself, or showed any hostility, those snippets would be displayed for all to see. Joel's prompting would be clipped from the footage, leaving me looking unhinged when I responded to antagonism my jury didn't see. I committed myself to remaining calm no matter what.

"I'm trying to help," I said.

"Help? Is that why you hired those goons? And drained Wendell's credits? You're trying to run this program into the ground. You don't deserve my help. And you're certainly not getting it."

"I'm not running anything into the ground. I'm a rat in a maze. Trying to do my part and get out of jail alive."

Joel didn't care about my problems. "You're not in jail. You're in reeducation." He snarled every word.

"You're right. Jail's easier. In jail you can see the walls."

Joel stood up to leave.

"You going to tell me where I can find Mandla?"

"Not my job," he said, coming around to my side of the table.

The program was structured like the simulation. If I didn't learn what Joel had to teach me, I couldn't pass. There was no second chance in this live lesson, and Joel didn't give me a single clue about what he had to offer. I had two minutes before he walked out the door and left me with a key component of my mission lost forever.

Light gleamed off a metal tube in his shirt pocket. Too big to be a pen. Too thin to be a cigar case. "What's that in your pocket?"

Disappointment sagged across his face. He shoved the tube at me with his left hand. When I touched it, he punched me with his right, snapping my head over the back of my chair. The seat tipped back until my body lay horizontal. My toes caught the lip of the table and held me teetering for an instant. When Joel saw my fragile recovery, he swept his foot around the back leg of my chair. The seat instantly flattened, and I went down hard, smacking my head on the tiles. The guy behind the counter gasped in shock, but didn't come around to help.

Joel stood over me with his legs straight. My aching head begged me to jam my foot below his knee and snap a ligament or two, but I had the slim camera in my hand and that was all I needed from him. I gestured to the security camera over the cash register with both hands, asking Wendell why he let this happen. Certainly he was watching in real time. Such brutality shouldn't have been allowed, but Joel wouldn't be disciplined.

"You're smart, but you're not going to make it," Joel said. "Our program is on the edge because of assholes like you. No way you pass reeducation. I'm going to make sure you get flushed."

"What about this Mandla guy?"

"He's your problem," Joel said and walked out.

He muttered something before he slammed the door. The guy behind the counter wiped his hands on his apron and looked across the dining room as I righted my chair and rubbed the back of my head.

"You okay?"

Seemed like another test. Could I keep my composure and be civil to the cook after being slugged?

I buried the camera in my palm and eased over to the counter. "I'm fine. My friend gets a little excited."

"Not a very good friend."

"I've got another friend I'm looking for. Name's Mandla. He's about five seven. Dark skin. Sells recreational pharmaceuticals."

He raised a finger. "There are others—"

"I'm not looking for drugs. Just my friend."

The cook apologized and let the conversation drop, but he sized me up, trying to figure out if I was an undercover cop out to make a bust. Clearly he wasn't part of my reeducation. He was one of the few real people I met, and if I'd had time, I would have been glad to spend a few minutes talking to someone who didn't have it in for me.

I left the pizza place with one hand holding my jaw, the other holding the camera. The cab waited in the same spot, the cabbie giving no indication which way Joel had gone, not that it would have helped to follow him. Farnsworth stood in the shadows on the far corner, and I crossed over to the liquor store to join him.

"Tough night?" he asked.

I waggled the camera.

"I heard. Nice work getting that out of him."

His earpiece was too tiny to spot, but it was no surprise the whole team was listening in no matter where I went or which team member I encountered. When you talked to one of these sadistic actors, you talked to them all. Sometimes live. Sometimes recorded. But everything you said was gobbled up by the voyeurs who tracked you day and night.

"How does this work?" I asked, extending the camera.

Farnsworth cooperated immediately. The button on the shaft started and stopped recording on a continual loop. A red light flashed when the camera started recording. The little device would hold an hour of sound and video then it would start overwriting the earliest part of the recording.

The Cat Bagger's Apprentice

"So I'm supposed to catch this guy in the act? I don't know anything about drugs. How will I know I've got what I need?"

Farnsworth told me there were two things that would sink Mandla. A marijuana conviction wouldn't do. I needed to film him passing hard drugs or gift cards.

"Gift cards? Don't they lead straight to the person who bought them?"

Farnsworth grinned at my naivety and told me that soon after credits were implemented, savvy store owners became the new money launderers. They sold a few gift cards to each manager in the city stores. The managers never took the cards. So when a customer purchased a gift card, he received the card purchased by a customer three or four cards earlier. When the cops tried connecting buyers with dealers, the data was complete nonsense. The stores enjoyed the protection of the dealers and did a brisk grocery and alcohol business besides.

"So all I need to do is find him and capture him exchanging drugs for gift cards? Then I'll be free?"

"That's not up to me. Find him, video him, then go home and let us know you've got it. Someone will pick up the camera."

I thanked him and he said, "Good luck," but our conversation wasn't over. He unclipped a microphone from his collar, dropped it into his glove, and cupped the glove in his hands to muffle the sound.

"Don't blame Joel. He's not a bad guy."

"I appreciate your help. Without it I would have been stuck."

"No problem. If you cross the park," he pointed diagonally across the intersection to a dark expanse of trees and what I assumed was grass beyond, "you'll probably find him hanging around the tennis courts. There are a few stores across the street he frequents."

Anything in reeducation can be an illusion, but I knew Joel wanted me flushed and that Nathan was gunning for Wendell's job. I wanted to believe I had it figured, but my foster father always said, "When you think you've got something mastered, that's when it jumps up and bites you." Those words had saved me lots of pain over the years, and that's why I stood and sized up Nathan Farnsworth a bit longer.

"Can I ask you a question?" Nathan said when I lingered.

I gestured for him to go ahead, and he said, "None of us believe you're going to go straight. You're a smart guy and you're making huge money on the outside helping people dodge taxes. It must have taken years to figure out your system because even now they can't figure out how you are hacking the database."

"Is that a question?"

"If you're that good, and you're making that much money, why not fly along through reeducation and get back to your life?"

"If you knew me, you'd know."

"This isn't extreme skateboarding. This thing will eat you alive."

"It's a rush, isn't it?"

"You're lucky you're not already dead."

Finally someone said it. "I'll be okay. Don't worry."

"You're out of your mind."

"Seems that way, doesn't it?" He wanted to say something, but I cut him off. "You've been a huge help. Now excuse me while I catch a bad guy."

He couldn't raise his voice when I walked away. All he could do was watch me cross the intersection toward the park. I was glad for his help no matter what his intentions.

Chapter Twenty-nine

The lights on Billings Field stayed dark in late fall, making the seven-acre park a haven for underage drinking, car dates, and drug deals. The ring of trees provided shade to baseball spectators in summer. During the fall months, the clusters of branches blocked enough light to throw the field into shadows. The long route around the east side of the park led up to the tennis courts where Nathan said Mandla worked. To approach along the chain-link border outside the courts meant walking in the thin strip of trees or along the street. Mandla expected his customers to come that way. He'd be alert to any approach and there was so little cover, it would be impossible to get within fifty yards of him without being seen.

The shorter route, on the opposite side of the field, offered a more concealed approach behind the houses and business on this side. It would be easy to draw even with the courts, but it was too far across the baseball diamond to record any evidence on video. If I'd had a lens with a powerful zoom, that would have been my choice.

I settled on stalking my way across the field itself. An unexpected approach that Mandla and his ilk weren't likely to be on guard against. The outfield was so dark, all I needed was to crouch and scoot across the grass to move without being seen.

Halfway into the field, my cell vibrated.

"Sneaky," Winchester said.

"Have I got company?"

"Charlotte is parked across the street from the tennis courts. She's been peeking through the bottom of the driver's side window since before you went into the pizza shop."

"Nice work," I said.

Winchester and his team were invaluable. I didn't bother asking how they found Charlotte. I guessed they'd put a tracker on her car while she visited me. They told me up front they didn't divulge their methods, so I didn't ask.

"What about Joel?"

"Haven't seen him, but Nathan is creeping through the trees on the west side of the park. By the way he's moving, it looks like he's gone off script."

"He wants me to pass," I said.

"Don't get cocky," Winchester said. "It's not up to him. If you get in trouble with the goon squad, that little snake will turn on you in a blink."

We hung up, and I kept low until I reached the edge of the infield. The crunching gravel might not have been audible over the din of traffic, but if things got quiet, I'd be stranded in the stone dust. I chose to back up and follow the grass toward third base and crawl in the grass along the foul line until I was close enough to capture a deal.

Dew soaked the front of my shirt and pants as soon as I started crawling. I picked up a coating of mud when I crossed the dirt strip that marked the foul line. One hundred feet from the furthest tennis court, my legs felt numb. Winchester and Koch must have been using night vision to see across the park because I was a lot closer and couldn't see anyone in the gloom. At least the darkness made me invisible to Mandla and his customers.

The court fence started way back in the outfield. Ten-foot-high chain link stopped tennis balls from lofting onto the baseball field and also barred any escape to the east. To get a decent view, I had to crawl the length of the infield while completely hemmed in on one side. That meant committing myself to taking the video and sneaking back across the field to the trees on the west side, where Nathan and Winchester were hiding.

The Cat Bagger's Apprentice

I wanted to ask Winchester how many guys were there with Mandla, but I could already hear hushed conversations somewhere around the basketball courts, so talking on the phone was out.

A car approached on the other side of the courts with loud rap music booming. I pushed up to my feet and scurried forward forty feet to the player's bench and crawled underneath. My dark clothes blended with the outline of the bench and the shadows in the dirt.

From my vantage on the ground, Mandla's team took shape. He walked to the net of the nearest court and stood surrounded by six men all with their backs to the fence. A man from the car stopped at the gate and was patted down by one of Mandla's guys before being allowed on the court.

Mandla had cheated reeducation once, and he didn't want to go back. Filming him from the grass was going to be impossible as was hiding on the tennis court. My only options were to give up and face the consequences with Wendell, or to fake a drug buy where I couldn't say what I wanted for fear of being recorded and flushed out of the program. I also couldn't be made for a cop by Mandla's gang for fear of being beaten to death.

Maybe I should have recorded the man from the car in the hope he flashed a gift card. The slim camera could have been sophisticated enough to capture his image or maybe Wendell had the technology to enhance the images I captured. I should have expected Wendell to be accommodating and accept almost anything.

What I didn't expect was for the group to stream out the exit between the tennis and basketball courts and to spread out along the backstop, blocking my quickest route to safety. I tried not to breathe, even though I knew someone had to have spotted me moving on the grass. I hoped they'd overlook me under the bench and move on to one of the stores.

That hope died when the dirt crunched behind me.

To turn and look meant giving myself away. To stay low was deceiving myself into believing I still had a chance. The footsteps came between first and second base. Mandla's men had me surrounded on one side with the high fence behind me on the other. If I turned and ran away from Mandla's gang, I'd have to follow the fence hundreds of feet before I could break out onto the street. One man waiting for me down at that end would have been enough to run me down and tackle me while I was breathless, holding me long enough for the rest of the gang to converge like wolves.

I hadn't made any noise, and I'd kept low. I wondered if Joel had tipped Mandla and his guys. If that had been him driving up to warn them.

My mission was a failure. Now that Mandla was ready for me, he could change locations or simply lay low. I couldn't wait days for him to resurface. By then I would have failed reeducation. Lying there under the bench, I thought I might not have much time left. What I thought would be a rush had my life hanging in the balance with no way out except the gun clipped on my belt.

Headlights flashed off to my left and my phone buzzed.

"Got you," I whispered. "Thank God you're here."

"We can clear a path this way, but you've got to clear our line of fire."

I scanned the streets for one of those dark Suburbans, but the vehicles on the edge of the park all looked like dark blobs from the bench.

The men kept moving, spreading and circling, three of them directly between me and my team, the others ready to intercept a retreat in any direction except toward the fence.

One man moved forward, and I saw my chance. I stood up, brushed the mud off the front of my clothes, and walked toward the pitcher's mound to meet the leader of the gang that had me surrounded.

I slipped the camera from my pocket and pressed the button hard until I saw the red light. I twirled the thing, filming the ground, the fence, the man coming to meet me, and then the shadowy group of men behind.

"Not cool," he said when he was close enough for me to hear.

"I'm cool," I said in my calmest, least-threatening voice.

"Definitely not cool spying all up in my shit."

The thug voice almost seemed genuine. It was too dark to see bandanas or gang colors on any of the guys with him.

"Not spying, man." I stepped closer with the camera on him. "Looking to meet up."

"What you want hiding here in the dark? You lucky my boys didn't take you down. Hear?"

I skirted to my left, giving Winchester a clear line to a few more of Mandla's guys. The two of us were twenty feet apart when he gave me his final challenge.

"You got five seconds," he said.

I couldn't offer to buy drugs because someone around that park was definitely recording everything I said.

When I didn't answer, he stomped his foot and turned his head. The signal tightened the ring of thugs. Eight, maybe ten of them stalked toward me in an ever-tightening semi-circle, weapons hanging low. I saw the flash of a knife and a pipe or a bat.

"I don't want trouble," I said with my free hand in the air.

"What you doin' with that?" He pointed to the camera.

When Mandla called out the camera in my hand, the gang arrayed behind him scurried into place, four of them directly between me and the van. None of the hands held a gun, but that didn't mean there wasn't one tucked inside a belt or holstered under a shoulder.

I stepped back toward the fence and the men converged, not running and not moving past their leader, but fanning in a circle to block my escape.

"We're going to have fun with you, pretty boy," the young guy with the bat said.

The black bats speeding into the park with their batons ready would have been a welcome sight.

I stumbled on the turf at the edge of the dirt foul line and barely caught my balance in the grass. Twenty feet behind me the fence lined the tennis courts. I'd backed my way off the baseball field and let Mandla's gang flank me on both sides, leaving myself nowhere to run.

I jerked the pistol from my belt and slapped the trigger.

Nothing happened.

Mandla saw my move, but couldn't see the gun. "Mess him up," Mandla said, and his guys raced toward me.

I clicked the safety and fired again.

This time red goo exploded from Mandla's chest. I fired three more times with the gun low then remembered to extend my arm and sight down the barrel. It didn't matter. Mandla jerked with the impacts of the first four shots and fell.

I whirled around the circle of men, looking for a gun and was met by a circle of panicked faces. They couldn't turn around fast enough. Two of them fell trying to change direction. I picked out the two closest and fired twice more, stopping then to conserve ammunition.

Gunshots stuttered from the edge of the park.

I hit the ground and flashed a look at my escape toward Winchester and Koch. Two hot-white circles of flash kept erupting where I'd seen the van parked. The men on the field scattered north and south and left me lying beside the fence alone.

Dozens of shots blazed.

They must have reloaded several times, but the two guns never silenced at the same time.

Finally, when I couldn't see another thug anywhere, I got up and jogged toward the van. The muzzle flashes stopped, but the white spots kept dancing in my vision. I couldn't see Winchester or Koch at the van no matter how many times I blinked and squeezed my eyes shut.

My phone glowed in my pocket, but I ignored it and kept running until I saw the headlights turn and race away. I stood at the edge of the trees panting, the camera filming the ground, the gun weighing down my right hand. Surrounded by counselors who'd caught the debacle on film.

Chapter Thirty

Ducking down on the ground with a tree trunk between me and Charlotte, I stopped to listen for trouble. A stream of headlights flashed between the buildings on the other side of the block, none accompanied by blue lights or wailing sirens. The gang members had fled the gunshots, most of them running into the trees north of the park. I'd run toward the van for help. My security team had left me behind, but I found myself in the most deserted acre for five blocks. For the moment I was safe.

Nathan Farnsworth could have been lurking at the edge of the field, but he didn't show himself. If he wasn't authorized to be there, he'd probably disappeared ahead of the cops along with everyone else.

I kept my head faced away from Charlotte's car. If she hadn't photographed me yet, I didn't want to give her the chance. Joel would have jumped at the chance to capture me and Mandla's body in the same frame. He'd been gunning to put me away for days and it wouldn't matter that I'd taken down one of the men Wendell said was plaguing his operation. Two good reasons to keep my head down.

My phone buzzed again. This time I opened the line but didn't speak.

"Move," Koch said.

At the same time, two headlights bounced over the curb into the park and raced out near the foul line where Mandla lay.

"Go west," he said. "Climb the fence and get down on the railroad tracks. Go two blocks north then climb out at the station and you're home."

The van skidded to a stop, tearing up grass. Two men scrambled out the back doors of the van, less than a hundred yards away. I'd paid for protection, and I didn't like being told to walk home in a neighborhood buzzing with angry gang bangers. Being in that van with Mandla may have been more dangerous than walking two blocks, but I wanted the ride and didn't understand why they wouldn't detour over to get me. Maybe shooting cops might have been beyond the scope of our agreement; though, we hadn't outlined clearly what our agreement entailed beyond keeping me alive.

Doors slammed closed, and the van raced through the outfield toward the pizza place. The phone connection ended, leaving me no chance to protest being left alone in the dark. The van jumped the curb onto Lagrange and the tail lights disappeared. They weren't coming back. All I could do was slink away through the shadows.

The earth dipped beyond the chain-link fence into a depressed, murky area where train tracks sliced underneath any street running east-west. I jogged over the sunken railroad ties mindful that a northbound train could catch me from behind and abruptly end my journey.

The steep banks on either side muted my footsteps on the thick wooden slabs. Cars passed overhead and voices called from the streets above, but none of the voices seemed alarmed by my presence, and no one followed me along the rails.

Two blocks later, I climbed out onto the pavement at the station and hiked over to Centre Street, muddy and exhausted, but alive, and as far as I knew, undetected.

The armed guy at my door identified himself as Colt. I didn't recognize him, but I was glad the door was guarded while Koch and Winchester disposed of Mandla. I stripped off my clothes, showered, and cleaned myself up to bolster my alibi when they came to find me.

When I turned on the monitor, I realized how ridiculous that was. The team wasn't interested in finding me. They'd been tracking me all along. They were busy trying to figure out what to do with me now that I'd graduated to murder.

The Cat Bagger's Apprentice

The monitor showed mostly feet since Charlotte had moved the toolbox off the chair. Several sets of legs moved in and out of view. The voices were mostly familiar, but when they got excited or spoke from a distance, I couldn't tell who was talking.

Wendell spoke defensively into the phone. I only heard his side of the conversation, but assumed he was talking to the mayor.

"No, Sir. We wouldn't have an op simulating gunfire in your city without authorization."

In the long pause that followed, no one from the team downstairs said anything. They were as intent on the conversation as I was.

"Yes, Sir. One of our relearners and several counselors were in the area. When the shots were fired, my people ran for cover."

Another pause. I realized the mayor probably hadn't even heard about the shooting yet, and it was probably the chief of police chewing out Wendell for staging a gunfight.

"The group on the tennis courts looked like gang members."

"We have no idea what gang they belonged to. We're psychologists not policemen. Our people focus on helping one relearner. Only one. We don't stop crime, and we definitely don't get in the middle of gunfights."

Brown dress shoes shuffled in the center of the group.

"I wish I could help," Wendell said. "We're scheduled to debrief shortly. If I learn anything about the shooting, you'll be my first call."

Wendell apologized three different ways before the caller finally let him off the phone.

"I can't believe you lied to him," the cabbie said.

A pair of work boots squared off with Wendell's brown dress shoes. The others stepped back. "That's the least of his problems," Joel said.

Chapter Thirty-one

"Let's start with you Joel, since you're so anxious to talk about what you saw." Wendell said from his seat at the center of the room.

Joel said he left the pizza shop and looped around the park to the east, staying on the street with a strip of trees and a few scattered homes between him and the playing fields. He saw me crawling around the infield toward Mandla on the tennis courts. At that point the plan had worked perfectly.

"You saw this all in the dark?" Wendell asked.

Joel's boots walked away and buttons clicked in the background.

I couldn't see the display from upstairs in my room, but Winchester told me they could track my ankle bracelet to within three feet. Joel must have punched up my travels so everyone could see that I'd walked right into the middle of the park and come face to face with Mandla.

"The red dot is Jordan. I'm in blue over here. Charlotte is in pink here on the road, and Nathan is orange here on the west side of the park. Mandla is purple here on the tennis courts and here he is about fifteen feet from Jordan in the middle of the baseball field."

I couldn't see anything on the screens, but hearing Joel, I knew their technology was enough to put me away. Winchester and Koch anxiously watched the monitor, ready to cover the door. They had rushed back after dealing with Mandla, expecting a raid was imminent.

"What happened when they came together?" Wendell asked.

"You tell me," Joel said. "You were here watching his feed, weren't you?"

The Cat Bagger's Apprentice

The old guy paced out of view. His footsteps echoed in the hall while the group clustered around the monitor to watch what he'd already seen.

"Holy crap," the cabbie said. "He shot him in cold blood."

The rest of the team maintained a stunned silence. They'd seen the shooting from a distance. The video confirmed what they already knew and forced an outcome none of them except Joel was ready to endorse.

Footsteps rushed into the room, came right in front of the camera, and stepped toward Wendell off screen.

"How is your team?" Wendell asked.

"Scared out of their minds," Farnsworth said.

"But okay?"

Farnsworth said, "A few of them thought it would be cool to rough Jordan up, but they didn't sign up for gunfire. I told them the men were firing blanks and I think they believed me."

"No one was hurt?"

"All accounted for. I think those goons wanted to chase them off so they could retrieve the body. I don't think they wanted more corpses on their hands. They had enough problems with Mandla. It's not every day you kill a reeducation counselor."

"Of course," Joel yelled from across the room. "We can find Mandla with his tracking beacon."

"Hang on," Wendell yelled back. He made Farnsworth assure him that the actors hired to be Mandla's gang wouldn't go to the cops. Farnsworth had made up a story about Jordan knowing the locals and told them not to say anything to anyone.

"We can't cover up a murder," Joel said. "We need to call the cops and send them upstairs to put a bullet in this guy."

"We're not putting a bullet in anyone. We don't even know Mandla's dead."

"You saw the video. Stop kidding yourself. Every minute you keep running this program you are putting us all at risk. That's a killer up there."

"If you feel unsafe, you're welcome to resign." Wendell's brown shoes walked over to the console and hesitated a few seconds. "Nathan, take Joel and follow Mandla's beacon. If you find a body, you call me. No police. No Agency. Call me and we'll figure out what to do."

Nathan made for the door immediately. Joel argued they should report Mandla missing, but they disappeared outside too fast for me to hear Nathan's response.

Wendell sent the cabbie to his post at the curb in case I decided to run.

Charlotte waited until the door closed, leaving her alone with Wendell and asked, "What are we going to say to Forty-three?"

"Nothing."

"We have to report him missing. He's assigned to our team. If he turns up dead and we didn't report it, we could go to jail."

"We can't go to jail, Charlotte. We run the jail," Wendell said.

Charlotte stepped back toward the camera. Even in sneakers and jeans, her sexy calves got my attention. The room stayed silent a few minutes.

I peered into the monitor, the volume maxed out.

Shooting Mandla should have ended my program, but Wendell balked. He had big trouble after Lindsay Francis and didn't want any more attention called to his program. He had to be considering making the call to Forty-three. The longer the silence went on, the surer I was that a gunfight was coming to my door. Winchester patted my shoulder and looked down on me like it was time to pack and run.

Wendell spoke first, "Could he have been trying to help us?"

"You're not serious?" she asked.

"Think about it. What if he killed Chad, Eli, and Greg? Our problems would be over."

"We can't justify murder."

"It's not murder. We should have terminated all three of them. You were certain. You practically begged me to. It's only a matter of time before they are locked up again, reprocessed, and terminated. Those three men are going to die either way. If he helps us, we stay open."

"Wow," Winchester said. He was so surprised by what he saw on the monitor he backed away and paced around in a loop. "I knew he was a zealot, but I never dreamed he'd let you get away with killing one of his own guys."

"Unbelievable," Koch said.

"What are you doing?" Charlotte asked, her voice tense even through the computer speakers.

Wendell sat at the console. We quieted and heard fast-paced clicking on the keys. "What time is it?" he asked.

When she said it was before eleven, he clicked out a rapid burst.

"Oh my God. You can't."

"The upload doesn't begin until midnight."

"Stop and think about this."

Her protests didn't slow him down. "What's going to happen when they find him? We're not the only ones who can track him. Or us for that matter."

"Relax," he said. "No one has reason to record our movements. If they do, we can say it was routine, we were following Jordan on a regular night out, and we had a heavy presence because he hadn't been out in a while."

"You can't."

"It's done."

Charlotte hustled out of the room toward the interior of the building.

I turned to Winchester and asked what Wendell had done.

"He erased their surveillance."

"Why would he do that?"

"He's covering for you," Winchester said, trailing off.

Koch pushed his way onto the keyboard. "He's not the only one we need to worry about. Any of them could make the call."

Koch worked the keyboard and brought up a series of cameras his techs had connected while we were all out of the building. He found Charlotte balled up in a corner of the hall with her arms wrapped around her knees.

Chapter Thirty-two

Charlotte sat transfixed by the text message from Sixteen on her phone.

Worried about you.

Why?

We're getting reports of gunfire two blocks from you. Is everyone okay?

Are you my guardian angel?

More Romeo than angel.

Sounds like a come on.

That would be sexual harassment. I couldn't do that. But checking in on you is legit.

I'm fine.

The rest of the team?

Everyone's fine. She lied. To protect Wendell or herself wasn't clear. She was fiercely loyal to her boss, but this was an opportunity for her to come clean and she refused without a second's delay.

Any progress with your pupil? He cooperating?

He's actually trying to help.

Really? Why the big change?

Too early to tell.

I'm impressed. You straighten him out and I'll buy dinner. Anywhere you want to go.

Chapter Thirty-three

"Who is Sixteen?" Koch asked Winchester.

"Someone high up in the Agency," I said, rejoining them from the bathroom.

We watched as she stared at her phone for several minutes without answering Sixteen's final message. She routinely charmed relearners into completing their programs and going on to a better life. Sixteen was much safer than the men she regularly worked with, so why not accept his offer for dinner when he could do wonders for her career?

"She's got the hots for you," Winchester said. "Maybe that's why she didn't turn you in. She wants you around a while."

A law and order woman like Charlotte wouldn't fall for a guy who shot a man in front of her. The bad boy image worked on some women, but Charlotte spent her life helping people learn to uphold the law. No matter how much chemistry we had, Charlotte would walk away the minute I finished the program. If it was up to her, she'd never talk to me again.

She stood up and entered one of the apartments that led across the building to mine.

"We don't have much time," Koch said.

Winchester agreed. "From now on we treat them all as hostile."

"Even Charlotte?"

"Easy, lover boy. She could turn on you in a second. They all loved Mandla. And just because Wendell is willing to throw his career down the toilet doesn't mean the rest of them will go sewer diving with him."

Koch agreed their run was coming to an end. They'd stay as long as they could, but it was time to start picking out drop points and rendezvous in case we needed to communicate after they were chased from the building.

Winchester pulled out a map and pointed out several spots along the train tracks where he could hide weapons or gadgets for me. He warned me to keep them hidden outside and to be wary of anyone who came through the door from then on.

A light knock at the door sent Koch scrambling to answer. I hid the map and closed the laptop, while Koch checked Charlotte for weapons and cameras. She sneered at me while he patted her jeans.

I said, "Hello," in my sweetest voice, getting up to meet her.

She pushed past me toward the bedroom. I let her lead the way and closed the door behind us.

"What were you thinking?"

I took the slim camera from my pocket and handed it to her.

She looked back in amazement.

"See for yourself. I tried to get him to admit what he was doing without incriminating myself. He wouldn't offer me drugs without me asking first. Once he saw the camera, he freaked. At that point it was him or me, so I shot him."

We circled each other in the small space between the bed and the wall, like wrestlers getting ready to grapple. Shock blushed her cheeks, and she kept canting her head as if changing her perspective would bring new insight into my psyche.

She stopped and locked eyes with me. "You killed him?"

"He was a drug dealer."

Her hands whipped to her ears so she wouldn't have to hear anything else I said. After watching the events unfold from her car and listening to the other counselors downstairs, the shooting couldn't have been a surprise, but she reacted like the horror was fresh. I studied her eyes for tears and saw none. Her face didn't betray whether this was another act from a trained performer or if she'd held out hope that somehow Mandla had survived.

"He was a counselor," she said.

"Oh shit." I grabbed the bedpost to steady myself, my eyes wide. I turned randomly around the room as if I had so much anger inside I didn't know where to direct it. Finally, I raked my hands through my hair and backed to the window, pressing myself against the glass to get as far as I could from Charlotte. "You! You did this to me."

Then I fixed my eyes on her like the prize she was. My last remaining bargaining chip. She seemed to understand what I was thinking and grabbed the doorknob, but didn't turn it. That door led to Winchester and Koch, trained mercenaries who would never let a hundred twenty pound woman escape. My torso blocked the only other exit. Charlotte stewed in fear, her panic button useless in her purse all the way back in the living room.

"Why?" I asked. "I trusted you. I risked everything to help you and you set me up. What was this stunt supposed to prove? Now the whole world is going to rain down on me. For what?"

She trembled by the door. For the first time since MacPherson, a program was beyond her control. She never should have come inside after I'd hired Winchester and Koch. I wanted to think she trusted me. Maybe even liked me. I could never see through the facade well enough to know what she felt, but my truest insights came when she was on camera downstairs with Wendell. What I heard then didn't fill me with hope.

"It would have been fine if you hadn't hired those goons." She pointed toward the kitchen. "We wanted to help you."

"Wanted to?" I said. "What about now?"

She didn't know what to say. The team was divided. Even Wendell, committed as he was to covering this up, had to be crafty to pass me from the program. It would have been much easier to send me swimming in acid and we both knew it.

Seeing her confusion, I knew that if I was going to save myself, I was going to have to get creative.

"Where's the body?" she asked.

"You don't want to make yourself that vulnerable do you? No body. No ballistics report. No murder."

"You can't make a counselor disappear," she said.

"You do it with relearners all the time."

Fear flashed through her eyes. She wanted to run to her boss and have me punished. Why couldn't she see how hypocritical that was? Wendell and Charlotte tormented criminals to see if they would fall in line, killing those who couldn't overcome their problems. The acid bath was a routine part of the job for Charlotte and Wendell, but when I killed a man I believed to be a criminal, I became a dangerous savage.

She barely moved. She had to be wondering if we'd used acid on Mandla. If we had, it wouldn't have been farfetched for Winchester and Koch to make the whole team disappear, including her.

I moved to the door, and she cowered back to the wall and then over to the bed. As I knocked on the door, she scampered to the window and tried to throw it open. The apartment windows were sealed to keep Wendell and his team out. The only one still working was in the living room and that window was covered by an armed guard day and night.

"Not a good idea even if you could get it open. We're three floors up."

Her chest heaved.

Koch opened the door. "What's up, Boss?"

"Charlotte wants a chicken burrito. Same for me. Get some Cokes and whatever you guys want."

Her eyes widened in surprise then narrowed with deepening fear. Mexican food was her favorite. After the strawberry rhubarb she knew it wasn't coincidence.

"It's late," she protested.

"Add some flannel pajamas, a tooth brush," I said. "Anything else you need?" I asked Charlotte.

She was too shocked to answer.

I motioned to the bed, and she tentatively stepped over and sat.

Chapter Thirty-four

"You'll never get away with this," Charlotte said.

"That's what my friends out there said about shooting Mandla. But look at me. I'm on a comfy bed sharing dinner with a sexy woman in flannel, sheep pajamas. What more could I want?"

She pressed on the bed with her free hand, holding her burrito in the other. She hadn't noticed until then that the cheap government-issued bed had been outfitted with a high end mattress.

"You can't lock me up in here." She kept looking at the heavy duty eye bolt Koch had driven into a stud over the bed. She suspected my intentions were far from honorable. I couldn't blame her, since I'd pinned her to the bed and kissed her once already.

"How is your detention any different than mine?" I asked.

"You broke the law."

"And you haven't?"

"You were sentenced here. I'm paid to help you." Her head bobbed gently forward.

"Now that you've moved in, you can give me lots of help."

She ignored me for the next few minutes, taking tiny bites of her burrito, sipping Coke, and avoiding eye contact. Our hands touched when she set her soda down on the cookie sheet we used as a television tray. She took her hand away casually, barely noticing.

"I'm not going to hurt you."

She focused her eyes on the floor halfway between the bed and the door to the hall.

"I need your help. I need to know what Wendell is going to do."

She wavered like a reed in the wind. Her glassy eyes pulled back from the wall, unfocused and slowly narrowing.

"How long before he starts listening to Joel?"

She didn't react to my question. I'd betrayed that I knew my reeducation team better than I should have, but she didn't hear me. She slowly crumpled forward. I pulled the cookie sheet out of the way before she toppled on my lap. It took finesse to shimmy out from under her without spilling the remains of our dinner, but I did and she fell toward the foot of the bed.

Winchester tapped the door and walked in as I stood and watched her snore. "Should I cuff her?" I asked.

"She's good till morning. The klonopin will have her snoring until then." Before I could ask about after effects he said, "Don't worry. She'll feel great in the morning. Now come out here. There's something you've got to see."

Three sets of feet appeared on the monitor. The only shoes I recognized were the worn brown dress shoes belonging to Wendell.

"Joel and Nathan are back," Koch said. "They found the bloody clothes and his earpiece."

"Did he make the call," I asked.

"I don't think he's going to," Koch said. "You're a genius. I never would have believed this if I didn't see it."

Wendell disappeared then came back into view and stood, saying nothing, the other men facing him, or at least their feet were.

Something plastic rustled.

"A garbage bag," Winchester said. "I don't freaking believe it."

He moved to Nathan and asked him to put the clothes in and wash his hands thoroughly. Then he ordered him to drop the earpiece in a sewer drain a few blocks past the park and drive the clothes ten miles away and dump them in a trash bin.

"This is insane," Joel screamed. "You're covering for a murderer."

Wendell didn't answer, but his plan seemed solid to us. Anyone tracking Mandla would think he came back to the control room and disappeared on his way home.

"This isn't just any murder. This is a counselor we're talking about. One of your people for God's sake!" Joel couldn't believe what his boss was doing and neither could we.

"You are to speak to no one about this. No one."

Joel stepped back off camera.

Nathan left with the bag to do as he was told. When he was gone, Wendell told Joel to take tomorrow off. Joel balked.

"We don't need Agency help to punish this guy. What can they do to him that we can't?"

Joel stood rigid. Even though we couldn't see their faces, it was clear Joel didn't trust Wendell to follow through on his threat.

"We'll make sure he pays for killing Mandla, but we need to put our case together first. Everything needs to be in order."

"What more could we possibly need?" Joel pleaded.

Wendell begged for time, and Joel left sounding skittish. He didn't promise his silence. The three of us watching the monitor were split on whether Joel would make the call for reinforcements without Wendell's consent. I could only hope he'd keep his mouth shut until I earned my life back.

The little old guy sat down alone. He didn't click the keys on the console because he had no view into my room, and he'd erased most of the data his team had collected. That left him no facts to report and a seven-day report deadline approaching fast. The poor guy had a lot on his shoulders. I wasn't sure if he was thinking about covering up the murder, the report, or something else until the phone in Charlotte's purse buzzed with an incoming text.

Her password was her birth month and day 1018.

```
I'm ok. I typed. I'm calling it a night.
Did he explain?
```

He gave me the camera. He says the shooting is on it. You can see what happened for yourself.

What now? We can't flush him without any data.

He wants to help. Maybe we should let him.

Okay. Let's talk in the morning.

You need to go up there. He wants to talk to you. I'm going to sleep in.

Good night. Sorry things have gotten so far off track. I appreciate your loyalty. I won't forget.

Wendell left the control room thinking Charlotte had gone home safe. He was in for a big surprise in the morning.

Chapter Thirty-Five

My heart hammered before I opened my eyes.

Charlotte was supposed to be asleep in my room with flannel pajamas protecting her modesty. I felt her there in the dark living room. Coming to explore our passion while the rest of the world slept. Her soft hands tugged at my socks. My groggy mind chugged, trying to understand why she'd go for my feet hanging over the end of the leather couch instead of sitting beside me and waking me more intimately.

I opened my eyes to dim lights illuminating the corners of the room. A large figure hovered at the end of the couch and I startled, pulling my feet back under the heavy comforter.

"Shh," Winchester said, reaching under the comforter to remove my ankle bracelet.

I rubbed my eyes and watched him walk the hall.

"Not moving," Koch said.

"What the heck's going on?" I asked.

"You're moving, but you're not moving," Koch said plainly, as if it made perfect sense.

"Maybe the satellites are tired," I said. "It's late."

The two men huddled by the computer and watched my beacon move around the room. They turned all the lights on to be sure nothing was moving around the floor. It was just the three of us. Charlotte was still snoring in the bedroom and yet, my beacon moved around my apartment and settled in front of the television, even though Winchester held my ankle bracelet by the table in the kitchen.

"We can't stop this," Koch said.

I didn't understand what was happening so I didn't answer.

"He's messing with the satellite data," Koch said.

"He doesn't have that kind of power," Winchester said.

"But he can control me like a puppet when he thinks I'm sleeping."

"What do you mean?" Koch asked.

"He's cloned my bracelet and shut mine off." The two of them looked at me, still confused. "The satellite can't tell if I'm on the third floor or the second floor."

"Looks like you're not the only genius around here," Winchester said.

"What now?" Koch asked.

"That depends. Is he helping me or hurting me?"

I told Winchester what I wanted, and we set to work moving the couch and drilling a hole in the floor with a manual drill that twisted its way into the floorboards a tiny fraction with each revolution. Below the carpet and the flooring, we passed through a ten-inch gap and then chewed through the drywall that formed the ceiling of the apartment below.

Winchester fed a thin wire camera down through the hole and twisted it until Wendell came into view. He sat on a couch identical to mine with a television and black box in front of him.

I motioned delicate footsteps with my hands so Winchester and Koch would realize he was working right below us and in the quiet, early morning hours, he could easily hear us moving.

"He puts in his hours. I'll give him that," I said.

"What's he doing?" Koch whispered harshly.

"Collecting his data," I said. My escapade that night had ruined his one chance to collect data on my case. He needed something for his report and apparently he'd chosen to do my lessons for me while I slept. The system would never know the difference, and if there was one guy who could manipulate the outcome of my lessons, it was Wendell Cummings. He designed the system. He created my program. And he was the one who would choose which data went into his report.

If Wendell decided to flush me, I was doomed.

Koch zoomed in so we could see the action downstairs more clearly. Winchester had to hold the wire in place, so we carried the laptop to where he could see.

My avatar stood on a sidewalk I hadn't seen in the simulation yet. Wendell guided me to help an old man rescue a kitten from a tree. The two of us, computer me, and the old man, talked for a moment and then I moved on. Later I helped the teacher in school and graduated the lesson. Fireworks erupted on the screen. Winchester gave me the thumbs up. Wendell had passed my second lesson for me while he thought I was sleeping.

We watched him work through two more levels. My avatar did chores around the neighborhood, and then I walked into the police station and gave something to the police. The video wasn't clear enough for us to tell what exactly I'd done, but the fireworks signaled another success.

I was going to get a passing grade in Wendell's report, at least until he discovered I was holding Charlotte captive in my apartment.

Chapter Thirty-six

"How dare you?" Charlotte stood at the mouth of the hall, hands on the hips of her sheep pajamas.

"Sleep well?"

"You had no right."

I turned and rubbed my finger along the incision at the base of my neck. "You want to talk about rights? Your friend Forty-three drugged me in a public restaurant then sliced me open. I needed you rested today, and I didn't want to cuff you to the wall, so we helped you sleep."

"Helped me?"

She hated being my prisoner, but kidnappings didn't get much friendlier. Winchester guarded the front door, but flashed a warm smile as she came down the hall. Koch nodded from his spot by the front window. We'd brought her pajamas. Fed her. Given her the only bed in the place. Aside from the fact we wouldn't let her leave, she got the royal treatment.

"How long are you going to keep me here?"

"We have some work to do. If you tell me the truth, and Wendell corroborates what you say, I'll let you go."

"Wendell's not going to let you keep me against my will."

If she knew he'd faked my black box lessons, she would have been a lot more cooperative. "Get dressed. I'll make French toast."

She raised up at the mention of her favorite breakfast, and I imagined I'd sent a tingle through her spine.

"How many times have you had breakfast with relearners?" The words soothed her a little. "Go take a shower and relax. I'll have breakfast in fifteen minutes."

I fed the team first, and they went back to their positions by the door and window. Charlotte came out in a new pair of jeans and a white cable knit sweater that hid her figure, but showed off her red hair nicely. Not a bad shopping job for a mercenary.

She sat and pulled her hair behind her shoulders.

I delivered two slices of French toast with a sprinkle of powdered sugar. She saw my attempt to get familiar and said, "I can't give you information about the program. It's against the law. I could lose my job."

"That's the least of your problems."

She cut off square little bites with her fork and dabbed them in syrup.

I sat across from her and waited.

"You're insane. You'll never get away with this."

"The jury's still out on that. Koch here thought I'd never get away with shooting Mandla, but here I am. And I've got you for company."

"Until Wendell finds out."

I laughed. "He let Mandla die. Are you so special he'll break you out?"

She didn't need to tell me how special she was in the Agency, but she also knew she wasn't going to get much help from her boss. That stuck feeling must have been terrifying. Otherwise she might have enjoyed her time with us.

"I can't talk about the program," she said.

"We both know the only way I'm getting out of here is by helping Wendell round up his problem children. I can't help you if you don't tell me who they are. And I can't trust you unless you and Wendell give me the same names without the chance to compare notes. Otherwise I might end up shooting another counselor." I'd already heard the names over the monitor, but she couldn't have known that.

Her eyes set and she clamped her lips together. Giving me the names would make her an accessory to murder.

"They should have been terminated," I said. "That was your mistake. They've had a few free months on the loose and now it's time to fix it."

"It's not the same," she measured me, unsure if I could be so callous about the lives of three men.

"What's the difference between a nerve agent and a bullet? You know they deserve to die. Think about Lindsey Francis. She'd be alive if you'd done your job."

Charlotte glared at me.

"Is that fair to her family?"

She wouldn't answer.

"I'm asking you nicely, but I'm not going to wait forever. You're dependent upon me just like your relearners are. We can drug your food. We can keep you awake. We can cuff you to the wall until you wet yourself."

Her predicament began to sink in.

"I didn't cause your problems, but you are going to tell me what I want to know so I can fix them."

She averted her eyes and went on eating.

Koch walked over and set the cuffs on the table.

"Why are you so messed up? What happened to you?" she asked.

"Always the head shrinker. You've got it backward. I'm not messed up. I'm here to help you."

I didn't know if it was the cuffs, or the futility of her work with Wendell, but eventually she started telling me about the three men who had brought Wendell's program to its knees.

Wendell was the pioneer of reeducation. He invented the black box as an educational tool years before the Supreme Court outlawed prison sentences for convicts. No one in law enforcement knew how to protect the citizens from felons without locking them up, so when Wendell designed reeducation and it seemed to work, the Agency quickly formed around him. It was a frenzy of experimentation and explosive growth for everyone involved. Wendell could have risen to the top of the Agency, but he wanted to be in the trenches with the relearners, where he could see the people he helped.

One program could only supervise a tiny fraction of the convicts, so dozens of satellite programs popped up to handle the workload. They followed Wendell's guidelines, but the new owners were in it for profit. Where Wendell only hired scientists committed to recovery, other programs hired anyone willing to work with convicts under the new rules. Those programs terminated seven out of ten relearners. Even in the early days when hardened criminals were the norm, Wendell only terminated four out of ten. And his recidivism numbers were still better than anyone's.

Wendell complained about the others all the time, but his real trouble didn't start until he took in Michael O'Connor.

"Who was he?" I asked.

She told me Michael was Wendell's son. Wendell didn't know who Michael was until he was already in one of Wendell's apartments, his program already in place and working.

"How could he not know his own son?"

"Wendell never dated Michael's mother. He helped her get pregnant because he thought that would help her."

With a baby she could get her own apartment and government support. It was supposed to be more of a sperm donation than anything. A helping hand. But twenty-five years later, Charlotte handed Wendell a DNA report that showed his son was in the program and that his grandson lived just a dozen blocks away.

It was a close vote. Wendell and Charlotte didn't want to terminate Michael, but he kept getting into trouble. It was obvious he'd never obey the law, but Wendell couldn't give up on his son and grandson. Finally Forty-three forced them to pull the plug and Wendell was never the same.

"So my guys were right. Wendell lost his nerve."

"He fell apart after Michael's judgment. We didn't work for six months. We've had twelve cases since Michael, but we haven't terminated a single one. When Lindsay Francis was killed, Forty-three warned us that this was our last chance. If we didn't help you, our program would close."

"So that's why he's letting me run rampant?"

She nodded demurely and told me some of the last twelve cases were causing real trouble. Forty-three interceded a few times with the local cops so their recidivism rate wouldn't totally tank, but he was out of patience. Something had to change in a hurry.

"But there's nothing you can do about guys on the outside."

It didn't take any more prompting for her to tell me the stories of the worst three offenders they had set free. I scribbled the names: Greg Frigon, Chad Bergeron, and Eli Botia. Greg and Eli dealt drugs not out of necessity, but because they felt everyone should be free to enjoy cocaine and heroin. That was where the Mandla story came from.

Chad had a temper when he drank and had destroyed more property in the last several weeks than Wendell could afford to reimburse. Chad had also killed Lindsey Francis outside a bar in Boston. That was why Wendell drew such a tough case this time and why he needed to come through.

Charlotte and Wendell desperately needed my help even if they were afraid to ask for it. They couldn't set things right while they worked for the Agency, but I was free to do what I wanted. I could fix most of their problems in a weekend.

Chapter Thirty-seven

Winchester casually announced Wendell coming up the stairs and continued making himself a chocolate shake. The key zipped into the lock and the door swung open. Neither of my protectors imagined the old guy would walk in uninvited, but he stepped right through the door and said, "We've got work to do today."

Winchester sidestepped to the fridge, gun drawn, and said, "Right there."

Koch tumbled behind my new leather couch and leveled his gun on Wendell's chest.

"Shoot me and you'll be dead by the end of the day. All of you." He sounded tough, but he didn't take another step. Deep rings hung under his eyes, and he looked unsteady on his feet from a long night completing simulations in my place.

Winchester gestured and Koch moved in. The junior man reached for Wendell's thigh and the old guy swatted his hand away, triggering a reflex from Koch that Wendell wasn't ready for. The soldier spun Wendell around and shoved him into the door. Poor Wendell didn't have the presence of mind to catch himself and his forehead whacked the door before his hands caught up.

He swiped backward at Koch, who twisted his arm up between his shoulder blades and continued patting him down.

"Is this really necessary?" Wendell asked wearily.

Winchester waved Koch off, and I led Wendell down the hall to the bedroom. "Whatever you have to say I'm sure you'll share it with your goons later."

"I have something I want you to see."

He plodded through the bedroom door with his eyes half closed until he saw Charlotte on the bed, both hands cuffed to the wall, a T-shirt stuffed in her mouth and tied around back of her head so she couldn't talk.

"How dare—"

Before he could finish, I grabbed him by the shirt and threw him out in the hall. I liked Charlotte too much to rough her up, and I didn't want Wendell to realize how well we'd been treating her. The gag covered much of her face and kept her from giving him clues about the three names she'd given me. I'd thought about putting her back in her pajamas and leaving her top unbuttoned, but I didn't want the old guy's fatherly instinct to kick in.

"You better not—"

"Don't worry, she'll be fine. Like you said, we have work to do."

Koch gave Wendell back his keys, and I stepped out into the hall with him. He looked down at the red button, scratched his head, and pondered why I'd held Charlotte and let him go.

Pressing the button might have made him feel better. He really would have enjoyed jolting me until I fell to the floor, but that wouldn't free Charlotte, and it wouldn't put me in a mood to treat her any better. He was helpless to save her without calling reinforcements and the report he'd concocted didn't support a distress call. I desperately hoped he'd submitted it already.

He followed me downstairs to the door Joel and Charlotte used to visit the control room. I gestured and he pretended not to understand what I wanted.

"You think I don't see your people use this door three times a day? Open up and show me where this goes."

"You're not allowed."

"I'm not supposed to do a lot of things, but you're going to take me back so we can talk about Lindsey Francis. If you want my help, you're going to give me everything you have, and I mean everything."

Violating the secrecy of his office was a small thing after what he'd done, but the little guy hesitated a long while at the door. I didn't explain any more, letting him come to the right conclusion himself.

He stalled, but he really had no choice. After a few minutes, he unlocked the door and led me across the gutted apartments full of spare appliances and woodwork. Things seemed to have settled in place, giving the impression the operation was extremely busy once, but now the flow of relearners had slowed to a trickle.

We came out to another hall, and he led me right on through to the reinforced door and down the hall to this very spot I'm standing in right now. He stared down at the Plexiglas partitions in the floor, slowing, then stopping just beyond the far partition. He held the remote in his hand, praying I'd step inside his trap.

I glanced down at the lines in the floor to let him know I saw them, then made a right turn into the jury room where thirteen chairs faced the viewing window. Wendell stood by the partition until I walked around to the other door and came out behind him.

I settled in the chair next to the toolbox. Across from me, rows of monitors showed views all around the complex. Mostly corridors and exterior views. None of them showed the inside of my apartment and the confirmation felt like victory.

I thought about shifting the toolbox or peeling off the camera and sticking it to a spot with a better view, but decided a view of feet was better than no view at all.

The old man sat at the controls and wheeled his chair around to face me.

"There is no disputing how bright you are, Jordan. What I don't understand is why you chose to go insane while you were in my care? Is this a game or have you really lost your mind?"

"I'm here to help you."

"You killed one of my counselors."

"You told me he was a drug dealer."

"That doesn't give you the right to kill him."

"What about Lindsey Francis? Did she have rights?"

"Who are you? A brother? Cousin?"

Sadness filled the old man's eyes, and he buried his face in his hands.

"You can't bring her back, but you can help the next Lindsay."

He shook his head.

"Three guys are plaguing you. I want the names, including the scum who shot Lindsay. Give me the names and I'll help you get back on track."

Wendell barely missed a beat. "Eli Botia, Greg Frigon, and Chad Bergeron." He confirmed the three relearners Charlotte identified. These weren't frauds. Wendell had said the names aloud when he didn't know I was listening. He didn't have time to coordinate another operation before I'd taken Charlotte hostage. The names were legit.

"Now the files."

He opened a drawer and shuffled through a series of file holders. I thought I'd won, but instead of paper files, he whipped out a semi-automatic pistol and aimed the muzzle square at my chest.

"Highly irregular to kill me without authorization."

The words came out faster than I thought possible. I had taken Wendell on for the rush. To see if I could break him, but in that moment when my foot started tapping the floor involuntarily, I knew I'd gone too far. There was no turning back.

"You've turned out to be quite problematic, Jordan."

"I've got your favorite person in the whole world upstairs. What do you think will happen to her if you shoot me?"

If Wendell had played his cards better and submitted a failing report that morning, I think he would have backed me into the Plexiglass box and gassed me without calling anyone to witness my judgment.

Instead, he sat thinking about his future. Charlotte. His program. His team. If he shot me it was all finished.

"I can fix it all," I said. "Without these three around, your numbers will improve and your program will come back."

He thought a bit longer, wavered, and eventually lowered the gun.

As soon as the muzzle pointed to the floor and the gun stopped moving, I stepped over and took it from him before he changed his mind.

He skeptically eyed the flash drive I handed him. "I want the complete files. Everything you've got including their tracking identification numbers and codes."

"Their bracelets come off when they graduate."

I rubbed the back of my neck and turned for emphasis. "You don't take these out, do you? That's how you know where these guys are. That's how you know they're the ones who keep screwing up."

He plugged the drive in then looked at the keyboard and monitor for several seconds. Another boundary crossed. Another rule broken. But Wendell was so far out of bounds it didn't matter anymore. He'd lost himself along the way, and even when I helped him and earned my release, he might never get over Michael O'Connor and Lindsay Francis.

I waited silently as the machine copied files, keeping myself still, the gun out of sight. Once he started, he worked right through. A few short bursts of keyed searches and mouse clicks and he transferred all the information I needed onto the drive.

He didn't ask why I didn't hack in and get the data myself. I could have broken in and done it once I had the names. It would have taken about the same time as waiting for Wendell, but my visit had earned me a bonus, a gun registered to Wendell Cummings, probably issued by the Agency.

He looked squarely at me when he handed over the drive. "Why are you doing this? Is someone paying you?"

"I have all the money I need."

He looked at me as if I was crazy. "Not anymore."

"I can get credits anytime. You should know that, Wendell."

"We shut down your accounts."

"You shut down five accounts. I can create a new one in less than an hour. Where do you think your credits went?"

He didn't have the energy to scream, and he couldn't understand why a smart guy like me caused him so much trouble.

"I'm going to hold you to your word," I said.

He didn't respond.

"I'm going to take care of these guys and you're going to let me go."

He tilted his head forward half an inch, probably not enough to show up on video, but enough for me to believe he'd set me free if I succeeded.

Before I let myself out, I heard wheels swivel. His elbows hit the desk, and his defeated head clunked down in despair.

Chapter Thirty-eight

The door from the control room dumped me in a back hallway with three locked doors. I could have hacked my way through keypads, but I'm no locksmith, so I tucked the gun in my belt, went out the front door, and walked across the lawn to my own entrance hall.

Once Koch let me in, I set the gun on the table and asked him to check it out, while I went to work on the files Wendell had given me.

The three young men causing Wendell trouble had records longer that I thought possible under the reeducation system. If you tangled with the law more than three times, you usually ended up swimming in acid. The worst of the three, a stocky guy named Eli Botia, had seven complaints in the months since he'd completed reeducation.

"How can this be?" I asked Winchester.

He reviewed the file and scratched his head. "This doesn't make any sense." Winchester told me that every time a graduated relearner had a brush with the law it was a black mark on the program. When those black marks added up, the government started asking for refunds.

"The really weird thing is that they're not readmitting." When I shrugged, he went on. "I've had a few guys graduate once and get in trouble again. They hired me because they were afraid. Word is that every time a relearner is admitted for a second time, the program leader flunks them. Every single time. They were right. You don't get three strikes anymore. Two strikes and you're all done."

"So why is this guy still breathing?"

"Beats me," he said. "We've stolen a few files and this one is legit. I've seen some lowlifes, but none close to this guy. Wendell should have buried him."

His pudgy face looked back at me from the screen. The file reported his weight to be two hundred ninety. A guy that big wouldn't be hard to find, especially with Winchester's help.

I slid the portable locator across the table. "Set him up, will you?"

"You have his code?" Winchester looked stunned.

He took the code sheet from the file and shook his head as he carefully punched in the long string of numbers. "This is too easy."

Back in the bedroom, Charlotte pressed her back against the wall and snarled when I walked in. I guessed she'd had time to think about what she'd told me and what I'd done. Being party to murder didn't sit well.

"I'm not a bad guy."

"You killed my friend yesterday."

"I did what I thought was right. If you hadn't deceived me, your friend would still be working with you."

"Are you blaming me for this? Really? You need to grow up and take some responsibility."

"Me? You're so invested in this psychological torture crap that you can't tell right from wrong anymore."

She grabbed a pillow and pulled her knees to her chest. I crossed the floor and sat at the foot of the bed. She shifted her knees in my direction to let me know I wasn't getting any closer.

"When am I getting out of here?" she asked.

"This place not good enough for you?"

She turned up her nose at the crumbling walls and ratty carpet. I'd come from four stately brick colonials in Brookline, but she had no qualms about dumping me in the same shabby apartment. Charlotte was on the side of justice. Relearners were beneath her, and it didn't matter where we were forced to live or what psychological games we had to endure. Maybe she thought this was the only way to help us. Or maybe she'd been doing it so long she didn't see how harsh reeducation was.

The scornful glare behind the pillow said nothing of the real woman. I knew about her family problems and the things she liked and didn't, but I couldn't tell if the real Charlotte was the sexy seductress or the supportive teacher. She was too good an actress to reveal anything she didn't want known. I worried that by locking her in my apartment, I guaranteed it would be the last place I ever saw her.

I showed her a picture of Eli on my phone and asked, "Who's this?"

She confirmed his identity and when I asked, she reiterated what I'd learned in the file. Eli was an unrepentant drug dealer and all around scum, who'd been arrested "a bunch of times." Thirty-seven according to the file.

"One more thing."

"Wait," she said. "What are you going to do?"

"Don't worry about that."

She perched forward over her pillow. "You can't."

She'd voted to terminate him, but now she wanted to save his life. If the man deserved to be punished, needed to be punished, did it matter who delivered the discipline?

"I need to know something," I said.

She began to protest again, and I cut her off.

"I was in the control room. Halfway down the hall, there are two thick lines across the floor. Is that some kind of trap?"

If you're reading this, you know the Plexiglas box is one of the most guarded secrets of reeducation. Winchester and Koch didn't know about it, because anyone who wound up locked inside never came back to tell them what had happened. I'm standing inside that box right now. Telling my story. So, you realize that someone will finally pull the trigger and decide that I've pushed too far. I hope you won't give up on me the way Charlotte has.

"It's where we pass judgment," she said.

"What about relearner court? Koch says it is brutal."

"Relearner court is a show like the rest of it. Nothing there matters. The judge and the proceedings help us keep relearners in line. That's all."

"So you're telling me that Wendell decides who lives and dies. If he gets me in that box, I'm dead?"

"It's not up to Wendell. We take a vote and then pass our reports to Forty-three. It could be him or someone else who decides. We're told when and how to pass sentence."

"Why the box?"

"It's the last chance for the accused to tell their story."

"Why does that matter?"

"Because Forty-three listens."

"So if I want to find Forty-three, all I have to do is get locked in the Plexiglass box?"

"You're insane." Her features lit with morbid excitement at the thought of Forty-three destroying me. She'd seen me shoot Mandla and hire goons to take her captive. Still, she didn't have an inkling of fear that I could take down Wendell's boss. I was looking forward to a rematch of the scene in the restaurant, even if Charlotte didn't think I had a chance.

"He's not God."

"What did he ever do to you?" she asked.

"Our business is between us."

"Is he why you hacked the agency? Or is he the one who stopped you?"

Anything I told her would have gone straight to Wendell, maybe higher up the chain. A threat against Forty-three would have brought everything to a screeching halt. I didn't want that. The day I met Forty-three had to be business as usual, and for that to happen, I needed to turn up the heat.

I told Charlotte I'd see her in a few hours and to ask Koch and Winchester for anything she needed. I closed the door to give her time to relax while I met Koch in the kitchen.

He handed me the gun and told me it was loaded and ready to go. That the action was clean and it would be reliable. I took Charlotte's phone from her purse and left it on the counter at the mouth of the hall.

"You sure you want to do that?"

"She's got to call him eventually."

Chapter Thirty-nine

"Listen to this," Winchester said.

I turned back from the door and came over to the computer. Downstairs, Wendell had been joined by three sets of shoes Winchester identified as Nathan, Joel, and the cabbie based on their voices. The three men came in together and surrounded Wendell in a semi-circle. Joel had been ordered to take the day off, but instead he seemed to have riled up Nathan and the cabbie to confront Wendell about the shooting.

"We can't ignore this. What if he does it again? What if it's one of us?"

"He's not stupid enough to shoot a counselor," Wendell said.

Joel lost his cool and started screaming so fast and so loud he overwhelmed the tiny speaker in our miniature camera. When he finally stopped ranting, Wendell explained that I was trying to help in my own way. That they had set me up to deal with Mandla. That they'd told me he was a drug dealer and that he'd acted like one. He made the shooting sound completely rational.

"Are you out of your mind? We need to do something about this. If someone else gets hurt, we're going to get sued."

"We're going to handle this. The four of us," Wendell said. "And when it's over, we'll decide what to do with Jordan Voss."

"Four?" Joel's feet shifted around left to right. He was looking around the room for something and then figured it out. "Where's Charlotte?"

Wendell told him that he'd given her the day off.

"Can you believe that?" Winchester said, so surprised he couldn't contain his whisper. "He's lying about the kidnapping. He'll cover anything for you. What's up with that?"

"You a long lost relative?" Koch asked.

I told them what Charlotte knew. That I wasn't in the database. That no one on the team had any idea who I was because I'd concealed my identity. Wendell wasn't giving me special treatment. He was frightened and didn't know what to do.

"He's completely lost it," Winchester said. Koch agreed.

The men downstairs had been arguing while we talked. When we quieted and focused on the monitor, Wendell and Joel squared off in the middle of the room. The other two had backed off, sensing trouble. If Wendell hadn't given me his gun, I would have been worried he'd do something crazy.

"It's not safe for your little girl, but you send us to get our heads blown off. I'm not standing by for this. If you're not smart enough to call for help, I'm doing it for you."

"Barry, we're going to have to initiate protocol—"

Joel's feet turned toward the camera and the cabbie. We heard a slight shuffle and then Joel's face fell into view. His face filled our monitor, blocking our view of everything else.

"Thanks, Nathan. I'm glad you understood what I meant."

"This doesn't solve our problem. We still need to figure out what to do about Mandla and Jordan."

"Let me worry about that," Wendell said.

The room went quiet after that. We couldn't tell if they started whispering or if they used hand signals to guide their work, but Joel's body dragged past the camera. Our view emptied, leaving only the counter and a chair visible onscreen.

"Holy crap," Koch said. "Did they kill him?"

We watched for another thirty minutes. Joel wasn't there when the group gathered again. They didn't talk about him, Charlotte, or the information I'd given them. Wendell told Nathan to follow me from a distance if I left the building, but not to get in my way. Wendell knew trouble was coming. He wanted my help with his relearners, but he didn't want his people getting tangled up in the details, especially if the cops showed up.

Winchester and Koch marveled at his tolerance. It seemed he was so desperate for help, I could do anything and he wouldn't stop me.

If I kept going, I'd eventually find his limits. I slipped off my ankle bracelet and went out the door to see if today was the day.

Chapter Forty

The cabbie wasn't at his post by the fence, and I guessed Wendell's orders meant I needed to find my own way to Eli Botia. The red dot on the monitor sat motionless eight miles east, somewhere in Mattapan. Taking a cab there meant leaving a trace for the cops to follow. Taking public transportation meant walking in an area where my white face wouldn't be welcome. For a moment, I considered taking several cabs, but the records would show where I went and changing cabs would only cement my guilt. I could have looked for an event nearby and taken a cab there, but I swallowed my pride and opened the cell phone Winchester had given me.

Thirty minutes later, I slid behind the wheel of a sedan solid enough to get me where I needed to go, but not so nice-looking it would disappear from the curb.

The sun had set over the tenements by the time I neared the dark building the map no longer labeled. The red dot had been inside for twenty minutes, and I slowed at the fringe of a neighborhood to consider what might be inside. Situated on a larger route, the building could have been a warehouse, but nestled into a neighborhood the way it was, it could only have been a school.

Chains blocking the entrance had been cut. Barrels rolled aside to allow traffic in. The parking lot held two dozen cars, covered in a black murk that assured me this wasn't a hometown basketball game. I circled around and parked at the far end of the lot, killed the lights, and watched.

Light leaked from a side entrance. The rest of the doors and windows had been covered over with plywood.

In my mind the old school was one of two things. A clubhouse for Eli and his crew to hang out and enjoy the spoils of easy money, or a narcotics bazaar open for business with the full knowledge of the local cops. In either case, going in meant confronting Eli among his friends. Mandla had been easy. I knew he was a counselor when I recognized his photo. If those guys pretending to be a gang had been real thugs, they would have opened fire and dropped me on the field. That encounter had been a dress rehearsal for tonight's first act, minus the danger. I had to be a whole lot more careful during my opening performance.

A Cadillac cruised into the lot and parked, straddling the grass at the edge of the walkway. A man and two women got out and followed the path toward the lights. Fifteen minutes later a group of young guys followed the same path. They looked too healthy for heroin addicts, too upbeat to be part of a gang.

A few more parties arrived. None of them fit either of my scenarios. They laughed and joked on the way in, more like a shopping mall crowd than a bunch of thugs gathering at a gang hideout. I'd assumed Eli would be working when I found him. Carrying a bunch of cards and on guard for thieves or cops. I trailed my way across the parking lot and when I made it to the door, I realized I'd caught him on a night off.

The wide hall to the left and right of the entrance was clogged with desks and chairs stacked on top of each other. Three layers of Graffiti covered the block walls in places where you could see through the clutter. The school had been abandoned for a few years, but light glowed from beyond a set of double doors, highlighting a couple walking toward me, carrying several small cardboard boxes.

Definitely not drugs.

They craned their necks as we passed each other. Being a natural blond was not an asset here.

I kept my eyes forward as I walked into the old gym. Folding tables covered the boundary lines in a wide U. The backboards and hoops had been removed and carted away. The bleachers now served as chairs for those who manned tables packed with gadgets. Shrink-wrapped boxes filled the space between vendors. The bright light in the former gymnasium forced me to blink. Either the sellers rigged a generator to the particular circuit for the gym or they'd figured a way to get the power turned on without the power company realizing.

The corner where the bleachers met the side door gave me cover to drop out of sight and check the tracker for Eli. His dot hovered at the far side of the gym where twenty patrons browsed with their backs to me. I made my way down the row of tables, casually noticing the new cameras, phones, and iPods. The truckloads of new merchandise in that room must have been boosted from a freight terminal. And there were too many customers for this to be a one-time thing. The market ran on a regular schedule, and that meant the cops knew and were looking the other way. I'd thought we stamped this problem out when we switched to credits. But people were resilient. They found a way around any system given enough time.

I kept moving to my right, upstream against the clockwise flow of foot traffic around the room. People kept stepping in front of me, and I kept stepping back, gliding along the back of the crowd for a better look at the big guy among the televisions.

Halfway across the gym, I saw the big guy hand over some plastic and hoist a huge brown box with the help of a smaller guy. They headed toward me, the smaller guy walking backward, Eli facing me with both hands secure on the bottom corner of the box.

With his hands occupied, he was defenseless. I could get within ten feet and drop him with a single shot, but then chaos would ensue. The other fifty shoppers could run or attack. Before I could decide which was more likely, four fingers dug into my bicep and pulled me into a gap between the tables. The gun in my belt was inches from my hand, but the rugged kid had better control of my arm than I did. His partner spun me around and slammed me against the wall.

"Whatever you're selling, we ain't buying."

"I don't want trouble," I said. "I stumbled on this place and I'm just checking it out."

"You got plastic?" The two of them blocked me into a corner between a gap in the bleachers and the locker room exit. The dark locker room was a dead end. The windows on that side of the building were all sealed. Doors, too. The maze through the bleacher supports led almost straight to the only working exit, but I had the feeling if I bolted underneath, there would be someone waiting when I reached the other end.

They could have been friends of Eli, watching out for him, or partners in the black market operation at the school. I couldn't be sure, but when I took a deep breath and relaxed my posture, they backed off a little. It may have been that Eli and his friend had carried their television across the gym and out the door.

I told him I had plenty of credits.

"That electronic crap's no good here."

"I just want to look around. Maybe I'll come back."

"You a cop, man?"

"Relax," I said.

He flicked open a knife so fast I didn't see where it came from then waved it in front of my face in a rehearsed ninja parlor trick that probably impressed his friends. Computer guys aren't known for bravery, and I'm no different. I wanted away from that knife as fast as possible.

"You don't want to kill me here. It would be bad for business."

He raised and twisted the knife, angling for my throat from two feet away. He wanted to scare me. Send me running for the door. I pulled back my shirt instead and showed him the butt of Wendell's pistol.

"I think I'll find a friendlier place to shop," I said.

They backed up and gave me enough room to skirt the nearest table and head for the door. Four guys trailed me through the hall and out along the narrow asphalt walk. They waited there even after I started the car.

The tracker showed Eli moving west. I cranked the engine and tore off in the opposite direction.

Chapter Forty-one

Looping around and catching up to the thug with the huge television in his trunk should have been as easy as weaving down the narrow streets and circling around the old school. The beacon headed north, but when I tried going that way, the subway tracks cut me off. I zigzagged my way west, hitting dead end after dead end until I finally found Norfolk Street and swung north over the tracks. Then my distance to the beacon started closing fast. I hadn't seen Eli's vehicle, but it had to be big to hold that television, and they'd probably be driving carefully so they didn't tip it over and break the screen. Stolen goods didn't come with a manufacturer's warranty, so if Eli broke his television, he was out of luck.

Cruising up Blue Hill Avenue, a familiar face peeked over the steering wheel of a blue sedan. Nathan recognized me from his spot at the corner as I passed. Wilcock Street zipped by on my left and I recognized the name from the file. The beacon had settled a few houses down. Eli was home unloading his television and he'd be busy with that for twenty minutes.

A series of three red cars forced me to wait at Johnston Road. When traffic cleared, I whipped around and parked, heading south on Blue Hill Avenue, fifty feet behind Nathan. I ran down the sidewalk right past his passenger side door, not bothering to hide my haste. Rounding the corner on Wilcock, I listened for the car door behind me, but it didn't open. Nathan followed Wendell's orders to the letter. He sat in his car and watched while I ran to the third house and turned up the walk.

The screen door of the first floor unit was propped open by a barbecue fork wedged into a gap in the floor boards. The heavier wooden door stood open a few inches. I pushed through and found Eli and his friend pulling staples from the top corners of the big rectangular box.

A bunch of us were crammed together in an instant. The two men working on the box didn't notice me, but the woman in a tight tank top behind them gasped. Their heads popped up. They faced me, but I already had the gun leveled.

My first shot punctured the big blue "70" on the side of the box, driving through the center of the screen so the unit would never display a single image.

"Don't buy stolen merchandise," I said.

Eli's face turned angry, and in that instant flash, I saw the danger Charlotte and the others saw. The reason they voted to flush Eli Botia in a pool of acid until his bones disappeared.

I shot him square in the chest, and he staggered back in disbelief.

His partner stayed rooted to the floor, but his eyes flashed all around the room for a weapon. I stepped up closer as Eli sagged on the box for support. "And don't sell drugs to kids."

My final shot came from three feet away, catching him square in the forehead and killing him as surely as any acid bath. I pointed the gun toward Eli's partner and warned him not to try anything stupid. Then I ran out front and down the steps.

Nathan's car tore down Blue Hill Avenue before I reached the corner. He'd heard the shots and wasn't waiting around for the cops to show up. I stomped the gas and raced him back to Centre Street.

One down. Two to go.

Chapter Forty-two

I might have beaten Nathan back to Wendell's control room if I didn't stop for Koch to help clean my fingerprints off the gun and the powder residue off my hands. When we were done, I crossed the front lawn along the length of the building and slipped in the short hall that led to Wendell's lair. I banged on the inner door and heard rustling on the other side, but it took a while before the door opened and Wendell greeted me from inside.

The police reports hadn't reached him yet, so he couldn't have been sure I'd killed Eli, but after what I'd done to Mandla, and hearing Nathan's account of the gunshots, Wendell seemed sure I'd fixed one of his problems. Though, he looked more perplexed than appreciative.

The old guy stepped back from the door and let me in. The first time I'd been down there it was just the two of us. No one needed to know that I'd seen behind the curtain. But this time, Nathan and the cabbie waited by the monitors. I think he led me back there so they could see me in person. That way it was harder for them to sentence me to die, not that it would matter. Wendell's team wanted me dead as much for what I might do to them as what I'd already done. The old man went to great lengths to keep them in check, and when he stepped back, I saw how far he was willing to go.

The man trapped in the Plexiglas box looked as surprised to see me as I was to see him. The partitions had been raised out of the floor all the way to the ceiling. When he saw me, he slapped the glass with his palm and said, "What's he doing here? What is this, Wendell? Are you insane?"

Wendell might have made some bad decisions, but he wasn't insane.

"I was wondering what that thing was for," I said. "Timeout for the loony bin staff? What did he do?"

Wendell ignored my mockery, opened the door to the jury room, and led me in. It was the only way through the space when the Plexiglass partitions blocked the hall. Wendell hurried through, saying nothing while we were alone.

Joel sneered at me as we came back into the hall on the other side. The cubicle offered no privacy whatsoever. Stuck in the hall, with no place to sit except the hard floor. Nothing to occupy his time except his thoughts. He blamed me that he'd been locked up, and he had to be worrying about what Wendell would do next to keep him quiet.

Wendell waited for me at the corner, pulling me toward the monitors with a four-fingered wave. I detoured back to the glass and pressed my palms to the outside of Joel's cage. The big man mirrored me.

"You won't get away with this, Jordan."

I turned my back and he banged the glass behind me.

"When I get out of here, you're going down."

No doubt he'd be dialing the second he got his hands on a phone.

Around the corner, the cabbie and Nathan Farnsworth stood uneasily between the rows of monitors and the back door. Nathan raised his hands when I came in as if to surrender.

The gunshots had broken Nathan. I couldn't tell where the cabbie stood, but the rest of the team was ready to end this operation first chance they got. They could torment and manipulate a relearner while he was helpless, all the while taking hero's credit for solving the crime problem. But when things got hairy, they were anything but heroic. They could talk their way out of trouble, but action didn't factor into the equation for these guys.

I pulled the gun out of my pants and unwrapped it from the T-shirt Koch used to remove my prints. Wendell stepped back when I tried to hand it to him, showing me his palms, refusing to get his prints on the gun. It clunked on the counter next to him.

"What did you do?" Wendell looked at the gun then me. The T-shirt wrapping completed the story, but he wanted to hear the words. By now,

Nathan had told him about seeing me run toward Eli's house before he heard the gunshots. Soon the police would confirm that Eli had been shot and killed in his own living room by a crazed vigilante. The instrument of his death belonged in this room. Too bad for Eli's friends that Wendell hadn't taken care of it privately.

"I did what you should have done."

"That's not up to you," Nathan said, braver now with the gun closer to Wendell than to me.

"Are you telling me you didn't vote to terminate him? Even if you didn't, by now you realize your mistake. He was a one-man crime wave."

Nathan was stupefied. His head moved subtly back and forth. I imagined his brain generating all sorts of arguments and his mental filter fighting them off to avoid divulging Agency secrets. He didn't understand how I knew about his opportunity to vote, no less how he had voted. He might have had a better idea if he knew I had Charlotte captive in my apartment.

The cabbie cowered against the wall, six feet from the door. He held his red button low in his right hand. The terror in his eyes suggested that was all he was capable of, pressing that button as a last resort when his team failed to contain me. When I left that room, Wendell was going to have a rebellion on his hands.

"One down, two to go. Then you set me free," I said, turning my back and walking into the jury room.

"You can't do that," Nathan yelled when he thought I couldn't hear.

I turned and opened the door again. Wendell already had his head in his hands. He had plenty to contemplate from the ballistics matching his gun, to his splintered team, to the two men he could save but shouldn't. I added one more complication to set the whole thing on fire.

"You can have Charlotte back soon. I'm almost done with her."

The cabbie looked like he was going to cry when I spun to leave.

Chapter Forty-three

Winchester welcomed me back. "How'd it go down there? Was he happy to see you?"

"Tell me you weren't watching."

"You know we were. The counselors are all spooked," Koch said. "We're running out of time."

Winchester went to the window, watching the street instead of listening to my debrief. Maybe he was doing both. Or maybe he'd heard enough over the monitor to know what was about to happen.

Koch had an edge for the first time. Most guys feared reeducation from day one. The stories of drugs and torture, men disappearing, it was enough to frighten anyone. Koch and Winchester made their living helping guys through the manipulation and deceit, so for Koch to be nervous, something serious had to be brewing. I knew I was close to the edge. I had been since I arrived, but I felt we were breaking new ground. Pushing boundaries Koch and Winchester hadn't approached before and that was why the first cracks in my protection team were starting to show.

Koch craned his neck for a long look down the hall to make sure Charlotte was where she belonged, then opened a window on the computer and whispered, "This is what your girlfriend has been texting."

She'd been busy while I was hunting Eli.

Her first conversation was with Wendell. She told him about the klonopin in her food and the files she thought I'd stolen from downstairs. Wendell didn't set her straight. She said she needed to get out of the apartment and back home. He asked her if she was being mistreated. If she'd lied he might have had more sympathy, but when she told him we were feeding her and pretty much leaving her alone, the old guy didn't offer to help. He told her they didn't have anything to report and that he couldn't call for help until they had definitive proof. He fished a few times for signs I was taking advantage of her. She didn't tell him about the kiss, but she warned him that the men in the files were in danger. She also said I had something even bigger planned. She hinted it was a grudge against the Agency or a personal vendetta against Forty-three.

Wendell told her he'd try to get her out and that was the last she heard from him.

She waited half an hour before contacting Sixteen. It was her first time contacting him, and her messages were vague. She hinted I was beyond control. That Wendell couldn't handle me. Sixteen pushed back, asking specifically what the problem was. She refused to say anything about Mandla or the files. He asked two more times, and when she didn't answer, he said to write back when she could be specific. He could help, but he needed to know why he was calling in the cavalry.

An hour later she sent a text to Forty-three.

Koch stiffened when we scrolled to the message. Armed to the teeth, combat trained, paid to be merciless, Koch feared Forty-three. When I saw Koch's reaction to the name on the message, I understood why he was afraid. It wasn't what he saw downstairs, it was the possibility of clashing with Forty-three.

She told Forty-three she thought he was in danger. He didn't return her message, and she sent three more, each one pleading a little more desperately, but offering no proof I planned to kill him. He finally answered an hour later, telling her that danger was a given in his role. Thousands of families wanted him dead because he'd sent their brothers and sons to die. His matter-of-fact tone came through clearly. He wasn't afraid of Jordan Voss or any other relearner snared by the system. He expected men to stalk him. He knew a dozen families had put a price on his head. If she needed protection, he'd come and help, but she needn't worry about him.

She wanted to tell him to come, but the only way to do that was to betray her boss and admit they'd covered up a murder.

When I looked up from the screen, Winchester and Koch were waiting.

"What's our exit strategy," Winchester asked.

"I've got that taken care of," I said.

"Killing Forty-three isn't a strategy. It's a death wish," Koch said.

"I didn't say anything about killing Forty-three."

"She got the idea somewhere. And you're not denying it," Koch said.

"We're on the brink here," Winchester said. "We're in for the full two weeks, but you've got to be realistic. If you keep taunting Wendell, you're going to wind up swimming in acid. I couldn't hire enough guys to save you from that. You've got to make a decision. Start playing ball or get out of here. We're behind you within reason. If this is a suicide mission, you can dig your grave alone. Sixty thousand credits isn't enough to die for."

Koch relaxed, waiting for what he thought would be a huge shift in strategy. My response made his jaw drop.

"I told Wendell I'm going to kill the three relearners he failed to terminate, and that's what I'm going to do."

"Not in a million years," Koch said.

"I'm sticking to my plan. I'm going after the other two guys."

"That's ridiculous," Koch said.

Winchester scowled and Koch stiffened. I was pretty sure I wouldn't hear more pushback from Koch, but if things got ugly, he might bolt.

"You keep me alive. Worry about Wendell's next move. What's he thinking? When is he going to pull the plug?"

"We're so far out of bounds I have no idea what he'll do."

"What would you do?"

Koch didn't hesitate. He told me he'd deliver a serious beating then described how he'd go about it. Winchester agreed a beating was coming, so the two of them set to work preparing to keep my rear end intact.

Chapter Forty-four

Winchester plugged in the codes for the remaining two relearners, and their dots appeared in opposite directions on the tracking screen. One north. One south. Neither of them within walking distance, but that made sense. The counselors wanted us to be isolated while in reeducation, and that wouldn't happen unless we were removed from our neighborhoods. Both men had gone back to theirs after reeducation. I still had the sedan parked out back, so the distance wasn't a problem. Actually, when Winchester handed me a SIG P229, I considered whacking both guys in the same night. The locator made stalking them almost too easy. And if I completed my mission, my deal with Wendell Cummings would be complete.

I decided to go south first and let things unfold. If the first hit was easy, I'd take a drive and try to make it a double play. If not, I'd come back to the apartment and wait for a better time. Winchester liked the idea and offered to have a car trail me in case I needed help, but I was fine.

Before I left, we watched Wendell and Nathan sit down and talk. The conversation was calm for the first time in a while. They spoke so softly that we couldn't hear them over the monitor. It felt as though they were planning something. We were all dead silent, and in the stillness, I heard something crack down the hall.

Winchester hadn't checked on Charlotte in an hour because they didn't think she had any way out.

I crept down the hall quietly to investigate, and when I got to the door, I heard a series of short squeaks on the other side and knew what she was up to. I opened the door a few inches and saw her straining against a butter knife, sweating out each quarter turn. The screws were deep into the window casing and there were a bunch of them.

"If you're eloping, I hope your boyfriend has a good ladder because it's a long way down, and that concrete is hard."

She snapped toward me, her face a mixture of exasperation and relief.

Two screws were missing from the right side of the jamb. Seven more and the window would have opened, but she was three stories up with nothing but a wisp of brown grass to break her fall.

I yelled down the hall for Winchester. He brought the screw gun and buzzed ten more screws into the jamb. If she wanted to stay up all night removing screws, she could, but after struggling so hard to back two screws out, ten new ones took the fight out of her.

"This place isn't that bad, is it? I gave you the upgraded bed."

"Kidnapping is kidnapping."

I ruffled the pillows and blankets until her phone bounced into view. "No one will believe you've been kidnapped when you've got this."

Her eyes filled with the kind of awe relearners got when they figured out they'd been manipulated so many times they couldn't tell reality from illusion. She must have realized that getting the phone had been too easy. That I'd wanted her to have it. She may not have figured out that we could eavesdrop on her conversations with Wendell and Forty-three, but she knew I was way ahead, and her bewildered expression was satisfaction enough.

She must have been replaying all the conversations she'd had on the phone that day, because she looked through me while I waited for her to catch up. She couldn't believe I'd made such a huge gamble by giving her the phone intentionally, and that made the whole scenario delicious.

"If this isn't a kidnapping, why don't you let me go?"

"I like having you here, Charlotte. And I didn't say this wasn't a kidnapping. I said no one will believe you've been kidnapped if you have your phone."

I patted the bed for her to come and take a seat, but she didn't budge from the corner near the window.

"I want us to get along," I said. "I like you."

"Are you insane? You terrorize me then want to be friends?"

I wanted a lot more than that.

"Terrorize? Please. It's your job to keep an eye on me. To help me resolve my family issues and get ready to rejoin the world. You're my favorite counselor and I want us to have all the time we can to talk and get to know each other."

"I can't be your counselor and your prisoner."

"You're my guest. I bought this bed special for you." I pressed my hand deep into the plush mattress for emphasis. She didn't come over so I went to the corner and boxed her in. She uncrossed her arms and pointed an angry finger at me.

"I know you like me." I put one hand on each wall, penning her in and leaning forward so our faces aligned.

"Like you? I'm here to fix you. You're a job. A broken loser."

I pressed up against her and her arm folded under my approach. "You don't believe that."

"I don't fraternize with convicts."

I let her mistake go. "I didn't steal anything. Didn't hurt anyone."

"Didn't hurt anyone? You shot Mandla."

"You shouldn't have deceived me."

She licked her lips subtly. Beautiful. Fiery. Wild. I had her penned up in the corner of the bedroom, and she didn't fight to get away.

In all the files and video I'd seen on the Agency computers, none of it would tell me what kind of men she liked. I hoped she had a thing for bad boys. Smart ones. She had a gift for giving men hope that even I couldn't escape in spite of all the games. Every relearner wanted a chance with someone so exquisite. Maybe I could have hooked her if she'd met me back home. We could have travelled in the same circles, and I could have impressed her with my stunts on boards and bikes.

She might have kissed me even then, but I didn't force it. I needed her to come to me. "Be straight with me from now on. I'll give you another chance," I said.

The Cat Bagger's Apprentice

Her mouth dropped open as I took the butter knife and her phone and backed away to the door. She was too stunned to speak. If she could have formed words, she would have called me an arrogant bastard. I'd heard it before and didn't necessarily disagree.

I waited a few feet outside the door for the bedsprings to creak. Sometimes when your emotions are all riled up it's hard to sort them out. Anxiety and tension can easily be confused for love and vice versa. From the outside, it was impossible to tell which of her coy looks were deception and which were real feelings sneaking through, but I believed we had a connection, and I planned to kindle that connection until they dragged me from that apartment to the Plexiglass box.

I traded Winchester the butter knife and the phone for the P229 and the tracker. I moved my ankle bracelet from the counter next to the stove over to the kitchen table so anyone watching might believe I was wearing it. Winchester understood what I was trying to do and agreed to move it a few times while I was gone.

Charlotte dominated my thoughts, and as I absently reached for the door, Koch grabbed my arm and jerked my elbow until it wouldn't bend anymore.

"Careful out there, lover boy."

Greg Frigon was a big time dealer. The guys around him would be on high alert this time of night. I couldn't afford to be preoccupied when a careless move could end my life. I shook off thoughts of Charlotte and slipped down the stairs, Wendell's cameras catching my every move.

Immediately out the front door, I took a hard left behind the withering shrubs and paused to let my eyes adjust to the dark. The car was around back, but I didn't want to give Wendell any unnecessary help by walking right to it.

Winchester and Koch had mounted a homing device in the trunk so they could follow my movements. I wasn't sure if Wendell was sharp enough to tap their signal, but I didn't want to prompt him to try. Better if I slipped away in the car without him knowing it was me.

Prickly branches clawed at my face as I pushed between the shrubs and brick wall, doing my best to stay out of the light on my way around back.

A hum of tires caught my attention and I instinctively ducked. It was the same disembodied noise I'd heard when the SUV stopped and six guys got out to pummel the blond guy they confused for me. I pressed myself flat, looking through the skinny trunks. A black Suburban blocked the street near the fence where I usually hailed the cab.

Another Suburban stopped sideways, blocking traffic at the far end of the building. Winchester's van was trapped in between. Without my ankle bracelet, I was invisible at night. I could have slipped around back and run, but I remembered Winchester saying his four men could take a carload or two of black bats. Better to duck back inside and fight alongside my protectors than run and get chased by a dozen angry reeducation cops on my own.

I scooped a handful of mulch and buried the P229 and the tracker in case things went bad then ran for the door and up the stairs.

Chapter Forty-five

"The old bastard finally called," Koch said.

"I need tactical support east," Winchester barked into his radio. "One minute until breach. One minute."

Koch opened a black case, racked the action of an MP5 and tossed it to me. "You've got thirty rounds, kid. Point and shoot. One at a time. Keep it that way." I wouldn't have known which lever to push to make the gun automatic and couldn't have controlled that many rounds at once if I did.

Koch had already thrown open the front window. Winchester burst past me with an MP5 slung across his chest and a hard case he struggled to carry. I had no idea where I was supposed to be. "With me, kid."

He threw open the front door and left it wide.

"Take that window," he said, pointing to the window facing the street.

I threw it open and kneeled at the corner as I'd seen Koch do.

"Other corner," Winchester said. "Less fire from the stairs."

I moved and watched Winchester pop the top of a metal canister then throw it down the stairwell. He threw two more before signaling in his radio that we were in position. A second later he said, "The girl."

She wouldn't be dumb enough to run out through a firefight, would she?

"Go cuff her so she doesn't get shot," Winchester ordered.

I scrambled inside, found the cuffs in the kitchen and ran down the hall. A foot shot out from behind the bathroom door, catching my shin and knocking me into a face first skid on top of the MP5. I whacked my elbow hard on the wooden floor, and the gun fired a single round right in front of my face. Metal parts poked into my ribs and I lay hurting.

Charlotte flopped on top of me and pinned my head to the ground with her forearm, her knees digging into my back. Her weight pressed the MP5 deeper into my ribs, the pain intensifying.

"What are you doing?"

"Getting out of here," she said.

"Not a good time."

I bucked her forward toward the bedroom, her weight lifting, but not high enough to tip her off my back. The cuffs had fallen a foot out of reach. Seeing them and knowing what I had planned only made her ride me harder.

"You're going to get yourself killed," I said.

I kicked up again, and she made a grab for the MP5. I caught her wrist and pulled it down under my chest. My next buck toppled her off when her arm refused to stretch. I slid the MP5 toward the bathroom and pounced on top of her, grabbing anyplace I could get purchase to hold her down, which wound up being an elbow and a wrist.

When my weight finally covered her, she couldn't lift me off. I worked to get hold of her arms so she couldn't scratch me. She kicked and bucked underneath me, stealing time I should have been covering the front window, but in the midst of it all, I couldn't help feeling turned on by the feel of her body beneath mine.

Wild eyed, on a quest to claw and scratch her way out, she tried every trick possible to escape. Still, deep down I desperately wanted her to have feelings for me. Even as I reached for the cuffs.

"Let me go," she screamed loud enough to be heard through Koch's window. I hadn't seen anything in her messages that asked to be rescued, but I wondered if she'd included a code word to summon the black bats.

She slapped at my face, and I caught her wrist. I used both hands to twist her arm around behind her. When I had a firm hold, I wrapped my free arm around her neck. She twisted and turned in spite of the pain, and I felt awful yanking her arm to keep her moving, but it was the safest way to get her back to the bed where she'd be out of the line of fire.

I pushed her onto the bed face first, let the arm out to her side, and fell on top of her. She waved her hand fiercely, but I managed to cuff it then feed the matching cuff through the eye in the wall and snap it shut.

Even cuffed she didn't give up. She swatted at me with her free hand, but she was trapped on the bed, my weight still on her legs. Once I caught her free hand, she was mine. I sat her up, took her jaw in my hand and brought my lips an inch from hers. Captivity couldn't tame her eyes, but she didn't squirm away. She sized me up, looking deep into my heart, daring me to take what I wanted.

The change in disposition was too abrupt. She was keeping me occupied so her friends could shoot their way in. How clever of her while under so much stress. Even knowing what she was trying to do, it was hard for me to leave.

Gunfire erupted in the living room and I was on my feet instinctively, running down the hall to find the MP5.

Koch fired out at the street, changed magazines, kept firing.

I ducked under the living room window, crawled through the apartment door and found Winchester manning my window in the hall.

"'Bout time, kid."

Chapter Forty-six

Winchester leaned into the opening, emptied a magazine on full automatic, then dodged to the opposite side of the window. I crawled to the vacated spot, hugging the wall all the way. Muzzles flashed everywhere along the street and I ducked my head back inside.

Winchester placed shot after shot, only ducking for cover to reload. "They're stuck behind the cars. Let's not let 'em get across the lawn."

I stuck my head out, lined the gun up and took a shot toward a guy behind the bed of a pickup. I shot again, not believing the bullets would punch through the metal sides, but firing just the same. I never saw the front sight, just the short barrel aimed in his general direction. They'd never told me how the two sights were supposed to look when I fired. Left and right were simple, just center the front site in the open space, but I never was sure how high that front sight was supposed to float.

Muzzle flashes chased me back inside.

Winchester shook his head at me, amused and disappointed by my form. He moved as one with the assault rifle. His cheek stayed planted to the stock, his eye at the base of the barrel. When he popped into view, it was just enough for the muzzle to clear the window frame. He searched for targets while looking down the gun, and when he found one, he fired.

I did my best to mimic him, but all I did was make a bunch of noise.

My third time out, I saw two bodies outside the communication van. They lay in the grass beyond the open doors. The men from the van had tried to run for the apartment, but they'd only covered ten feet.

I clicked the trigger three times before realizing the gun was out of ammo. The action was open, but I couldn't relate the open action to an empty magazine without thinking. Thinking was difficult when twelve guys fired at you every time your head popped up.

I hadn't counted, but that's how many there'd be. Two Suburbans full. About the maximum Koch and Winchester said they could handle.

I'd seen Winchester reload six times. The magazine was easy to find in the big case, but it took a few tries to find the release that dumped the one already loaded in the gun. I shoved the new one in, poked my head out, but to my surprise the gun sprayed thirty bullets all over the yard. Well, mostly at the buildings across the street because once it started firing, it bucked up higher and higher until I was shooting at helicopters that weren't there.

I changed magazines again and kept an eye on the smoky stairway.

The only ways in were that stairway and the windows. Those were all screwed shut except the ones we were firing out of. These cops might have had better luck with a roof assault, but they were fixated on the front door.

The gunfire hit a lull, and I caught a sly look from Winchester.

"Why now?" I asked.

"You started a shit storm, kid. They're here to clean up."

"That's not encouraging."

Winchester fired three quick shots and darted back. "Your ballgame, kid. You're the one playing with fire."

I had my own reasons for the tornado of trouble I'd caused. I thought about Winchester and Koch. The risks they were taking for sixty thousand credits. But it was more than that. Like me with Wendell's flunkies. It was the rush we all were after.

When I finally looked outside again, twelve dark figures hustled across the lawn. They sprayed up at our windows without taking aim, running as fast as possible to get to the door beneath us.

Why they didn't go around back, I couldn't be sure, but Winchester had said they were SWAT dropouts. Their tactics surprisingly simple.

I fired my entire clip at the approaching mob, not sure if I hit anything or not, but Winchester and Koch dropped four of them on the lawn. I took aim and made a careful shot at one of the bodies. It didn't flinch. Either the guy was already dead or I'd missed.

Most of the guys who reached the wall, hugged it and hid beneath the overhang at the floor beneath us. Some barged in through the door and started up the stairwell toward us.

Winchester got on his radio. "T minus thirty seconds." Then he dropped another canister down the stairwell and hit the floor. I saw him covering his ears and did likewise, facedown, unsure what was going to happen until the explosion rocked the floor.

My ears rang. Winchester yelled something at me, but I couldn't hear. He ducked for the window and started shooting furiously.

That was when I saw them. On the rooftop across the way, three guns started flashing in a measured series of shots. The guys who had been flushed from the stairwell by the explosion ran out onto the lawn in search of cover and were pelted by fire from across the street. All but one dropped within twenty feet of the house. The last guy almost made the street, but fell face first a dozen feet short of a sedan wracked with bullet holes.

The others, stranded behind the shrubs, dropped in place. Two put their hands up and walked toward the street and were unceremoniously nailed by sniper fire from across the street.

"Clear up," Winchester said into his radio.

He tossed me a magazine. I caught it as Koch sprinted down the stairs into the smoke.

Winchester told me to do something, but I couldn't hear him. He tried explaining with hand gestures, then grabbed me by the shirt and dragged me over to the monitor to watch what was happening downstairs.

I saw three pairs of shoes and couldn't hear a thing.

I moved to the window and saw organized chaos on the lawn. Winchester's soldiers dragged twelve bodies across the lawn and piled them into the Suburbans. There had to be twenty men out there hustling to clear the battlefield. The Suburbans raced away. The communications van disappeared, and soon Winchester and Koch returned to find me listening to a terrified exchange between Wendell and Nathan.

Chapter Forty-seven

The computer speaker wasn't loud enough to overcome the ringing in my ears, so I watched three sets of feet and wished I'd shifted the toolbox back up on the chair so I could have seen what was happening. The rifle reports might not have penetrated the brick walls, but anyone watching the monitors had to notice ten minutes of muzzle flashes in the dark.

The brown shoes paced and circled. I couldn't hear Wendell's voice. It could have been a long speech or a brainstorming session to figure out what to do with me. I pressed my ears closed several times to quell the vibrations to no avail.

Winchester asked for a fan, but my apartment didn't have one, so he propped open the door downstairs and threw open the windows on every landing to let the smoke rise up and out of the stairwell.

Koch scooped up hundreds of metal casings from the floor and dumped them into one of their hard cases then swept the area by the windows so clean it looked like nothing had happened.

Koch asked me if Charlotte was okay and I jumped from my chair. All the way down the hall I wondered if the assault on the front door had been a distraction so someone could climb in the back and get her out, but when I threw the door open, she lay there on the bed, still cuffed to the wall. Her expression fell flat when she realized it was me.

"Expecting someone else?"

"What happened out there?" she asked.

"A scuffle on the front lawn. It's settled now."

Somehow she knew it had been black bats out there. She might have called them, but she certainly didn't know the plan. She'd spent an hour or more loosening the screws on that back window, and they hadn't even tried to come in that way. We hadn't seen anything on her phone to suggest she'd called for help, but I had to be sure. If she had made the call, the game was over. They wouldn't stop coming until they flushed me out. If it meant knocking the building down, they'd do it.

"Did you call the cops?"

She shook her head gravely. I asked again and she threw up her hands. She wanted to be rescued, but she wasn't the one who'd called. I went back to the kitchen and found that Wendell was busy downstairs trying to answer the same question.

"Two carloads of armed police didn't just show up. Someone called them. Who was it?" Wendell didn't mention that they were soundly defeated and that he had little chance of ever controlling me without a full scale military assault. He fixated on finding the traitor because Nathan and Reggie were men he could control.

Joel couldn't have called because he was locked in the Plexiglass box. Charlotte hadn't, unless we'd missed a code in her text messages. If there was a traitor, my money was on Nathan. He wanted Wendell's job and proving him incompetent was a big step toward getting it. Wendell kept questioning Nathan and the cabbie, but after another ten minutes, he gave up and sent them outside to hide the evidence of the gunfight.

We watched from the window as the two of them made passes back and forth across the lawn with large spotlights, looking for anything out of place. They picked up small items and bagged them. Most likely shell casings fired as the men crossed the grass.

When they got to the street, they saw a big problem. Two cars the black bats had been hiding behind were riddled with bullet holes. The owners probably had insurance, but when Nathan called Wendell, he ordered tow trucks to take the cars away. He made another call to someone tasked with contacting the owners and replacing the vehicles before the police got involved.

The Cat Bagger's Apprentice

Nathan and the cabbie hunkered down in the street, collecting handfuls of empty casings. They packed heavy bags into Nathan's trunk while the tow trucks hauled the cars away. Fifteen minutes later, they made a final sweep of the area and headed back inside.

They hadn't been gone two minutes when the first cruiser arrived to find the curb in front of the apartment complex empty. The cop circled the block once, then came back and drove up and down Centre Street, returning every two or three minutes.

The guy must have been confused. He was looking for a battle zone, and all he'd find, even if he took the time to look thoroughly, would be a few shell casings Nathan and the cabbie missed.

He sat in front of the building a few minutes.

"Probably thinks his buddies are pulling a prank," Winchester said.

Another cruiser pulled up alongside. The officers talked, and together, they drove into a driveway across the street and knocked on the front door. They stayed inside five minutes, surely hearing the story of the gun battle from the neighbors.

They went back to their cruisers, sat a while longer then the phone rang downstairs and Wendell picked it up.

"No, Sir, we didn't hear anything."

The long pause on the phone meant the cops on the other end weren't buying Wendell's story.

"We are all here," Wendell said. "We're working on a technical issue in the control room. We're fine. Nothing wrong on our end."

Wendell assured the caller several more times and even offered for them to come downstairs and see him if they wanted to. They finally hung up, and a minute later the cruisers drove away.

When they were gone, Nathan brought in a heavy bag of shell casings and they took turns inspecting the empties. I didn't figure Wendell for a ballistics expert, but he kept picking up handfuls of casings and letting them cascade back into the bags.

"These guys don't fool around," Nathan said.

No one answered. Every one of my counselors was terrified. Exactly why I hired Winchester and his team. Their firepower gave me the upper hand, and at that moment I was in charge.

"Those cops are going to disappear just like Mandla," Nathan said.

We couldn't tell what Wendell was doing, but he didn't answer. He must have been torn between the good I could do for him by killing the men he failed to terminate, and the problems I could cause on the outside if he let me go. It should have been an easy call. My identities helped working people. Those other guys deserved what they got for taking advantage of people, but Wendell couldn't make a decision. It felt as if he'd completely shut down.

Two feet walked in front of the camera and joined the group. Our view became two jean pant legs and a light gap between them.

"Impossible," Wendell said. "That thing is supposed to be escape proof."

"How did you get out," Nathan asked.

Heels clicked in the hall and everyone went silent. Joel joined his teammates and our view cleared. All four of the men backed away in a semi-circle, slowly pushing back to the workspace in front of the monitors.

"What kind of circus is this?" a voice boomed.

No one answered.

I looked at Koch and Winchester. "You know who that is?"

Neither man spoke.

Koch gently shook his head and watched the monitor.

A few seconds later, our feed went black.

Chapter Forty-eight

For the next hour, Koch and Winchester barely spoke. They suggested I uncuff Charlotte and feed her, which we did. I asked them what they thought was happening downstairs. All I got from Koch was, "changes". They didn't speculate about the man who'd found the camera. They kept quiet, checking the windows, and strangely, I caught them taking stock of the furniture and appliances they'd delivered. I spent my time watching the feeds from the hall cameras and wondering what had happened to Wendell and his team.

The door to my apartment opened without warning. It shouldn't have been possible for him to surprise us, but the man stepped in without a sound and stood inside the threshold, owning the space.

He'd gotten upstairs without appearing on my screen. For a moment I ignored him, focusing instead on my view of the hall and wondering how he'd gotten up the stairs without me seeing or hearing him. He had to be the same guy who found my camera downstairs. He had to have a way to capture the feeds to locate a camera so small. And if he was that smart, he probably looped the output from Wendell's hall cameras somehow and then walked up the stairs without worrying about being seen on our monitor. This guy was smarter than Wendell. A lot smarter.

Winchester and Koch had taken charge of every person who'd entered the apartment since they'd arrived. This time they stood motionless, arms by their sides in the most non-threatening manner possible.

The guy in the doorway had a military haircut. A bullet proof vest bulged under his jacket, and he openly carried a pistol on his hip.

He walked to Koch, gestured for his pistol then dropped the magazine on the floor and racked the action to clear the chamber. The live round bounced around the floor, and Koch was so nervous he didn't look down to see where it went. When the gun was empty, the man set it on the table in front of me. He did the same to Winchester. Just like that, the team that had defended me against twelve black bats had been disarmed. Without a shot. Not a single word spoken.

"You must be Forty-three."

"And you are a huge pain in my ass."

He sat down across the table from me and snapped the computer closed so he could see me better. He folded his hands, looked straight into my eyes and said, "Playtime is over."

Koch and Winchester stood by, hands at their sides, waiting. Forty-three was big, but the two of them could have taken him. I guess it wasn't so much taking Forty-three as the repercussions.

Forty-three turned to the men and said, "You've got thirty minutes to take what's yours. After that, it's mine."

Koch nodded toward the computer.

Forty-three unplugged the power cord, lifted it as if he was going to hand it to Koch, then turned and smashed it on the edge of the table. "The surveillance in my buildings is here to accomplish my mission. You will not tap into it again."

Koch said, "Yes, Sir." Then took the smashed computer and dropped it in a hard case, ignoring the bits of smashed glass that fell on the floor.

Winchester went into the hall and talked on the phone in a low but urgent voice. Soon after, a large engine came across the lawn and right up to the building. I couldn't see what kind of truck it was because I didn't dare get up from my chair.

Men scrambled in the door less than two minutes later. Ten, maybe twelve of them. They started unhooking the appliances. Lifting my leather couch. Lugging the cases. They descended on everything Winchester had brought all at once. The place was about to be bare, but that was the least of my worries. Forty-three knew how to run a reeducation program, and he wasn't going to fall for the mind games I'd played on Wendell.

"You have something of mine," he said.

I desperately wanted to ask for a lease or a rent to own deal, but didn't dare make the quip. Instead I got up slowly and led him to my room.

Charlotte stiffened against the wall when we walked in.

"You cuffed her?" He walked over to the hook in the wall and gave it a yank. Then looked at her wrists for marks.

She had a faint red line on her left.

He walked over, right in my face and barked, "You bastard," then slapped me hard across the side of the head.

"I didn't want her to jump."

He loaded a shoulder to punch me, but held himself back. Instead he opened his phone. "Get Nathan and Joel up here immediately." Then hung up.

He introduced himself to Charlotte and told her to relax for a minute while he took me back out to the kitchen. "You take another counselor hostage and I'll kill you myself. Understand?"

No answer could have made up for what I'd done.

He pointed me to a seat at the table, and I listened as he checked on Charlotte. His deep voice carried down the hall, "Are you okay to continue?"

Charlotte's voice was too soft to hear through the door.

"Careful who you're listening to," Forty-three said. "Some people can't be trusted. Especially in this business."

He meant me.

As he sabotaged my relationship with Charlotte, I turned my attention to the moving crew, who performed as efficiently as army ants, taking things out in a long line, the stairs completely occupied with furniture and appliances as they went down. The stairwell emptied until the team turned around and came up again for the remains.

Forty-three reappeared with a device in his hand and a glare at me. I didn't understand what was happening until he knelt down and raised the legs of my jeans. He didn't ask where my ankle bracelet was. His phone tracked it down for him in the cabinet by the sink.

"Need me to drill a hole through your tibia or can you manage to keep this on?"

I raised my hands in surrender. He was the nastiest hard ass I'd ever met, and he wasn't done. Joel came in with a suitcase. He left it on the kitchen table, then went down the hall and retrieved Charlotte and walked her to us.

"We're going to fix this together," Forty-three said to Charlotte, meaning me. "Your program is historic. It would be a shame to let someone con you into making a mistake that ended it forever."

Charlotte followed Joel, seeming more embarrassed than relieved at being rescued.

The hard ass had destroyed my progress with Charlotte in a few words. I was back to square one with her, and she might never listen to me again.

Nathan eyed me from the door with his arms crossed, and I got the feeling Forty-three had given him an incentive to take me down. Maybe promised him Wendell's job. Of all the counselors, Nathan was the one I felt would sell me out. The others were in the business to help people. Nathan wanted status and my shenanigans gave him a sure path to a big promotion as soon as Wendell was out of the way.

When Joel and Nathan walked out, the place was empty. My team gone. My counselors gone. It was just Forty-three and me.

He told me to strip and I refused.

"I know you have thumb impressions sewn into your clothes. No more easy money for you. You're going to live within your means from now on."

He watched me strip and led me across the hall in my briefs to a room exactly like the one I'd woken up in six days earlier.

"I should have had Charlotte do this part. Let her get even," Forty-three said as he tossed the case to the floor and let it settle at my feet.

I smiled. I would have liked that.

Chapter Forty-nine

"They can all see me right now, can't they," I said, standing in my briefs with the suitcase at my feet.

"You've attracted a lot of attention. I think the whole Agency is watching."

"That's not fair. How can I graduate if every person in the Agency is trying to take me down?" From the beginning I'd banked on Wendell's emotional problems. As long as he was the gatekeeper, my transgressions remained hidden. If he hadn't destroyed the evidence of my failures, I would have been flunked already, but even Forty-three had to report to someone, and that guy didn't let him kill relearners without permission.

He pointed an accusing finger at me. "You're your own worst enemy."

"So Wendell called you for help?"

He shook his head.

I shrugged and he read my unasked question.

"I will not let you make a mockery of the Agency. You won't hire private security guards. You won't tamper with Agency equipment, and as of now, you will use no cameras, telephones, or computers. Don't even use the microwave except to cook."

None of those things were technically against the rules. Forty-three didn't suggest a punishment if I broke his rules, but the militant obedience shown by Winchester and Koch meant this guy wasn't to be messed with.

"Keep the ankle bracelet on, and don't leave the premises without Wendell's permission."

He sounded strong, but he couldn't have been serious. Imprisonment was outlawed. They couldn't keep me in this tiny apartment until they were done with me. "I'm supposed to sit in this room?"

"No," he said, and went to the door.

Wendell had been waiting outside and came in when he was invited. He gawked at my lack of clothing and turned to Forty-three, but didn't ask how stripping me nearly naked would help.

"I was hoping you'd be a redhead."

"Easy on the redhead," Forty-three said, poking me hard in the chest. "If you see her again, you better have these on." He handed me a shirt and a pair of jeans from the case.

Wendell's expression sunk deep in guilt for subjecting his most trusted aide to my advances. Forty-three could have fired him on the spot for not reporting her abduction, but he chose not to. I knew why, and that secret was the only thing keeping my hopes of success alive.

I buttoned and zipped my pants and sat at a kitchen table identical to the one across the hall. Forty-three sat across from me with Wendell closer to his side than mine.

"Time for shenanigans is over," the big man said. "Wendell is going to keep you on a short leash."

A smile must have cracked my lips because he stabbed a finger toward my chest but couldn't quite reach. "Fool with me and things are going to get ugly. Ask Wendell, he'll tell you what happens to relearners who think they're above the system."

I wasn't sure what he meant. Without Winchester and Koch to guide me, I was left guessing.

"I'm going to be watching every minute I'm awake. In the few hours I do sleep, two people from my team will keep an eye on you. If you screw up, I'm coming down on you hard."

Wendell's shoulders scrunched up toward his neck, making him look even scrawnier than he was. His tongue lashing from Forty-three an hour earlier was probably even more severe than mine. His life's work was at risk, and I had a feeling the moment we were alone, he'd let me have it.

"We're going to let you start with a clean slate," he looked at me and Wendell. "As of tonight," he said to me, "you will be assigned lessons and you will complete them earnestly. And you," he turned to Wendell, "will report what you find no matter what it says about our friend here. He passes or fails based on what he does from this moment on."

Forty-three must have rejected the simulation work Wendell completed for me. I wasn't sure if that meant Wendell had to create a whole new simulation or if I'd be tested more stringently on the programs I'd already seen. Either way, Wendell's computer simulations were a snap for any gamer. Navigating his virtual worlds was like being stuck on level one indefinitely.

"You two have some things to work out. I'm going to leave you to it."

Forty-three paused to give Wendell a chance to speak. When he didn't, the big man walked out the door and didn't look back.

Wendell shifted his chair more directly across the table from me. The deep lines under his eyes showed the strain I'd put him under. Emptying his accounts. The shootings. The battle on his front lawn. The cops, the mayor, even his own Agency was coming down on him. He should have hated me for it, but I didn't see hate in his eyes. The old guy was bogged down, slogging through this crisis like any other setback. He must have been near his breaking point, but somehow, frazzled as he was, he maintained control.

"You're lucky," he said.

"I don't feel lucky. Being free would feel lucky."

"Being dead would feel worse."

Chapter Fifty

So much for working things out. Wendell barely said anything after Forty-three left. Once he reminded me to work on my lessons, he rushed out the door without saying anything about our deal. If Forty-three heard what we were conspiring to do, he might have flushed us both, but for me, killing the remaining two thugs seemed the fastest way to earn Wendell's blessing.

No doubt the room was wired. Maybe we could have discussed our deal in the bathroom, even if both of us going in at the same time would have looked strange. Wendell could have written me a note or hinted in code, but he did neither of these things. Was it possible he'd keep looking the other way if I tried to finish? And would he be happy when I did? Or did Forty-three's involvement completely change the game?

The only thing I could do to make Forty-three happy while I was in reeducation was to fail. But what did Wendell really want?

I sat on the cheap couch, wondering how fast to do the lessons. If I finished too soon, Wendell would have to come up with something more challenging. If I didn't try hard enough, Forty-three would pressure him to fail me.

Everything became more difficult under the microscope, but I still had some leftover advantages from my days with Winchester and Koch. Our pressure forced Wendell to make some big mistakes he didn't want exposed. Forty-three must have known things were going off track, but he couldn't have known how much Wendell was hiding. That was my leverage. My ticket to roam freely and keep pressing until I passed. Tonight wasn't the night to sneak out. I needed to at least pretend to follow the program for a while.

At one A.M. I clicked on the television and started the black box with the intention to pass the simulation for the first time. My goal wasn't just to pass, but to set the record time for relearners. The program that appeared may have been a little easier for me because they couldn't track my family. For most guys, the first time was freaky. They turned on the black box, and they appeared on screen as a kid in their old bedroom. Wendell was a master at recreating a world so familiar that relearners believed it was them on the television. Not so for me. The room on the screen could have belonged to any little boy. Virtual me jumped out of bed, put his clothes on, and ran downstairs without emotions cluttering up the place and slowing him down.

I tried to open the front door, but it wouldn't budge. I hunted for buttons on the remote, but the point of this game wasn't finding key combinations, it was behaviors Wendell wanted me to learn. I was thinking like a gamer and not a kid. I'd forgotten to eat my breakfast. That was why the door wouldn't open, so I maneuvered little me to the kitchen and sat in front of a bowl of cereal. It disappeared when I sat. From there I ran upstairs and brushed my teeth. Then the front door opened and a green line appeared outside.

When I reached the schoolyard, I went to the center of the playground and kept close to the teacher. I scooped up the first dropped item almost before it hit the ground and turned to the teacher. She stayed right by my side after that. She accepted a wallet. A watch. An apple. Three books. And then a bag of candy. Then the screen went dark and fireworks erupted.

I missed the record time by four seconds. I cocked my arm to hurl the remote, but stopped myself. Whoever set that record must have been one of the programmers. Another relearner couldn't have beaten me because none of them cared enough to try that hard. Giving in to anger wasn't going to help my cause. Forty-three wanted me to get mad so he could capture my outbursts on video and use them to put me away. I needed exemplary behavior to survive and that is what I vowed to show them.

The next simulation featured a cat stuck in a tree and a little old man trying to get her down. I completed that one ten seconds off the record. The champ must have known exactly where to go and what to do because I wasn't burning much time. Little me ran every step of the way, and with the green line on the ground, it was impossible to get lost.

The next three simulations substituted the cops for a teacher. I helped them bust a drug ring, stop a counterfeiter, and find a bank robber hiding in a garbage bin. The goals of the simulation were painfully obvious, and I ran my character as fast as I could, but still couldn't beat the champ. I wondered if the guy even existed. If they just set the box to lie and tell me whatever I scored, someone had beaten me by four or six seconds. That's always what it seemed to be. A handful of seconds lost somewhere along the way.

The machine ran out of lessons shortly before three A.M., and I proudly shut the television off. I'd been asked to do the simulations, and I'd nearly set the record in every one. The results didn't jive with my prior rebellion. If they were sophisticated enough, they might have realized I was gaming them. That I was performing only to be passed, but that had to be part of every reeducation program. Any idiot who wanted to go free could work hard at a video game for a few hours.

The next day would bring something more. I curled up on the lumpy bed, wondering what that was. When my head hit the pillow, those thoughts were replaced by violent dreams I couldn't escape. It could have been the naked vulnerability of being on camera without my security team, or it could have been an overdose of subliminal images spliced into the videos. I had no way of knowing which. All I could do was run through the swamps, mazes, and battlefields of my dreams.

Chapter Fifty-one

"Let's go, Cinderella." The voice was familiar, but different. Nastier.

My body jolted and I fought to keep my eyes closed. The arm rocking me didn't care I'd been up working until almost three. I cracked an eye open and the light glared so brightly I shut it tight.

"Sleepy time is over. Get your butt out of bed the way you did on those videos." He'd seen my simulation performance from a few hours earlier. He might even have watched it in real time.

"Playtime's over, Blondie. It's time for the real deal."

"What time is it?"

"Six thirty. Time for breakfast and a real lesson."

I groaned and buried my head in the half-empty sack that was supposed to qualify as a pillow. Less than four hours of sleep and Nathan wanted me to start another lesson. My shoulder stopped rocking and I nestled under the blankets. Warm. Happy. On the edge of dozing. And then water splashed on the back of my neck. Ice cubes clinked and fell from the glass and slid down my skin to the sheets. The sudden change from snug warmth to freezing cold jolted me up. I rocketed out of bed and steadied myself six inches in front of Nathan. He stood with his arms by his sides waiting for me to strike.

He wasn't going to defend himself. He was going to let me punch him for the cameras. Tricky to annoy me while I was sleeping to test my self control. The viewers back in an Agency office wouldn't know that I'd only slept a few hours. All they would see is my assault, conveniently spliced onto a highlight reel of mistakes. That would have been the end of my reeducation bid and a promotion for Nathan.

Forty-three's visit changed everything. When I came to reeducation, I'd been pitted against Wendell Cummings, a broken down old guy on the edge of a nervous breakdown. It wasn't fair for Forty-three to put Nathan in charge of my punishment. He was going to pressure me worse than I'd pressured Wendell, and I hadn't planned on that.

He stood outside the bathroom door while I showered and dressed, pounding every sixty seconds to rush me along. The whole process took less than five minutes, so I assumed it was all show for the cameras. He'd splice out separate shots of him pounding and edit the times to make me look lazy and slow. Fixing the uncooperative image he was creating would be nearly impossible without access to those cameras.

Breakfast waited on the table. A bacon, egg, and cheese sandwich on an English muffin. He'd gotten that right, down to the pulpy orange juice. I ate the sandwich in four bites, gulped down the juice, and followed Nathan outside to find a box of garbage bags and a metal-tined rake on the front steps. He smiled thinly and swept his eyes along the length of the two hundred foot building. The expanse of lawn stretched from the picket fence on the north, to the side street that bordered the south end. I guessed the lawn was bigger than a football field. The good news was there were only a few scattered leaves, and the sickly turf had almost no thatch to be removed.

"You're never going to work on computers again," Nathan said. "You've got to learn to do what you are told. Do you understand?"

I'd never done manual labor before, but I could certainly rake a lawn. Any idiot could do that even on three hours of sleep. I reached for the rake, but Nathan didn't release it. He wasn't done giving instructions.

"Have you seen a Japanese sand garden?"

I had.

"This is an important building, and we need it to look its part. What you're going to do today is remove the debris. Leaves, dead grass, and trash go in these bags here."

I reached for the rake again. Instead of handing it over, he turned it in his hands and scraped perpendicular to the walkway. "When you are done, I want it to look like this." He stroked over and over again, meticulously forming perfectly straight lines in the dirt without letting the tufts of grass throw them off course. "There can be no footprints. No irregularities. The lines must be true and continuous from end to end."

Finally he handed me the rake as a light drizzle began to mist the air.

"You can come inside when you're done."

He stepped to the landing as water droplets coated my arms. The sun barely brightened the sky that early morning, but the air was nearly fifty degrees, warm enough to be comfortable if you kept moving.

My plan was to remove the debris first and complete the artistic work second. That way I could haul the trash bags around without worrying where I stepped. Raking toward the curb seemed the most logical, gathering debris where it would be bagged and ready for pickup, rather than hauling it around from wherever the debris accumulated enough to fill a bag. Even if he ordered me to move the bags, I could carry them along the sidewalk without ruining my artwork.

My parallel lines scraped up more thatch than I'd expected and the two-inch gaps between tines proved poorly suited to dragging the dead grass along, so I swept over the same areas several times before getting them clean. The first three-foot-wide swath to the street took nearly ten minutes and produced a small mound of thatch and a few leaves. The lawn stretched out almost two hundred feet to the left and over a hundred to the right. The simple first step would take another three hundred minutes if I didn't tire, and that didn't include filling the bags and cleaning the end near the street once the piles were picked up.

The next few swaths wore on my arms. Blisters started forming at the base of my thumbs where the rake rubbed the back of my hands. Gloves would have helped, but Nathan was nowhere in sight, and going in to find him would have been viewed as disobedience. My hands felt better on the next swath, but the rake grew heavier, my vision fuzzy. Rain plastered my hair to my head, but the cold didn't penetrate my hazy thoughts.

The bastard played dirty. Forty-three knew Wendell would never flunk me, so he fired Nathan up to use any means possible. He wanted that job badly enough to drug me so I'd quit his project halfway. It didn't matter how woozy I felt. People watching the video would only see that I'd quit before I raked a third of the lawn.

At the end of the next swath, I trudged back to the edge of the mulch, planted my feet wide apart, and leaned into short strokes, using the rake to balance myself when I wobbled, pulling the debris along inch by inch. My progress slowed to a crawl. A professional landscaper would have pulled me aside, seen my condition, and sent me home sick. The job demanded great vigor, but Nathan didn't care about the job. He'd designed it for me to fail, and the rain added nature's blessing to his ill intent.

I soldiered on. With each unsteady step, I committed myself to outlasting Nathan. The tufts of grass waved in my failing vision. The rake felt fat in my dull grasp. I moved slowly backward toward the street, stopping when I ran into something solid behind me. Nathan's hand on my back.

"You didn't think you were going to run around shooting the place up and then graduate? Did you?"

I didn't waste the energy to answer.

"The lines need to be parallel to the building, not the walk."

I nodded and pulled the rake again.

I don't remember collapsing, but I never walked off that grass. Nathan might have stopped me from finishing his job that day, but I didn't quit. I gave him nothing he could use against me, and for that I was proud. Drugging me might have been payback for the klonopin I'd given Charlotte, but he wasn't that loyal to his teammates. Nathan wanted power, and I was his major obstacle to moving up the chain.

Chapter Fifty-two

I woke up on a lumpy mattress with the saggy old pillow under my head. My brain told me I was wet, and the pain in my chest reminded me I'd fallen on the rake with my face on the soggy ground. I remembered lying in a puddle unable to get up. My face was dry now and the rake was gone.

Someone had picked me up and carried me upstairs then changed me and put me to bed. It didn't feel like victory, but I'd won the first round with Nathan Farnsworth. I'd kept working in spite of the drugs. Unfortunately, from then on I couldn't trust any food or drinks in my apartment. How long could I go without eating? Could I work with my hands during the day and eat nothing? Not possible. I might work all day without eating, but I had to drink.

My only choice was to stash supplies where Nathan wouldn't find them.

Before I moved, I slipped off my ankle bracelet and left it on the foot of the bed. To anyone watching only my tracker, I was still asleep.

The back parking lot lay still under the dim watch of the streetlights for a solid five minutes. The clock on the microwave read 2:00 and that fit with the dark stillness outside. The rusty fire escape looked less trustworthy than Farnsworth, but safer than using the apartment door and risking the cameras in the hall. Without my ankle bracelet, I could run and they'd have to hunt me down the old fashioned way. I wasn't planning to get away, just to do some shopping and slip back without anyone knowing. Starvation wasn't an option, so in my mind, I was doing my best to obey the rules.

The metal groaned and shifted with each step down the ladder, the anchors threatening to pull away from the bricks and drag me to the ground in a tangled pile of scrap. The supports bore my weight better with my feet closer to the brick facade. I kept them there, each step tentatively tested before lowering my full weight. The ladder held steady. Rusty flecks of paint pricked my palms, but the ladder bore me safely to the shadows at the base of the building.

The twenty-four-hour drug store two blocks south was my target. The shortest path led right past Wendell's control room. He had to have cameras all around the outer door, so I detoured into the parking lot, ducking and weaving through cars until I reached Park Street. I cut across Park and through the back of the lot on the corner. When I slipped out onto Centre Street half a block south, I was in the clear.

No one hoofed out of the control room after me. No cars followed me from the parking lot or the street out in front of the building. And no black Suburbans crawled along behind me.

When I saw the red and white sign and cut into the parking lot, I felt home free until the car door popped open and the head of red hair poked out. The ankle bracelet was back in my bed and yet, Charlotte stood directly between me and my goal, two blocks away from the building. Had they drawn me here with subliminal messages in my videos? Did she know from previous relearners that this was the place to go for late night snacks? I was impressed. More so, I was curious to see how she would treat me after being held hostage.

"Sleep all day. Play all night. Sounds like vacation."

Her inviting voice sounded like a trap. If I bolted across the street, I could have disappeared around the park, but one call from Charlotte and the whole Agency would be scouring every backyard for me.

"A guy gets hungry after working all day."

"Or thirty minutes." She laughed, enjoying the pain I'd suffered at Nathan's hands. "Aren't you supposed to be confined to your room?" She fingered the red button on her keychain. It was a show of force more than a threat. I doubted she had pressed that button three times in her whole career.

"Can't trust the food in there."

"If you buy food on the outside, they'll be in your room waiting when you get back, bracelet or no bracelet. Every time you make a purchase it sets off alerts all over the place. You're supposed to be in bed, remember?"

Forty-three had taken the rest of my latex fingerprints. I could make new ones back in Brookline, but I'd seen all my gear listed on the warrant. A hundred grand in technology, rusting away in a locked evidence room. Impossible to access. Impossible to reproduce before I starved. I was at Charlotte's mercy, and she delighted in having me under her thumb.

"Want my help?" she asked, fondling the button more openly.

I asked her what it would cost me, and she said enough cooperation to make her look good. A story no one else could have gotten. I had no choice but to agree and we went inside.

Chips and candy dominated the display space. Twelve-packs of soda were a find. No way Nathan could contaminate those without me knowing. I could drink straight from the cans, and if they were out of my sight, even for a moment, I could throw them away. I imagined him trying to replace my cans with his own drugged soda and bought a marker to identify mine.

Three bags of peanuts held enough calories to keep me going, but the brittle plastic wasn't secure. I grabbed them anyway and browsed through an aisle of chips and crackers. Tasty even if they were low in nutrition. Around the corner I found chili and soup. Sealed containers. Heavily preserved, low quality meat, but lots of protein and calories. An armful of cans would last me for days and the metal would resist Nathan's attempts to mix something into my food.

The basket weighed twenty pounds by the time I reached the center aisle and headed for the checkout counter. Charlotte waved me over to a register near the photo processing area.

"This is Christy, the store manager. She's going to help us with your credit problem."

"No problem at all," Christy said. "A lot of people get caught short. We can wait two days until your payment comes in."

I thanked her and pressed my thumb to the scanner. I'd never seen a company delay payment. It didn't seem like it should be against the rules, but by delaying my payment, Christy helped me defeat one of the Agency's best tracking mechanisms. If I needed to press my thumb to buy something, that meant I was in that place at that time. In two days, a notification was going to come through the system and look like I was standing in this CVS when I could be anywhere. If I knew exactly when the transaction would post, it might have been an opportunity for me, but I couldn't ask the manager with Charlotte standing there, so I let it go.

Loaded down with plastic shopping bags on the way to the car, I reconsidered what I knew about Charlotte. She deceived the manager as naturally as she walked down the store aisles. Women were excellent deceivers. If counselors didn't have to restrain violent offenders, the reeducation programs would have been filled with them.

On the ride back, I wondered if she'd tell Wendell and Nathan about our shopping trip or if they already knew somehow and were planning ways to switch out my chili and Coke with something to make me pliable.

We hiked up the stairs together. She paused to look at the door to my old place. Where I'd held her hostage for two days. Surprisingly, her expression didn't sour. She followed me into the new place, sat on the couch, and opened a notepad like I'd been following her script for an hour. Maybe I had been.

Chapter Fifty-three

"Tell me what you did to the database."

We sat on opposite ends of the couch. Not because we were planning to get cozy, but because there wasn't another comfortable seat in the entire apartment. The fire from her captive days had been replaced by intense curiosity. It could have been a desire to prove to Forty-three and Wendell that she was over being kidnapped and could still do the job. Or maybe it was just her way of showing she was back in control. I reminded myself that you could never trust what you saw in reeducation, especially if it was coming directly from a counselor, so I didn't get excited about the blue eyes beaming at me no matter how much I wanted Charlotte to be interested.

I didn't deny meddling with the database because I'd vowed to be good to my word. Instead, I asked her specifically what she meant and of course she had only a rudimentary understanding of databases and could only ask why my parents didn't come up when she searched.

"I doubt my parents want to be found."

"Most relearners' parents don't want to be found. Who wants to discover they have a grown child who's a criminal?"

"I'm not a criminal."

"So, why are you hiding your family?"

She was too black and white a thinker to consider I was right. She was kind, though, and for the next thirty minutes, she didn't call me a criminal again. I held up my end of our bargain by telling her about my family.

My father worked for the government as a theorist. Helping to predict the effects of various programs, so the feds could control something as dynamic as the United States Economy. When I called him cocky and arrogant, she accused me of being bitter and told me I needed to confront my father for the problems he'd caused in my life.

I moved on to my mother's work as a medical researcher, playing God, intervening when God decided it was time for someone to die. She was as intelligent as my father. Both overachievers. I had them to thank for skipping so many grades. For being the only kid around who had a Ph.D. five years before he could legally drink.

Charlotte inched toward me on the couch.

My admission of weakness gave her something to latch onto. Something to fix and I understood why she relished her role. Her intense personality, her commitment to solving family problems, her flashes from cold and distant to coy and enticing, they all came from the same place. Charlotte had unresolved issues with her parents, and she would never have a chance to confront them for the pain they'd caused. She lived her therapy through her clients. That's why she prodded me to talk to my parents the way she wished she could talk to hers.

She asked if I blamed my parents for my problems and sat back anticipating my answer as if I were about to give her the winning lottery numbers.

"I make my own choices."

"But your parents developed your sense of self. The way you frame and attack every problem you face."

"I don't blame them for my choices. I blame them for theirs."

She sat forward, waiting.

"They gave me up," I said.

She inhaled so suddenly I heard her shock from three feet away. She may have had other relearners who'd been adopted, but she expected them to come from poor households that couldn't afford to support another child. My parents simply didn't want the burden, and that was hard to digest spontaneously as we sat on the couch.

With no time to tamp down her emotions before we talked, she couldn't hide her reaction. My adoption touched her the way it only touches someone who's been abandoned. I'd seen her on the MacPherson tapes. Since then I wondered how she could support Wendell after his failure with Michael, but she never showed a hint of disappointment toward him.

She moved closer and gently rubbed my shoulder.

Intimate contact I expected to last a few seconds continued on while I told her about my father's republican ideals. How they had conceived me young and went on to great careers because they never had children weighing them down. They may have had regrets now that they were getting older, but that was no consolation to a child who grew up in a foreign household to parents who gained dominion in court.

She urged me to meet them. To talk my feelings through. I told her that I'd found them in the database and changed it so they couldn't find me.

"It hurts to think someone didn't want you," she said. "But that doesn't mean you should write them out of your life forever."

"Were you adopted?" I asked.

She met my eyes and nodded, tears building. Unlike me, Charlotte had adoptive parents who kept the secret from her until adulthood. She'd grown up believing to be the daughter of a kind, middle-class family and then, at twenty-four years old, that image was ripped away from her. I believed her tears were real, and as she wavered my way, I wanted to pull her close and bury her head in my shoulder.

"So Wendell is like a father?"

She leaned toward me but stopped abruptly. "How do you know Michael O'Connor?"

"What do you mean?" I asked.

"You could have killed Forty-three, but you didn't."

I waited for more.

"If it's not about Forty-three, then it's about Wendell and Michael. We haven't terminated anyone since. Why don't you tell me what your angle is and maybe I can help."

"I never met Michael O'Connor. I promise."

Chapter Fifty-four

She stormed out at quarter to four and I watched her climb into her car and drive away, leaving me alone in a dark apartment. Too early for Nathan to come and put me back to work. Too late to get any sleep. My ankle bracelet was still on the bed, and no one had come for me. Had I gotten out and back without anyone realizing I was gone? As far as I knew, the only counselors around were in the control room in front of the monitors. Probably only one person. Most likely sleeping at this early hour.

Maybe I should have thought longer about Greg Frigon, but he was squarely on my path to freedom, and I couldn't let him block my progress long because I was running out of time.

I slipped out the front door, along the line of shrubs and dug in the mulch where I'd left the tracking device and the P229. The top two inches of mulch had absorbed most of the rain. The tracker seemed damp, but it showed Frigon's location sixteen miles south along Route 138 in Stoughton.

I slipped into the sedan in the back lot, rolled past the control room, and headed south on Centre Street. Every light on the main roads was lit solid green on my weaving path down to Route 95 and south toward Canton. Winchester could have given me a hot sedan, thinking I'd only need it a short time. Travelling the highway might have been a huge risk as was parking it in the lot behind the complex. But what could the cops do? The penalty for boosting a car, or cheating on taxes, was the same as murder. Everyone got reeducation. The programs were probably a lot tougher on killers than car thieves, but the idea put me at ease in the light traffic speeding down the four-lane highway.

The Ponkapoag exit was most direct, but more than that, the drive down Route 138 led me past fewer cops. A quiet drive with only early commuters hurrying on their way to jobs where they were that reliable first guy. The one with the keys that let everyone else in. Started the coffee. Got things humming. Those people would never notice me.

The blue dot on the locator stayed steady. Frigon was into drugs according to his file. He'd have guys around him providing security. The building on the map looked big and square, an apartment building probably. His guys would have apartments on lower floors, keeping watch on anyone who went up. But at that time of morning, the thugs would be sleeping after a long night doing deals and causing trouble. At that time I could walk in if I was quiet enough. When I took care of Frigon, all Hell would break loose, but I'd have a few seconds of confusion to get to the car and get out of there.

So I thought.

Rolling by the big square sign for Alex's should have given me a clue why Greg was in the area, but I raced on toward the blue dot a quarter of a mile south without thinking. The one club didn't define the town more than any other business. Or at least it shouldn't have.

Most commuters were still asleep, so when I passed the blue dot and hit the brakes, there was no one behind me to honk or swerve. In hindsight I should have kept going and looped back to the little neighborhood behind the motel, but I hooked a hard left onto the sleepy street with my tires squealing.

No heads poked out when I parked. Most folks were gearing up for a battle with the snooze button and didn't care much that I'd rolled up outside. The windows in the neighboring houses stayed dark as I walked a dirt driveway through a cluster of trees. Staying in the trees, I could dodge to one yard or another if any lights came on, but none did.

A low cement wall separated the backyards from the rear of the motel. From there, a paved strip with a single row of parking spaces led up wooden stairs to the second floor rooms in back.

The tracker led me to room 217. Winchester hadn't said how accurate the device was. Whether the blue dot would appear in precisely the right room or if it might register Frigon on the second floor when he was in the room below. But when I eased up outside the door, I knew I was in the right place.

Two men hollered a chorus of "Yeah baby."

At nearly five A.M., I still hadn't made the connection, but I figured out how I'd get inside without breaking the door down. I pushed the tracker into the back pocket of my jeans and readied the P229 in my right hand. Safety off. Ready to go.

I pounded on the door. "Manager," I hollered.

"Go away," they said from inside. Two distinct male voices.

"Open up."

"We'll keep it down, just go away."

"Open up now or I'm calling the cops."

The room went quiet. I listened for feet heading to the bathroom, but heard nothing inside. After a pause, footsteps approached the door, and it opened a crack. A man's face appeared in the space. His bare chest lower in the gap.

"We're getting complaints about the noise. I need to—"

I kicked the door mid sentence, hitting the hood square in the face, knocking him down. I had the P229 centered on his forehead in an instant, but he wasn't Greg Frigon. A lackey or a body guard. Maybe just a friend. I had no way to know if he dealt drugs with Frigon, and I certainly couldn't shoot him for making too much noise in a motel room.

A canvas bag lay behind the thug on the floor. An overnight bag big enough for a riot shotgun and a handgun or two. In Frigon's business, it was more likely loaded with guns than not, so I pulled it away. The discarded shoes at the foot of the bed caught my attention. Sparkly red platform heels. A transparent pair. One sparkling silver.

Frigon stood at the edge of the bed behind a black woman with bleach blond hair. The contrast of deep dark skin and bright hair looked so poorly matched it was comical. Then I noticed the other two women. Completely naked and not the least bit concerned about me seeing them that way.

Frigon stood connected to the girl, amazed at my intrusion. One of the girls lay back in a chair so high on drugs she didn't seem to realize I'd come uninvited. The other two women watched the men for a clue to what was about to go down. Their glances gave no hint to where Frigon and his buddy had their guns hidden.

I shifted the gun to Frigon, grabbed his friend by the hair, and yanked him to his feet.

"You have no idea what you just stepped in. Get out of here before I kill you." Even naked at gunpoint, Frigon believed he was boss.

I shoved his naked friend out the door and slammed it behind. Without clothes or weapons, all he could do was run for shelter in their car, which I hoped was locked and would take a while to break into.

"You think you're going to get away with this?" Frigon asked.

Two of the women sensed what was about to happen and spread out to the sides of the room. The high girl lay obliviously in the chair. The artificial blonde cowered behind it as if wicker could stop bullets. The other squeezed into the corner by the door. All three of them had a clear view of my face in the dim light coming from the bathroom. Later, when Frigon's friends asked, they'd be able to identify me, but I lived sixteen miles away. They were street hoodlums not cops. I wasn't worried about them tracking me down based on my face.

I skirted around behind Frigon and pressed the muzzle to the scar at the base of his neck, his head a few inches from the mattress.

"My guys will kill you in two days," he said.

"That's forty-eight hours more than you have," I said and pulled the trigger, blowing him off Wendell Cummings' radar.

Chapter Fifty-five

The girls screamed at the bloody mess and scrambled away from the bed until they were pressed against the far wall. "You didn't see me," I said. "It was an old hippie who couldn't get drugs." They wouldn't look at me as I waved the P229 around, and they were too stunned or too high to listen.

The guy from the door was a bigger problem. Why had Greg brought this one guy along? He could have been a body guard, but the girls' clothes littering the floor convinced me these were strippers from the club who'd traded sex for drugs. Greg brought one guy because he didn't want to buy girls for his whole crew. The naked guy was probably a friend.

I rushed out feeling good about my chances to get back to West Roxbury without Greg's gang finding me.

Down the stairs, the naked guy leaned against a black Grand Cherokee, poking a wire in the weather stripping of the passenger's window. He fished around, but had no luck before I came up behind him.

"You want to live?"

He stopped working the wire and turned cautiously.

"Go along with the girls. Finger someone else." I waved him to the room where he could find his clothes and hustled off through the trees. If I'd shot him, I never would have seen him or his friends again, but it wasn't right. My deal was for the three guys in the files. I didn't have the right to shoot anyone else.

I bolted for the trees with my head down to hide my features from the nosy faces that should have been pressed up against the glass watching my

The Cat Bagger's Apprentice

escape. But the windows remained dark. Even as I jumped in the car and shoved the gun underneath my seat, not a single face appeared anywhere along the block.

The five of them had been partying in that room for hours. Maybe the gunshot wasn't that loud outside. Maybe the residents were tired of calling the cops about commotion at the motel. But the dead guy would stay up there until someone called the cops. The girls wouldn't do it. They'd take off and let the housekeeper stumble in on the horrifying scene. I couldn't save her from that gruesome vision. Even if I had a phone, I couldn't make the call.

My electronics had all been taken away, save the tracker in my pocket. I worked it free as I zipped north on Route 138 and found Frigon's blue dot missing. My shot had destroyed it. That would set off an alarm in a monitoring center somewhere. They'd know Frigon had been killed or had his implant removed. Either way, the Agency was about to come running, and I had to get out of there.

Traffic was still light on Route 95 with only the hearty early morning souls braving the roads. The fading moon followed me up Centre Street and distracted me enough I almost rolled up on the three black Suburbans parked out front. I made a hard right on Park and ditched the car down the street from the train station and left the gun under the seat. The tracker showed my final target was at home.

For a second I thought about driving four miles over to find him, but Chad Bergeron led a fifty-member gang and his place at the end of Louise Road was protected by enough guns to stop Winchester and Koch. The police report said it took five Suburbans filled with black bats to bring him back when he walked off. The men gave up without a fight, so there was no telling if the firepower was enough to get him out or if he decided against making his home the epicenter of a horrific gun battle.

I clicked off the tracker, slid it into the glove compartment, and headed back to the apartment to find out why so many cops were outside my place. Up along Hastings, a man with a briefcase parked his car and hurried into a cozy breakfast place. The sidewalk was clear from there to the corner.

Lights strobed off the building on the opposite side of Hastings, blocked from hitting me by the two-story building on the corner.

Stepping into the open on Centre Street might have been foolish. I wouldn't have gotten very close, but in the age of tracking devices, the guys who passed for cops had gotten lazy. Gone was the gut instinct and bravado of the guys in blue who died when the Supreme Court sent the prison doors swinging open. These new guys might have let me walk down the sidewalk and disappear without noticing me. Might have, because I never got that far.

The black panel van in the lot behind the book store had a satellite dish that might as well have been a sign for Winchester and Koch. I turned across the lot and patted the door twice before it rolled back.

"I thought they confiscated your pass to Disneyland?"

"This is a public park, kid," Koch said, offering me a hand into the back of the van.

"What's going on?" I asked.

"They've got this problem child," Winchester said. "Keeps getting off his leash and walking around in the middle of the night."

"Don't they all do that? Those ankle bracelets come off like nothing."

"This guy's special. They don't need the ankle bracelet to track their people. That is just a sign the relearner is playing by the rules," he said. "But you know that already. That scrambler you bought or whatever you've got to block your signal, that's worth a million credits. Every relearner in the country would pay to have one of those."

"I don't make a habit of being on this side of the law. I certainly wouldn't help thousands of criminals walk free. Not for a million credits."

The two of them looked at me in awe, and I stole a second to check out the monitors showing the perimeter of my building. Every exit was covered by armed men. At least one man stood at every corner. The front entrance and the door to the control room swarmed with a dozen men each. Impossible for me to get inside without being seen unless I dropped from the sky or tunneled in from underneath. Neither was happening on my timeframe.

"I've walked away before. What's the emergency?" I asked. I didn't believe they could have known about Greg Frigon. Even if they did, they couldn't have assembled so many men so quickly.

"They get a lot more interested in enforcing the law when Forty-three is around."

"He's not still here?"

"Virtually. He's paying a lot of attention to your case."

I wanted to ask my two protectors why they'd given up without a fight, but I knew Forty-three was special.

"He's never shown up to a case before. Not short of judgment," Winchester said.

"What's the chatter from the team?" I asked, and he told me Wendell was covering for me with Forty-three. He didn't want to lose his program and made a lame excuse about my bracelet falling off while I was sleeping. Forty-three wasn't buying it, but he wasn't closing Wendell down either.

When he wasn't begging Forty-three for slack or telling the black bats he could find me on his own, he spent the rest of his time screaming at Nathan. That morning the cabbie had been on duty, his name was Reggie. He'd fallen asleep and didn't notice when I walked out. Since my ankle bracelet stayed in my bed, he had no warning that I was on the move until Nathan came in early and discovered I wasn't in my apartment.

He'd called Forty-three and started the circus on Centre Street.

They replayed the conversations for me. I never would have believed the little guy could get so angry if I hadn't heard it myself.

"How'd you record Wendell's call with Forty-three? He just said he's coming to work." There was no video, but for once we had both sides of the conversation. "You tapped his phone?"

The pride in Winchester's eyes said it was true. He asked if I wanted his help getting back inside. If I went in with all those police watching, my hit on Greg Frigon would be too easy to put together. I told Winchester I needed a distraction, and he had a device that fit the bill perfectly.

Chapter Fifty-Six

"You can send a message and make it look like it came from anyone," Winchester said.

I typed in Wendell's number and keyed a message.

```
There's an old friend waiting for you at 860
Washington Street, Stoughton.
```

Winchester smirked when he saw who I'd sent it from and when I asked for a ride back to Stoughton, he started the van. It could have been my message or the sixty thousand credits that made him want to help. Either way, we stopped at the sedan so I could lift the gun from under the seat, then we swung south for my second trip to Stoughton before seven o'clock that morning.

Winchester anticipated the traffic jam all around the scene at the motel, circled around, and came in on a side street. When we parked facing the wrong way, the satellite dish on the roof helped us blend in with the news crews already on the scene. Winchester watched through the windshield while Koch watched the action on a monitor in back, zooming his camera around the scene to catch important bits like a veteran news producer.

Yellow crime scene tape surrounded the motel and even from the street, we could see cops nosing around behind the building. They scoured the ground for evidence, but there had only been one shot, and it was fired inside the room. Maybe their reports were sketchy. Maybe no one had called it in. The poor housekeeper must have been horrified.

The Cat Bagger's Apprentice

"He doesn't come up on my tracker, so Wendell is going to have no idea what he's in for," Winchester said. "I bet he's expecting to find you here. You, by the way, also don't come up on my tracker."

"When he sees the cops, he's going to hope you're dead," Koch said.

I grunted and scanned the crowd on Koch's monitor.

A Nissan Altima pulled a U-turn and wedged itself in on the corner across from us. Wendell Cummings stepped out and slipped through the crowd toward the officers. I grabbed the gun and reached for the door handle.

"Where are you going?" Koch asked.

He didn't like my idea to plant the gun in Wendell's car, even though it was just across the street and we had seen him leave it unlocked. Winchester hadn't been there when I told the girls the killer was an old hippie. I didn't have Wendell in mind at the time, but his long straight hair made him a ringer for a hippie constrained by a daytime dress code.

"The cops won't hassle him over a dirt bag like that. They've probably been begging him to take the punk back. Why would they complain if he whacked him? They all know he has the power. The program is just a formality."

"Are you serious?" I asked.

"Cops aren't stupid."

We'd wasted a twenty-minute trip. My grand distraction was supposed to bring all the cops running from Centre Street to put Wendell behind bars, but it amounted to a few gallons of wasted gasoline and put me no closer to getting back inside my apartment than I was before.

Wendell was among friends. Guys who saw him as their only hope in a world where they couldn't catch a thug and lock him away for more than two days. They shook his hand as he joined the circle at the back of the ambulance. He didn't need to show ID to get in under the tape. The celebrity of justice was immediately surrounded by a crowd of supporters.

A minivan double parked ahead of us, directly across from the scene. The two rough-looking guys up front waved off angry drivers forced to wait to get around. The cops didn't react right away. They were all clustered together. Some with Wendell. Others with the blonde from the motel room. As the men jostled around in conversation, an opening cleared between Wendell and the girl. The moment she saw him, her finger shot out in his direction.

I wished I'd planted the gun.

The other girls stood up and pointed at Wendell, too. They couldn't have known who he was. They followed my rough description to the first guy on the scene who matched it. Unlucky for Wendell, Greg Frigon had been causing him a lot of heartache. Unluckier still, the guys in the minivan saw the fingers pointing and zeroed in on him. The girls might not have known Wendell Cummings, but the thugs in the van did. Unlike the cops, the thugs weren't fans, and they weren't going to let Wendell kill their leader and walk away.

The side door rolled open and a gun stuck out. The shaved head behind it looked ridiculous with a tiny strip of hair on top. The huge tattoo on his neck spelled something starting with "SU" in shoulder-to-chin letters.

"Gun," Winchester said, the van already starting.

Koch rolled the panel door back ten inches and locked it in place. He grabbed an MP5 from a hard case and shoved me toward the back of the van where the bullet-proof panels would protect me.

The moment the action snapped back, the van lurched forward.

Luckily, the rear door didn't open or I would have rolled out the back and dropped to the asphalt.

A horn blasted. I stretched for the monitor, but could only guess what was happening outside. We'd stopped well before pulling alongside the minivan. The horn alerted the thugs to our presence and drew the attention of every cop across the street to both vans. Our horn. Why?

Whether the gang members saw Koch in the back with his MP5 or not, they weren't stupid enough to engage forty alert cops. Their first shot would have been a death sentence for every thug inside the minivan. The driver stomped the gas, and the minivan rushed down Washington Street in a blur of tan metal.

"What was that?" I asked, wondering why Winchester blew the horn.

He ignored my question and started rolling while Koch pulled his door shut and hid the MP5 behind some gear. We stopped even with the scene for a cluster of cops who had run out to chase the minivan. One of them crossed to Winchester's window. Winchester rolled it down and whispered with the cop. It wasn't an argument about him pulling into traffic. No one outside the van could have seen Koch's gun, but the conversation lingered for two minutes with traffic piling up behind us.

When he finally drove away he said, "Wendell Cummings is important to the United States. Without him we wouldn't know what to do with real criminals."

That was a huge surprise coming from the guy hired to protect me from Wendell. Winchester didn't sound like a mercenary. He was capable and well prepared, but he had too much of a conscience to be on my side to the end.

Chapter Fifty-seven

Winchester let me use his special phone again, and when we arrived at CVS two blocks from the apartment, Charlotte was waiting to collect me. Instead of getting in her car, I went inside and bought a two-liter bottle of Coke and a can of Chili. I'd been gone long enough for Nathan to trade out my food for something he'd tainted. I was being paranoid, especially since it was all in sealed cans, but being drugged without your knowledge a few times will make you question everything. The team was paid to manipulate me and when I got in the car, I didn't even trust Charlotte.

"Where did you disappear to?"

I looked down and checked my ankle. "I just went for a walk," I said. "My ankle bracelet must have fallen off while I was sleeping."

"Nice one. Sure, it just fell off. Like I've never heard that one before. We've had people combing the streets for you since five A.M."

"Well maybe if you didn't drug me first thing in the morning, I'd be able to sleep at night. Then I wouldn't be out hiking in the dark."

"Stop talking. I hate when guys lie to me."

She avoided looking my way when she pulled into traffic, but she couldn't help shaking her head when she saw the big black cars parked out front and the guys in tactical gear patrolling the lawn. The hybrid zipped around back of the building and parked across from the control room door.

I guessed she was reacting to the huge waste of money spent to find me. "I don't get it either," I said. "The whole thing is a money pit. Why anyone thought we could manage criminals without jails is beyond me. Not that I belong here, mind you. Without this whole farce, I'd be back in my living room programming and making a good living. Reeducation is a circus and someone needs to pull the tents down once and for all."

"Are you trying to pull the tents down?" She looked at me now that the car was stopped. "Reeducation works when people follow directions."

"Like Greg Frigon and Eli Botia?"

She slammed the car door and clomped across the parking lot, not waiting for me to follow until she paused, holding the control room door. With black bats all around, I needed to keep up. If they saw me without a counselor, I'd have been in the back of a Suburban in no time.

Her reaction bothered me. I couldn't tell if it was anger for bailing me out even though I was destroying her program, or guilt for what she was about to do. Every part of reeducation was dangerous, but the control room was where the game ended. Being invited in was ultra scary. She hadn't done anything to coax me in, and in reeducation when you thought you were doing something of your own free will, you had to wonder.

Two steps short of the door, I was certain it was anger in her eyes. She was helping me in spite of being mad. The instant I caught the door with my elbow and walked inside with my arms full of food, doubt began to creep in. Joel and Reggie waited by the monitors. Wendell was still in Stoughton, but these three could have locked me in the box and kept me there until the rest of the team arrived.

I stood riveted one step inside the room as the door closed and the light dimmed. Without my camera down here, I had no idea what had been going on. Joel was probably still trying to lynch me, and Reggie was probably still quiet about his leanings. If the vote had already been taken, I was doomed. The faces gave no hint what was in store, but it certainly wasn't a surprise graduation party.

Joel pulled a chair away from the desk and wheeled it back to the opening where the toolbox camera had been and patted the seat.

I shook him off. That opening was four short steps from the Plexiglass box. In a wheeled chair with my hands full I'd have little chance of stopping myself if he decided to spin me around and shove me between the partitions.

"So you're nervous now?" Charlotte taunted.

"Cautious," I said.

"You're not cautious. You're stupid," Reggie spat.

A condemnation from him was dangerous. Joel had been out to flush me from the beginning, and Nathan had been trying to trip me up on film for days. If Reggie joined Nathan and Joel, Charlotte would be the only one between me and the acid.

"I finished my lessons," I offered more weakly than I'd wanted.

"That's B.S.," Joel said. "You know it is, so don't pretend you made some great effort playing a video game for a few hours."

Something poked me in the crotch when I shifted my feet, and I remembered the P229 stuffed in my pants. If anything could get me into the box, getting caught with the gun that shot Greg Frigon was it. I stayed still and watched the counselors circle each other.

I felt as if they'd each made their decision. They were waiting for something or someone before they took the next step. Joel was the angriest of the group, but he was no more eager than Nathan.

I faced him and strode forward with a confidence I didn't feel. "You're not going to teach me anything. I received my Ph.D. before I was sixteen."

"We're not teaching you, genius. We're testing you. We need to decide if you can stop stealing tax money. From what I've seen, the answer is no."

"Ever consider the tax policy might be bogus?"

"A couple more days and it's over for you." Joel wasn't even listening.

"You're just going to keep calling up the chain and ratting me out until you get your way, aren't you?"

"Who told you that?" Joel glared at Charlotte. "If you want to throw your career away for some pretty boy, go ahead." Then Joel stormed out with Reggie right behind. Charlotte turned and followed.

It took a second to realize they'd left me alone in the control room. I could access anything in the Agency, but the one thing I needed at that moment was in the tool box in the corner. I poked my head around the corner to be sure they'd really gone then stuffed the keyhole saw underneath the back of my shirt where the jacket concealed its contour.

Chapter Fifty-eight

Charlotte met me in the hall outside the control room and led me up the stairs, warning me that I was in trouble a dozen times on the way. How could I not be? I'd killed three people and broken every rule on the books. Instead of going to my apartment, we should have stayed downstairs for my final audience with Forty-three.

The saw poked me with every step, working its way down my shirt, inching closer to a slide to the floor where Charlotte couldn't miss it. I stayed behind her on the stairs and walked slowly in the halls so she'd lead the way. As soon as we got inside the apartment, I put down the bags and excused myself to the bathroom to get rid of the saw and the gun. When I opened the door, I heard her voice behind me in a one-sided conversation.

"I'm not undermining."

"We didn't need the cops."

"What were they going to do that we can't?"

Wendell didn't push her that way. It had to be Forty-three, and by her meek tone, it was clear that he was angry.

I quickly wrapped the saw and gun in a towel and went out to thank her for helping me get home safely, but the living room was empty when I got there. It wasn't like her to leave abruptly, so I poked my head into the hall. No sign of her on the stairs. She must have left the second I moved away from the bathroom door. Odd she'd ditch me after coming all the way up, but I decided to use the free time to hide the gun where no one would find it.

The place was so sparse that hiding it in a drawer or closet was out. My first thought was to cut a hole in the drywall behind a picture and stick the gun inside. I paced around the apartment, pretending to think, and for the first time, realized there wasn't a single picture hanging on the walls. I also knew—even though they were too small to see—that there were cameras in every room except the bathroom, and maybe there was even a strategically-placed camera in there. Forty-three had proven he wasn't shy about showing relearner nudity.

The bathroom mirror was fastened too hard to the wall for me to loosen with a butter knife. Finally, I gave up, ate my chili, and returned to the bathroom for an "official visit". There beside the bowl, a narrow crack in the linoleum went right through the flooring. It could have been the building shifting or a previous relearner with similar ideas to mine. The keyhole saw fit perfectly in the slit and in minutes I hacked a fist-sized hole. Ten inches lower, a slim piece of drywall was the only thing separating me from the apartment downstairs. A bigger hole would let me exit my apartment without the cameras seeing me leave.

I went to work with the saw again, this time I sliced away all the flooring between the joists. When I finished the wide rectangle, the smaller circle in the center made a great handle to pull up my trap door. Then I went to work on the drywall below. The powdery board cut almost too easily. My biggest challenge was keeping the saw straight to make a square hole I could fit through. Several inches before the blade reached the final corner, the piece bent in half and folded toward the floor. Once I cut it off, the whole thing fell.

The apartment below had a workbench installed right under my bathroom. The piece of folded drywall hit the bench and cracked into a dozen pieces with only the painted side holding it all together. I lowered myself down and gawked in amazement at the lengths Wendell employed to control his relearners.

The contraption right before me was hard to miss, but it took me a while to figure out why anyone would install manual valves on a wastewater pipe. The rig quarantined sewer water into a five gallon tank. The storage tank hanging above the bench had a valve on the bottom and a pipe that rejoined the sewer line. My apartment was set up to drug test my toilet water. Not a problem for me, but a relearner with a drug problem would never escape scrutiny here.

Further down, the bench formed a raised U that created a platform underneath my kitchen cabinets. The ceiling gave way to a recess that went up into the floor. A series of hinged panels opened to the backs of my kitchen cabinets. The craftsmanship was first class, and even if I'd gotten down on my knees and crawled into my own cabinets, the panels were so tight when locked in place that I never would have found them.

On the floor against the wall, lay a pile of chili and soup cans that matched mine. I walked over and found my tiny black marks on the bottom corner of the labels. Nathan and Wendell had switched them out since the previous day. Amazing they could copy the soup cans that quickly.

I wondered if they'd subliminally maneuvered me into buying certain brands, or if they'd made up their cans after I'd purchased mine.

Going back toward the bench, I noticed the wires coming from above and realized that Wendell and his team could install hardwired cameras anytime they wanted by poking them through the drywall from down here. They didn't need to sneak into my room to monitor me. That game that I thought I was winning, finding the cameras with my laptop and removing them—that whole competition was a fraud. An escapade for my benefit. I don't know why Wendell allowed it to go on for so long. Or why he didn't have views of my room on the monitors when I went down to the control room. Had he known I would force my way in? Or could the whole control room setup be a dummy for another place where the real monitors were?

The multi-level thinking made me dizzy. As I stepped away from the bench below my kitchen, I felt no matter how clever I thought I was, I would always be a step behind as long as I lived here. I should have gone back to my apartment then, but I couldn't help exploring.

The rooms toward the front of the building housed appliances and building supplies. Back here, the space was dedicated to snooping on relearners. The open space I'd burrowed into extended across two apartments to where the building jogged at the end. The apartment exit led to the hall where Joel and the others took the stairs down to the control room. If I got around the corner on this level, I'd be directly above the control room, maybe even the jury room and the Plexiglass box.

I pulled a bunch of flattened cardboard boxes away from the wall near the rear windows, found a short two-by-four and punched through the drywall with the butt end of the stud. The keyhole saw would have made a neater cut, but the two-by-four finished the job in seconds. The drywall on the other side popped off in big rounded chunks, revealing a small closet on the other side. Opening the door slowly, expecting a middle-aged woman with a rolling pin, I stepped into another unfinished space that stretched to the back of the building. It made sense. Wendell didn't want someone living directly above his control room. The vacancy gave me free rein to walk to the back wall and pace forward to where I thought the Plexiglass box was.

I figured twenty-five feet. My test hole through the floor proved two feet short of the partitions. My next hole opened a man-sized space in the floor directly above Wendell's trap. If he locked me in, I could climb my way to the ceiling and punch my way through the drywall. With the flooring cut away, I could crawl out of the Plexiglas box and stun Wendell and Forty-three. They might have enough cops around to run me down, but the shock would be well worth the chase.

My pride faded and something prickled the back of my neck. I thought I'd been inside the belly of the beast undetected, but something about that moment felt wrong. I hurried to cover the hole with an old chair. I closed the closet door and covered the other side with the cardboard boxes. The hole in the ceiling would have taken an hour to fix with a good set of tools and then it wouldn't have looked right until it was compounded and painted. I had no choice but to leave it open and cover the hole in my bathroom floor with a towel.

Chapter Fifty-nine

The most uncanny thing about reeducation is the timing. It's no mystery that you're being watched. Everything you do and say is monitored and recorded from the time you are placed in custody until you are released. Maybe even longer. The weird thing is that while they can see you, you can't see them. You never know who is going to knock on your door, or what they've done while you've been asleep or outside.

That day when I finished camouflaging the hole in the bathroom floor and stepped into the hall, the immediate knock unnerved me. I hoped Charlotte had come back to talk. I hadn't showered, even though it must have seemed to my counselors that I'd been in the bathroom for almost an hour. My armpits were ripe from running, sawing, and climbing. And I still had the gun tucked in my pants even though I'd tunneled out of my apartment to get rid of it.

I ignored the knock and rushed to my bedroom for clean clothes and to fold the gun inside a spare pair of jeans. The warm shower of water splashed over me for less than a minute. Time enough to soap the important spots and wash my hair. I used the towel and carefully bunched it up at the edges of the hole so it didn't fall through and hurried to answer the door.

Charlotte wasn't on the other side. The smile I craved was replaced by a sneer and an arm holding an orange jumpsuit.

"You didn't have to shower for me," Nathan said.

I fingered my wet hair, took the suit he offered, and pulled it on over my clothes. The Coke and chili on the table hadn't been touched. Another handful of credits wasted. I couldn't eat from those cans when I got back. Nathan might not have switched them, but I couldn't take the chance.

We went through the door and downstairs. As we passed the second floor, I remembered I'd left the saw on some boxes above the control room. My breath caught as I imagined Joel finding the hole in the ceiling and calling Forty-three. I'd done worse things. Whatever their reaction to my venture into their secret space, it couldn't have been worse than the job Nathan had picked for me.

The orange jumpsuit was his first attempt at humiliation. Maybe I'd mentioned my Ph.D. one too many times. Maybe he just wanted me to give up and run. As we drove out of West Roxbury toward Boston, people in adjacent cars stared. Then we parked and walked into South Station, the busiest train station in Massachusetts with twelve platforms of trains running off to our right and bus, subway, and airport connections under a single roof. We headed into the massive lobby with people streaming in and out even at lunch time. Every head turned as we skirted a cluster of metal tables. Women clutched their children as we passed the small bakery and entered a narrow concrete hallway toward the restrooms.

A brittle old man waited for me with a mop and instructions on how to avoid disturbing the patrons. Twelve urinals lined the walls, each generously sprinkled yellow with a matching puddle on the tiles below. Men came in, feet wide apart to avoid the puddles, and sprayed.

I avoided their eyes, pulling the stringy fibers over the tiled floor to reduce the stench before I got to the worst part of the job. Men used the urinals then departed, never meeting my eyes. One guy stiff-armed me as he walked in, taking the open urinal I was about to mop underneath.

White rubber gloves protected me from whatever diseases lurked on the porcelain. I kept my hands to the spray bottle, the scrub brush, and the rag I used to clean the urinals. Still, pictures of squiggly bacteria and viruses danced in my thoughts. I finished the first few urinals as quickly as I could, holding my breath as I worked, turning my head to inhale. Doing what I was instructed and no more, moving down the line toward the door and freedom.

The Cat Bagger's Apprentice

The disdainful looks shook my confidence. My eyes stayed low, avoiding the suited men who rushed in and out on the way to sales meetings and lunches. Nathan stood cross-armed at the entrance, reveling in my displeasure, and then I realized his goal was to tear me down. From that moment on, I attacked the job with vigorous brushing and pleasant greetings for my customers.

Someone had to clean restrooms. I'd never considered such work until I had the mop and brush thrust into my hands. If the men talking over the urinals spent a day cleaning bathrooms, they might have improved their aim and their attitude toward me and my orange suit.

When I finished the urinals, the old gent directed me to the stalls. I gave them the best cleaning they'd had in years despite the smell. We moved from there to the ladies' room, which, contrary to my expectations, made the men's room look inviting. From there, we visited ten more bathrooms in and around the station. That night I might have dreamed of dirty toilets, but I didn't give Nathan Farnsworth the satisfaction of seeing me retch.

Nathan's smug look faded in the face of my sunny attitude, but when he dropped me in front of the aborted Japanese sand garden, the superior smirk returned. My forearms hurt too much from mopping and scrubbing to wonder what Nathan was happy about. Walking the path reminded me of raking in the rain, and I wanted to collapse. But even more than rest, I wanted to shower off the bacteria clamoring at the surface of my skin.

The hot water couldn't cleanse the day's images from my mind, but it soothed away my stress until I stepped out clean and lifted my towel. I rubbed my hair back and forth a few passes before I realized something was wrong. The hole I'd cut in the floor was gone. Linoleum covered the floor in a single piece. No seam anywhere. And when I pressed on the spot above my trapdoor, it held firm.

It was like I'd never been down there. But the saw was gone. I'd seen the cabinet doors and the wastewater pipes. I hadn't dreamed it. Hadn't made it up. I stumbled into the kitchen so shocked I almost drank a can of Coke.

Chapter Sixty

I started walking south toward CVS for yet another round of Coke and chili, one I planned to eat the moment I got home. When I saw a neon sign down the end of the next block, I turned east on Park Street. I don't know how I could have known the restaurant was there. The sign was little more than a neon glimmer. Maybe I'd stumbled past when running from the cops. Or some subliminal message of Wendell's directed me there. I guess by then I'd given up trying to figure out how they were messing with my brain.

When I saw prime rib on the menu, the rumbling in my stomach demanded to be fed. The vinyl booths and decades-old fixtures lacked the ambiance I was used to, but a good meal would hit the spot and restore a few ounces of self-respect. It had been a long time since I'd relaxed and eaten a meal without worrying about what might be mixed in. Even choosing my own restaurant and eating with a dozen other diners in the room, I still had the feeling I'd been manipulated into coming here and that my food couldn't be trusted, but what choice did I have?

The waitress beamed friendliness while she took my order, the kind of aggressive happiness that can't be denied without looking foolish.

"You're not one of those criminals, are you?"

I asked her if I looked like a criminal and she said I didn't.

"Can't be too careful," she said and headed for the kitchen.

The exchange made me miss Charlotte. I'd seen her in pictures and videos, but these last weeks were my first chance to sit with her, touch her, and breathe the same air. The waitress didn't look or talk like her. Charlotte was much smarter. Sexier. There was a resemblance somewhere. I wrote off the mental connection to more mind games.

The crunchy cucumbers in French dressing helped me forget Wendell, Charlotte, and their mind games. Crisp lettuce and Vidalia onions reminded me of my old life, and when I sliced into the pink prime rib, I could have been back home in Brookline, relaxing after a day of skateboarding and video games.

After my dishes were taken away and it was awkward to linger any longer, I touched my thumb to the scanner and headed up Park Street for another round of torment.

The sun had long set and the stream of pedestrians on Centre Street had slowed to a trickle of hearty souls unafraid to be in my neighborhood after dark. Most windows in the old building were black. Vacant apartments and areas Wendell and his team used to spy on the precious few residents they did have. Not a single figure crossed in front of a window while I watched, and for a second, I wondered if I was the only real resident in the place. What a waste of taxpayer money. A prison that size would have housed two hundred men.

A black Altima made the corner in front of me, cruised half a block, and turned in behind the building. I hurried across the street to get a glimpse of Wendell. I hadn't seen him since the crime scene in Stoughton, and I wondered if the murder improved his spirits or left him even more frazzled. Forty-three's pressure could have convinced him to call off our deal, but we hadn't had a chance to talk privately. Maybe I shouldn't have assumed he still wanted to go through with it, but only Chad Bergeron was left on the list now. One more shot and Wendell's mistakes would be rectified.

He might not have seen it that way, and he probably didn't know about the men who'd brazenly tried to kill him on Washington Street, but the only way to know how Wendell felt about me was to look him in the eye.

The brake lights went out, and the car door closed weakly in a space near the street. His footsteps sounded on the pavement about the time I reached the front corner of the building. I didn't want to alarm him, so I detoured to the scraggly shrubs that lined the foundation and hustled around the back.

I made the back corner of the building when he was ten feet from the rear entrance. He walked normally, head down as usual, his mind busy with schemes to salvage what was left of his program.

Tires squealed behind me as the tan minivan skidded to a stop at the mouth of the parking lot. Wendell looked up casually as the side door slid wide and an automatic weapon poked out and started firing.

Wendell stood shocked, only five feet from cover, but too panicked to work his key and dive inside to safety.

The front door of the van opened and a smaller gun joined the fray, popping one shell at a time.

I reached for the front of my pants and came up empty. The gun was hidden upstairs in my jeans. I stood in the middle of the attack, unarmed and without cover except for a lone tree and a car too far off to my left to be useful. The guys in the minivan didn't know it was me who shot their friend, or they would have turned and gunned me down easily. Instead they concentrated their fire on Wendell, who stumbled along the bricks, miraculously unharmed.

The man with the rifle switched magazines, and I noticed the tall letters tattooed on his neck.

Glass broke overhead and bursts of rapid fire rained down from a third-floor window. Two more sets of gunshots echoed from the far end of the parking lot, where two uniformed men ran clear of the building and stormed toward the minivan, themselves uncovered in the open as they ran to save Wendell at the door.

Wendell stumbled around the corner and fell out of sight.

The minivan pulled away, a few last shots zipping toward Wendell before the door slid closed and the gang disappeared.

Being the closest, I turned and ran for the corner, "Are you okay?" I yelled, my steps rushing to close the fifty yards between my captor and me. I certainly didn't like the incompetent boob who'd been holding me captive for a week. But I'd put him at risk when I duped the girls into fingering him.

I didn't mind killing criminals, but I didn't want to kill a guy who spent his life trying to make the world a better place.

His feet lay motionless as I passed the locked control room door.

I'd almost reached the corner when the door flew open behind me and voices shouted for me to freeze. I thrust my hands in the air and said, "He's right here."

"Down on the ground."

I dropped to my knees. Seconds later a hard muzzle poked into the back of my head, and the man holding it told me that if I moved, I'd die. His partner rounded the corner in front of me and checked Wendell for injuries. The two uniformed men from the parking lot jogged over and joined the cluster around Wendell, breathing heavily.

Feet shifted behind me and pain swallowed the back of my head. My vision flashed solid white. My jaw throbbed. I tasted blood and everything went black.

Chapter Sixty-one

The front of my skull felt as though it were in a vice. Constant pressure above my eye ached deep into my head, and when I opened my eyes, glossy wood dominated my view. Sitting up didn't improve things. The windowless room had a dim overhead light somewhere behind me. Even the modest light sent pain radiating to the back of my head and down my neck.

My hands were cuffed in front of me, held down to the table by two recessed metal hooks a foot apart. Even an accomplished criminal would have no chance of picking those cuffs. I resigned myself to sitting until someone came to talk. The wait lasted only a few minutes.

"How's your head?" Nathan asked when he closed the door.

"Was that you who hit me?"

"Not this time," he said. "I was busy."

The haughty attitude cried out for a punch in the face. I couldn't do anything with my hands cuffed and as he circled me at the small table, I realized his role was some twisted version of bad cop. It was his job to break me down and make me lash out. So far I hadn't, but in that room I wanted to hurt him more than anyone I'd met in reeducation.

"You're making this too easy for me," he said.

"What are you talking about? I cleaned bathrooms all day."

"We know what you're up to."

"I seriously doubt that."

The Cat Bagger's Apprentice

He scoffed at my conviction. "You really are deluded, aren't you?" He came around in front of me so I could get the full effect of his condescending stare. "We are masters at monitoring criminal behavior."

"Real masters." The words blurted out. Not a great idea for a guy who'd pushed things as far as I had. Sitting handcuffed in a locked room within walking distance of the Plexiglass box and an acid bath, I couldn't help antagonizing Nathan.

"We know everywhere you go. Everything you do."

My ankles were hidden under the table. I wasn't sure if I had my ankle bracelet on or not. I left it on my bed routinely to go outside and no one had ever stopped me. I'd just come from dinner. I wouldn't have left the building with it on, so I guessed it was buried in the blankets on my bed.

Nathan saw my mental gymnastics and said, "We don't need your ankle bracelet to know you went to dinner tonight after Forty-three specifically told you to stay inside this building."

Dinner had been a rare delight in my last few days.

"No one defies Forty-three. I have no idea why you're still alive."

"You'd kill me over a steak?"

"A steak?" He leaned over the table so he could look squarely in my eyes and told me about my venture into the apartment below mine. They wanted me to see the cans on the floor and the wires leading upstairs. What I hadn't seen were the cameras watching me while I was down there. Nathan was confident he knew every move I'd made since I woke up in that apartment. Not my new apartment. My first apartment. Cameras had been following me since my very first day of reeducation.

It wasn't possible. I'd ditched my ankle bracelet. Switched cabs. Hired guys to hide me away in that apartment. If they'd seen everything I'd done, why didn't they flunk me when they had the chance?

Nathan had to be lying, but where was he headed?

"You can't flunk me, can you?"

He stood up straight and I knew I'd touched a nerve. This was still Wendell's program, no matter what power Forty-three had given Nathan. It was Wendell's call to end my program and no matter how guilty Nathan thought I was, he didn't have the power to terminate me.

The anger in his face was answer enough.

"You think you can sneak off to Stoughton without me knowing?"

I gasped. Couldn't help it. I'd taken my bracelet off for sure. Taken the car Winchester had given me. Winchester himself said I didn't show up on the tracker. I'd done my best to beat Wendell's technology, and I wanted to believe I had, but then how did Nathan know I went to Stoughton?

"Not so smart now, are you?"

I strained so hard to figure out how they'd followed me that I almost didn't hear him say I was getting one last chance. That I was on the edge and he was going to let me have a look at what was to come.

"Push your chair back," he said.

I complied and he knelt down and unlocked the shackles that had held my feet down. The answer to my quandary looked up at me. Forty-three had replaced my shoes so I wouldn't have access to the false prints I had sewn inside. So, why couldn't he have hidden a tracker in my new sneakers? They were the only pair I had. I wore them everywhere I went.

I almost thanked Nathan for helping me realize my mistake.

He led me into the hall and I waited to see where in this little place they hid the acid bath. The Plexiglass box was obvious, and I assumed the acid bath was somewhere nearby. I was so focused on the rooms at the far end of the hall, I almost fell over when he jerked me toward the outer door.

"Where are we going?"

"To see your future."

Chapter Sixty-Two

"Do we really need these?"

"Even you're not stupid enough to attack a counselor," he said and unlocked my cuffs. "And if you run, we'll see every step you take."

He might have been right for a few more hours, but soon his leash would go dark for good.

We drove south in silence toward Stoughton then took Route 1 south toward Walpole and the old Cedar Junction Prison.

Nathan delighted in telling me the story of my future.

Reeducation started because the Supreme Court outlawed extended prison stays.

I told him I didn't need the history lesson, but he was adamant, and after he ignored my first few protests, I just sat there and listened while he drove.

Wendell Cummings had been working on a black box that would teach a variety of lessons to high school drop outs. It was special because it taught moral lessons intertwined with basic subjects, and at the same time, the box monitored students and provided feedback in several ways.

When "The Ruling" came down, Wendell was recruited to teach criminals how to behave in polite society. He structured a program that succeeded beyond anyone's expectations, but there were still men who were either evil by nature, or so damaged by their past, they couldn't be allowed to live with other polite humans.

Nathan lied and told me reeducators weren't allowed to kill convicts, but I already knew about the Plexiglass box and the acid bath, so I didn't give his next statements much credit.

He said the cat baggers were the last resort. They operated in abandoned prisons, cracking the cases reeducation counselors couldn't.

I didn't believe a word of it. I'd heard the stories about the cat baggers, but anyone who'd met a graduated relearner knew this was just an evil fairy tale concocted to scare us into compliance. We were still ten minutes from the prison, so I prompted him to go on, even though I knew he was lying.

They were called cat baggers for one of their early tactics. They'd drug a relearner, tie him to the bed or blind him, then rile up a bunch of feral cats in a bag and let them loose in his small room.

The cats mauled many men in the early phases, but somehow word must have gotten out because men started killing the cats. Some enjoyed smashing them with books or their toilet bowl cover or anything else they could find.

The cat baggers graduated to harsher psychological methods. They glued relearners' eyelids shut. Kept them in the dark for days without food and denied them sleep.

The men behind the curtain in the prisons had the same tools Wendell and his team had, but their goal was not reform but extermination. They terrorized lost souls until they couldn't take it anymore. At night the windows on the upper floor were left open so the men could end things on their own terms. It was done that way to ease the bureaucrats' conscience. If the men committed suicide, the program wasn't really killing them.

Convenient that his story about relearners killing themselves at night matched with our arrival at the prison after dark. He pulled past the old visitors' parking area and drove right up to the welcome center where families came to see incarcerated loved ones back when the prison was open. The steep outlines beyond the high walls remained dark.

"Think you can scare me with this B.S.?"

"Call it B.S. if you want. Keep going the way you're going and this is where you're going to end up."

The Cat Bagger's Apprentice

"Give me a break, Nathan. These ghost stories are supposed to scare us straight. Anyone who knows anything about reeducation knows the cat baggers are a myth. If anyone's torturing me, it's you making me clean toilets and rake grass after pumping me full of drugs."

"Suit yourself."

"We both know the end of the road is an acid bath. You can stop pretending and take me back now."

Nathan buzzed both our windows down and waited.

"Cut the theatrics, will you?"

A distant scream howled from one of the windows. The guy sounded desperate. I would have bet it was a recording.

"What if we used the myth to cover reality?"

"Nice try."

The scream came again, followed by another and a hard thump to the ground. I'd heard about this act. If I hadn't known it was coming, it would have been terrifying.

"You're going to enjoy it in there."

Nathan couldn't have known then, but I did end up at Cedar Junction Prison and I enjoyed my time there very much.

"Why waste the time and money? Execution is much easier," I said.

"Lots of people want a crack at those who've harmed them. Cops. Victims. We let them have justice. And then sometimes, once in a great while, we let someone get away."

"You're—"

"It's amazing what happens to crime in a neighborhood after a scarred and battered thug shows up and breaks down in tears when he sees a cat."

"The people would never let you get away with that."

"The people want to be safe. They don't care what happens to criminals. As long as they're gone from the streets, people don't ask questions."

I gestured for him to turn the car around.

"What if the myth is really true? Are you willing to risk that?"

I got out and slammed the door. Nathan's jaw dropped as I headed for the open gate.

Chapter Sixty-three

Knee-high grass grew through the cracked asphalt, brushing my legs on the way to the gate. A frost heave in the center of the entrance blocked the gate from closing, holding it open wide enough for me to slip into the long holding area. Chain-link stretched out on both sides and overhead, preventing anyone from getting into the prison yard without the far gate being opened from the inside. The inner gate stood open, and I walked through the sally port to the buildings that grew straight up out of the paved yard.

The screams had come from the left, so I wandered off to the right, behind the welcome center and toward the main prison buildings in the center of the compound to see if I could get behind the puppeteers. A bumper and a rounded quarter panel peeked out from a sharp concrete corner. Angling around, I saw a minivan in the moonlight. It resembled the one the gang members used in Stoughton and again at my reeducation apartment that day, though I couldn't make out the color. The tinted windows revealed nothing of the inside. No one would sit in the van this late in a dark prison yard, but still I didn't dare move closer.

I stepped quieter then, watching for loose stones as I crossed the asphalt yard. High blank walls and locked doors slowly herded me to the left side of the prison, closer to where I'd heard the screams.

In the distance, car tires rolled on the asphalt. An engine revved as Nathan Farnsworth abandoned me inside the prison walls. I hadn't heard him get out of the car, but if he'd locked the inner gate, I would have been trapped. I should have run then, but I was too curious about what I'd find to go back. I kept moving left, continuing around the main building that once housed the cell blocks and underneath an overhang that connected a nicer-looking building that once housed staff offices.

Three black Suburbans parked around back where they couldn't be seen from the gate. The engines were cool. Not a light anywhere to indicate where the men from the vehicles might be. A fence cut across the rear yard, stopping me in a corner beyond the overhang. I couldn't go further back into the prison complex without climbing a high fence or going inside one of the buildings.

An entrance in front of the cars attracted me. The door was cracked open a bit, and I couldn't help thinking the cars had been parked there to attract me, but I couldn't fight my impulse to expose Nathan's lie. The door opened into a wide stairwell with windows on the outside that let in enough moonlight to lead me up to the third floor.

A wide corridor bridged the overhang the vehicles had driven underneath and on the far side by the wall, the hall turned left and right. Where the rest of the prison lay silent, this wing was alive with scuffling and moaning. Part of me wanted to call out the charade for what it was. To hit the lights and storm around looking for explanations, but my rational side kept me quiet as I slipped to the first door.

The rooms along the corridor had been walled staff offices for prison administrators. The original locks had been supplemented by a series of heavy bolts on the outside. The metal scraped as I pulled the first one free, the sound echoing off concrete walls. Something inside the room scuffled away fearfully.

Two more bolts and the door opened.

"No more. Please no more."

Blood covered the man's face. He sat on a stool with his hands and feet chained to rings cemented into the floor. The only light came in from behind him, but the shaved head with the narrow patch of hair on top matched the shooter from the minivan. He couldn't have finished reeducation. He was free two hours earlier. Already he cowered the moment the door opened.

"We didn't know who he was," the man begged. We both knew he was lying, but he was desperate to escape another beating.

His window was closed, but he couldn't use it while he was chained to the floor. It would be days, maybe weeks, before he was ready to jump.

I moved on to the next room, pulled back the bolts, and stepped inside to find another man in similar condition. The next three rooms held the rest of the crew from the minivan. Not arrested. Not remanded to an apartment and a set of reeducation counselors. Locked up and beaten. No one would find them here. The rumors about the cat baggers kept everyone away from old prisons. That gave the black bats time to do their worst. From what I'd seen of them on the outside, they must have been hellish tormenters behind closed doors.

Charlotte had said attacking a reeducation counselor was a zero tolerance crime. Standing there before the bloody men, I felt lucky to have gotten away with holding her in my room.

The long corridor headed me toward the outer prison wall, a long way from the stairwell and my escape. Eighteen black bats from the Suburbans could have easily chained me down with the others. I should have run, but I couldn't help moving down the corridor and opening one of the last doors.

This man had no chains.

"No more. Please." His voice barely a whisper, his body sprawled on the floor. His clothes tattered. His hair hanging down.

"I'll do it," he said, crawling toward the open window.

I wanted to tell him no. That I wasn't one of them. But all I could do was gape as he clawed his way across the floor.

He rested at the base of the wall, gathering the strength to pull his weight off the floor. I couldn't watch him plunge to the asphalt, so I turned and ran, leaving his door open as I sprinted for the stairwell.

The myth had come to life. I didn't stop running until I was through the gate and halfway out to Route 1A.

A dark sedan waited for me along the cracked drive.

Chapter Sixty-four

"Hey, stranger," Charlotte said when I opened the door. "Fancy meeting you here."

I was too shaken to flirt. Didn't even think about grabbing the knee of her tight jeans. Her smile welcomed me, but her appearance at the prison reminded me that my counselors knew exactly where I was, whether I wore my ankle bracelet or not. For the first time, I wanted reeducation to be over. As much as I craved Charlotte's attention, there were a few things I needed to do, and at that moment, I wanted her to get me back to the apartment fast, so I could do them and end the nightmare.

"Have a good time?"

Her voice didn't have an ounce of sympathy for what I'd just seen. She was probably assigned to pick me up and play good cop when Nathan left, and she enjoyed seeing me shaken.

"Do you know what goes on in there?" I asked.

"I do." She drove north without saying more.

I couldn't imagine Charlotte being party to torture. She had a kindness in her eyes that couldn't be faked, and I wanted to think the innocence I saw in her smile was real, too. I could accept that she knew Nathan was bringing me there to trick me into following the rules, but to think she knew men were being tortured in those dark rooms made me shudder.

Could her psychology training have removed her conscience and shrouded her true intentions with a pretty and inviting mask?

"You're letting him check off boxes," she said.

"What are you talking about?"

"We can't terminate a relearner because we don't like him. We have to report progress, and when things aren't working out, we need to try several interventions."

"The cat baggers are one?"

"The last one."

"Why are you telling me this?"

"I like you. I shouldn't. I mean, I'm not supposed to, but I do."

I smiled at her. "Sometimes there's no helping it," I said, wondering if my kiss had pushed her into dangerous ground.

Her bittersweet smile professed her angst for a prohibited attraction. Maybe I shouldn't have believed anything from someone so practiced at deception, but I needed the longing in her eyes to be real.

"So, why are you letting him win? Why won't you let me help you?" She sounded desperate.

"He's not going to win," I said.

"How can you say that? He can take you to a vote any time he wants."

"And he couldn't before?"

"It would have violated protocol."

"Killing people doesn't violate protocol?"

"You've wanted this all along. What are you? Suicidal?"

"Answer my question. Why didn't I get rushed to meet Forty-three after I killed those people?"

"Because if we reported it, they'd shut us down."

"So you'll do anything to keep your doors open."

"We're doing good work here."

She turned off Interstate 95 and headed up Centre Street in silence. We both knew she should have reported me to Forty-three long ago. I wanted to believe she kept me alive because she loved me, but in the short time we had together, I'd never be sure what she really felt. In spite of all I had to do, I desperately needed the truth from Charlotte.

"Keep going," I said. "Take the next right."

She asked why.

237

"Let's not go back to my apartment. They hear everything there." I guided her to the parking lot around the corner, and she swung in and cut the lights. I got out and walked around to her door. More than likely her car was bugged, but once we got outside, our conversation was just for us.

She stepped out and right into me. I closed her door and pressed her back against the rear window, my arms on each side of her slender form, corralling her against the car. She didn't have time to survey the lot, so I wasn't sure if she knew the black van was behind her.

My chest tightened. My breath came in short puffs. I tried to stay analytical, but the kiss came out of nowhere. She tilted forward and I met her. Our lips mingling, her warm tongue tickling mine.

"Is that what you wanted," she asked when we came up for a breath.

"I need to know something."

She giggled and told me she'd never kissed a client.

I pressed her to the car again. More urgently this time.

"If you're trying to buy my vote, you're doing a good job."

"Why didn't you stop me?"

"What do you mean?"

"You let me kill those people. Why didn't you stop me before anyone got hurt?"

Her eyes hardened. She knew our stop was about more than an illicit make out session. "No one could have predicted what you'd do."

"Really? I killed a guy this morning. Are you telling me you didn't believe yesterday that I'd do it? Didn't I ask you for three names? Didn't you see the files?"

She slapped me hard. I felt the heat rising in my face, but didn't back away. I grabbed her hands and wrestled her until she faced me again.

"Was it the job or not?"

"You asshole. You're blaming me?"

"You had a part in it."

"That's not going to save you," she said.

"Your mistakes won't save me. That's for sure."

"Mistakes. What's wrong with you? Wendell and I did everything we could to help you." She realized then she was at my mercy. Her key fob with the red button was still in the ignition, and she wasn't strong enough to wrestle free from my grip. "I should have let you fry."

"You should have, but why didn't you?"

She fought herself while I watched. Whether she couldn't decide between love and duty, or whether she couldn't understand why I was hot and cold, I'd never know.

"Why?" I asked, finality in my voice.

"I couldn't throw it all away," she said, tears streaming down her face.

"So you let me kill two people?"

"Three. And how could we stop you?"

"You could have turned me in."

"How? After you killed Mandla, we were in as deep as you. You are dragging us down with you."

"Because you didn't report me."

She couldn't say the words.

"You wanted to save your job, so you let me kill two men. You knew I was going to kill Eli and Greg. You could even track me when I went to do your dirty work. Still you let me."

"That's not fair. We had no idea you'd kill Mandla. Or any of them." We both knew the last part was a lie.

Winchester came around behind me.

"You bastard. What are you doing?"

I held her hands while he cuffed them together then I locked her car and handed Winchester the keys.

"Where are you going?"

I turned my back.

"I hate you. I can't believe I kissed you after you killed my friend."

"There's nothing wrong with your friend," I said, then hustled down the dark sidewalk to my place.

Chapter Sixty-Five

The gun was exactly where I left it, but I couldn't imagine Nathan and his buddies leaving it for me intact, so I dropped the magazine, pushed down on each bullet, and pulled them free to check that each had a primer and a slug. I couldn't verify the shells had powder, so I decided to scramble them up, put them back and try a test shot as soon as I was out of the city.

If Charlotte was right about Nathan, he was getting ready to count his votes and haul me off to the Plexiglass box. Maybe the trip to Cedar Junction was the last step in his plan, but as long as Charlotte was with Winchester he'd be a vote short. I had no idea what constituted a quorum, or if Nathan even cared about protocol now that I'd seen the cat baggers' work. I hoped Nathan would spend a few hours looking for Charlotte before he came after me, but I didn't wait to see if he would.

I opened the door a crack and listened, expecting them to be out there ready to haul me away. Feet shuffled and voices whispered at the bottom of the stairwell. No surprise. They were ready for me. Maybe they'd suspected I'd taken Charlotte again and that was the last straw. Or maybe it was just time. They had the stairwell blocked off. I considered the fire escape for a moment, but that route would make me an easy target.

I went back inside and headed for the bedroom. They could have rushed up the stairs after me, but I didn't stay in the apartment long enough to find out. As soon as I reached the bedroom wall, the furthest into the apartment, I kicked a hole in the drywall and kept kicking until it was big enough for me to push through.

I came out the other side covered in white dust and weaved through the adjacent apartment and right out the door, without stopping to brush myself off. They didn't expect me to break through the wall, so when I hustled down the stairs, no one was waiting for me in the other stairwell. I burst out the door and broke into a run across the failed Zen garden. Two guys in dark clothes exploded from the door closer to my apartment. Another came around each end of the building at a dead run.

I made the sidewalk forty yards ahead of them, jagged for the corner of Hastings with them yelling behind me. I could outrun them for a while, but every cop around would be tracking me soon. No way I could outrun the whole force, not even in the car.

The corner of the brick building provided cover. I stopped, pulled the P229, and leveled on a red car across the street. The slug smashed the back window, flew through the car, and punched a hole in the window on the other side. I'd aimed for the shiny rear quarter under the streetlight, wanting to bury the bullet in the car so it wasn't flying unchecked across the lawn. I'd missed by a good foot and a half, but I had my answer.

The men hit the deck and crawled for cover behind the other cars on that side of the street. I jogged down Hastings with a bigger head start and the knowledge that the P229 was still firing live ammunition.

The black van was gone from the lot. I wondered if they'd been tracking Charlotte, too. If they'd taken Winchester into custody to cut off my lifeline. Or maybe Forty-three got tired of his meddling and hauled him off to Cedar Junction with the gang members. None of that could have happened so fast.

I needed one last thing from Winchester. Foolish of me not to have asked when I handed off Charlotte for safe keeping. Now I was on my own. Unsure if I'd get any more help from Winchester and whether Nathan had his quorum or not.

I cut through the parking lot on a diagonal, not really hoping to find the van hidden away in the trees, but it would have been a welcome sight. The thin trees and tiny backyards provided perfect cover for my flight down past the restaurant where I'd started my night and to the train station beyond.

The Cat Bagger's Apprentice

A long purple train sat before an audience of scattered cars and even more scattered patrons. A few people crossed the platform far to my left and boarded the train near the little hut that sold snacks and tickets. I snaked through cars to a clump of trees off the end of the platform at the rear end of the train. A thick hydraulic hose served as the perfect hanger for my sneakers, the laces fastening them securely in place for the trip to Boston.

The angular stones spiked into my stocking feet, and even when I made the asphalt parking lot, tiny stones jabbed me so hard my eyes watered, but I couldn't afford to slow down.

The departing train would have taught me what I needed to know about my pursuers, but they were already coming down the row of cars on Park Street, sticking to cover and moving slowly, but making enough progress to trap me well before the train departed. My question about the tracking devices in my shoes had to go unanswered for a while.

I started the car and tore off for Hastings, hanging a hard right on Centre and rushing north before even turning on my own tracking screen to find my target. Halfway down the next block, two black Suburbans skidded to a stop, blocking both lanes, men jumping out behind the engine blocks and rear corners, guns flashing, bullets flying.

I yanked the wheel left, skidded into a bank parking lot, and jammed the gas in my stocking feet. The men from the Suburbans clambered back into their vehicles. They disappeared from view when the car fishtailed. If they kept tracking me visually, my sneaker ploy couldn't work. I needed to steer them toward the train tracks and lose them closer to where my sneakers would pass, but I couldn't risk turning around, even as beautiful as the thought of fifty agents chasing an empty train was.

I kept on the gas across the mostly vacant lot and swerved hard onto the side street, clipping a Volkswagen on the outside of my skid, before righting the car and stomping the gas right down the middle of the street.

From there I zigzagged north. Cut across VFW Parkway and kept to the tiny neighborhoods until a series of dead ends forced me to turn on the tracker to check the map and find my way out. A huge park was the culprit. It forced me west down Independence Drive. It may have been the time I lost looping around, or they may have been tracking me and waiting for me to circle around the park for South Brookline, but when I got halfway down Independence Drive, two Suburbans pulled out of driveways and blocked the road. Behind them, cruisers strobed the whole neighborhood blue.

I slammed the brakes and spun around, hit a hard left away from the park, and sped through two stop signs for freedom. Grove Street was blocked. No doubt the circle was blocked. If I kept driving in circles, every cop within twenty miles would have me surrounded.

I headed south down Russett Road, knowing I was going to be playing bumper cars with a bunch of cruisers and Suburbans on VFW Parkway if I came out that end.

The clothing store on my right was a break. The place was locked up tight. Lights off. Parking lot empty. Not knowing how to pick a lock, and not having time to fiddle around before the cops closed in, I drove the sedan right through the front doors and into the aisles. The bottom half of the door broke free and rode on top of the hood. The metal frame between the huge plate glass windows crumpled as I passed through. The store windows smashed and I wound up fifteen feet inside, under a pile of debris so heavy I had to roll down the window and climb out to escape the wrecked car.

I shucked my clothes in the main aisle and dropped them on the tile floor. Shirt. Pants. Socks. Underwear. I ran for the back of the store without a stitch of clothing, carrying only the gun and the tracker, moving into an area that might have been a trap, but at least it was further from the clothes that had betrayed my location for the last day and a half.

Racks of suits and dress shirts spread out in every direction. I grabbed a package of undershirts. Ripped off the plastic wrapper and wrestled to pull a single shirt free, flinging the cardboard backing when it finally came untangled. The nearest table held stacks of dark sweaters, cashmere by the feel. The one I chose hung loose, but it was a good enough fit for the little time I had. Further back, I picked a dark suit with pant legs six inches too long. I tucked them under and kept going. Found some dark socks and stiff leather shoes. The pants slipped down my waist until I cinched them tight with a belt I found near the counter at the back of the store.

In a few minutes, I'd stolen an expensive outfit I'd need to throw away because it would never pass in daylight. It was completely unsuitable for my mission that evening, but I guess thievery was like that. When times were desperate, you had to take what you could get.

A few moments later, out the back of the store, I graduated to carjacking when I pointed the P229 at a guy in a black Nissan. He gasped when I zipped away, probably thinking he was lucky to be alive. From there I cruised through the night, undetected by Wendell and the nasty cops who backed him up.

Chapter Sixty-six

Once I climbed in the Nissan and made a wide circle west of Brookline, the cops I passed just kept driving. They couldn't see my face in the dark, and now that I was finally rid of the clothes, they couldn't home in on my signal. I was like any other guy in a suit driving around town as long as they didn't look closely enough to recognize my face.

Locating Chad Bergeron with the tracking device implanted in his neck was a lot easier than killing him. The file I'd left back in my first apartment, showed photos of the road to his place. Men sat out on porches day and night and, according to the notes, they hid automatic weapons beneath card tables and wicker chairs. The road ended at a reinforced gate. Anyone stopping there found themselves surrounded by a dozen armed men with nowhere to hide.

Chad Bergeron was why Wendell needed me. Chad didn't even try to hide his savagery. Instead, he readied himself for war and tempted the authorities to come get him. But, Bergeron was just a street hood with a tracking device in his head, and I could follow him until he ventured away from his goons.

The locator showed him at his place. The same spot he was every time I turned it on. I wondered if he was trapped in there. If every Agency man around had a bead on him. If that was the case, this wasn't going to be another drive-through killing. I was going to have to work to get to Chad Bergeron, and I'd need luck to get out without being caught.

The Nissan wasn't big enough to ram the gate, and even if I managed to get through, I could never fight my way inside with a single handgun. I needed a quieter way in, and I found it by skirting the edge of a massive custom home nestled into the woods on Dudley Road.

The place backed up to a huge conservation area with green trees packed together for acres. Five or six windows in the big house were lit, but that didn't mean anyone was home. This far back in the woods, the lights were probably meant to keep people from sneaking down the driveway. But not me. I stashed the Nissan in some trees behind the pool and headed across the narrowest part of the forest that connected this little neighborhood to Chad Bergeron's place.

The smooth leather soles of my stolen shoes were all wrong for walking in the forest. They slipped on every pine needle and cracked every branch my weight came down on, but there was no one out there to hear me. And luckily, I didn't come across a river or a swamp where the stiff leather shoes would get sucked off in the mud. The briars got thick in low spots, and I had to change direction a few times, but the locator directed me right to the house at the end of Louise Road.

Once I could see the lights burning ahead of me, I moved from tree to tree, using natural cover and darkness to hide my approach. I tried not to crack branches on my way, but several snapped. Fortunately, the only guy I saw patrolling the grounds came around the back lawn in a slow loop and disappeared a minute later.

I kept moving forward in the darkness until I hunkered down behind a brush pile with only a short lawn separating me from the back wall of a two-story colonial. Bergeron was at the back of the house. I guessed he was in a second-floor bedroom, but couldn't tell for sure without getting closer. My plan was to break cover and scale the tiered woodpiles at the back of the house, climb the porch roof, and flip myself up onto the balcony outside what had to be the master bedroom.

Bergeron could have been a mob boss judging by the security out front, but the clapboard siding and the clumpy lawn argued otherwise. He was into something big to hire this much security, but appearances weren't important to him. He must have had credits to burn, but he holed up in an average middle class home. I could have walked away from all that security, but I was sure the moment I put a bullet in Bergeron, I'd win my battle with Wendell Cummings.

Three guards looped around back on a path about fifteen feet from the rear wall, each carrying a short rifle. When they disappeared, I had two minutes to make my way inside. I didn't waste a second.

I broke cover on the lawn, hoping Bergeron didn't have a dog lurking in the shadows. If he did, it didn't react in time, because I hopped up the woodpiles like a ladder, pulled myself on the sloped porch roof, and stalked around under the balcony. I checked the locator one last time, and it showed Bergeron fifteen feet away on the other side of the room. All I had to do was get through the balcony door. If I shot him before he shot me, all I had to do was run into the safety of the trees, and my reeducation challenge was over. My inner voice screamed danger, but I was too close to stop. One good shot and I'd win.

Voices started talking around front. I could have frozen and waited for them to come around, but hung like a figurehead from that balcony, I was impossible to miss. I hauled myself up, catching my hands on the balcony floor and swinging three times before I caught my foot between the banisters. The motion dislodged the locator from my pants and it bounced off the porch roof, tumbled down, and landed hard on a kid's bike or something below in the dark.

Voices hurried my way. The only way to stay alive was to swing over the railing and get inside the door. I clawed my way up and found the sliding door locked.

The glass door bucked in its track when I pulled. Once. Twice. Then the cheap lock snapped and the door slid open. The commotion had to have alerted Bergeron, but I had no choice. I'd lost my tracker. Alerted his guys. This was my only chance. I swept the curtains aside and leveled the gun at the figure in the bed in the corner.

The place was empty. One lamp. One bed. One lump under the covers. What underworld figure lived like this? I didn't have time to wonder. I had to shoot and get out. Get back to Wendell and claim my freedom.

I leveled the gun and fired. I hadn't seen Bergeron, but who else could have been in that bed? The lump giggled as the slug passed. I fired two more times and turned for the balcony without looking to see who I'd hit.

Chapter Sixty-seven

"Want to see who you just killed, Jordan?"

The voice gave me chills. I stopped with the balcony door ten feet in front of me. The voice was so loud I expected to see the man in the middle of the room. He wasn't there when I turned. I took a single, hesitant step toward the bed.

"Drop the gun first."

The smooth walls gave no hint of a speaker or camera. The voice could have originated somewhere in the house or back at Agency headquarters.

Every nerve in my body told me to bolt. The single interior door led toward the center of the house. No doubt there were five or ten guys waiting down there. The only other exits were one window on each side of the room and the balcony door I'd come through. Even if I managed to get out, the men on the ground would certainly have the house surrounded after hearing the shots. They had rifles to my one handgun and there were more of them outside than I had bullets. If I tried to shoot my way out, I wouldn't make ten yards ducking bullets on the lawn.

"Do you really think you're going to get away from me?"

I took another step.

"Drop it." The voice grew angry.

I bent down and set the gun on the floor, noticing the stains and scuffs on my brand new suit.

"Go ahead. Take a look."

The Cat Bagger's Apprentice

I stepped across the room. Pulled back the sheet and found a mannequin lying where I'd expected Chad Bergeron. Around his neck he wore a tiny transmitter that had been calling me here for over a week. That's why Chad never moved on my tracker. The decoy wasn't alive.

A deep graze sliced across the mannequin's chest. Had this been Chad, the hit would have caused him pain, but done no real damage. Another bullet hit more squarely, a killing shot through the side of the ribcage that would have devastated his cardio vascular system and killed him within five minutes.

When I turned away from the decoy, three partitions crashed down from the ceiling all at once. The largest sheet of Plexiglass cut the room in half, separating me from the gun. Another crashed down in front of the window, sealing me into the room until my captor decided it was time to go. The third cut me off from the interior door, completing my cage.

I'd known to look for partitions coming up from the floor. Even in my rush, I might have had the sense to dive out of the room had I seen them, but these had been hidden in the ceiling, painted over and disguised so well I could have spent a day in the room without finding them.

"This is cheating," I said.

The voice laughed.

"We had a deal. I completed my end. It's over. Now let me out."

"Chad Bergeron is very alive," the voice said.

A set of cuffs dropped from a small trap door in the ceiling.

"You think I'm putting those on, you're nuts."

"You're in a box, Jordan. Smart as you are, you have to know I've planned more than one way to restrain you. Would you prefer gas or a Rottweiler? I'm fine with either."

"You can't dump me at Cedar Junction. People will notice."

"That scared you, didn't it, computer boy?"

I turned away from the voice and went to the window. Three armed men waited outside. They weren't taking chances with me anymore. Not even with the Plexiglass cutting off my escape.

"You never believed in reeducation, Jordan. Said it was a farce. That criminals gamed the system to get free. Now you've seen for yourself. You don't know what's real and what's not. Whether you should call the governor and report the torture you saw, or tip your hat to a well-conceived deception."

I didn't admit my fear, but he'd been watching me every moment. He'd seen my face when I ran down those dark corridors to escape the cat baggers. He knew I still couldn't tell what had been happening inside that prison. The coincidences of that day began needling me. It was Winchester who spotted the van full of gang members and the gun. The leader stuck his face out when it wasn't necessary, giving us a full view of his Mohawk. They'd appeared again at the apartment. Shooting lots of shots, but hitting no one. All for my benefit.

When I saw them chained and beaten it could have been makeup. Most certainly it was. The naked guy was the clincher. He was in Greg Frigon's gang. Had he known where to find Wendell he would have come shooting, but I never saw him after that morning. Not on Washington Street. Not outside the apartment. And not at the prison. Naked guy wasn't there because the men I saw were actors. Wendell had shaped my reality even when I thought I was spinning his world out of control. The old guy had more spunk than I'd given him credit for. Or maybe he had help.

"Time to go. We have an appointment to keep."

He waited until the cuffs were secure then two more partitions lowered to form a tunnel from my cubicle to the door leading downstairs. I balked when the partition in front of me rose, clearing the tunnel entrance.

"So many choices," the voice said. "Gas. Dogs. Armed police. Which will I choose?"

I put up my hands and followed the tunnel to the head of the stairs and down through the front door. Clear partitions bridged the gap between the porch and a waiting truck. All four sides fit so snugly to the rear of the truck, I couldn't have broken out unless the truck lurched forward. Not that breaking out would have done me any good. A dozen armed cops watched me through the partitions on each side of the truck and I was wearing cuffs. Unarmed. Defeated.

I boarded the sheet metal container to find my clothes from the suit shop folded neatly with the handcuff keys laid on top. My sneakers had been retrieved from the train. My ankle bracelet neatly circled the strap I'd been wearing on the inside of my knee. Even my phone waited in the neat pile of my belongings on the lone bench at the front of the cargo compartment. The rear door closed, and the truck waited for me to change for my meeting with Wendell Cummings before starting our journey.

The voice stayed with me for the trip. I imagined him sitting up front, watching me on a monitor and gloating over his success. The trap had taken considerable planning and money. The guards had done a convincing acting job. They seemed intent on keeping me out of the house when I was in the woods, but once I broke cover, they stayed out of my way so they didn't scare me off. The beacon was the unfair part. I'd worked hard to eliminate Wendell's mistakes. The beacon was my only connection to the men he had mistakenly set free. Cloning the signal to lure me into a trap wasn't right.

I wasn't a cop. I couldn't be expected to round up three hardened criminals in a week. I had to rely on the beacons to find the men I was looking for, and the longer we drove back toward the control room, the angrier I got about being tricked.

"Time to call your lady friend."

"That won't do any good," I said. "She's with Winchester."

"Not now, she's not. I cut her loose five minutes after you dropped her. She's gone home for the night. Call her back in."

I typed the text message I knew would bring her running to the control room. The voice hadn't told me how soon we'd arrive, but a minute after I sent my message, the truck turned and backed up, bumping over the curb and rolling back to a stop.

The door rolled up, revealing a dark night, and the familiar parking lot behind my apartment on Centre Street. A dozen cops mingled among the cars, ready to take me down if I decided to run.

"You're really going to shoot me if I run?"

A cop dodged around the corner on cue and shot me from thirty feet away. With nothing to hide behind and nowhere to run, I was a sitting duck in the sheet metal box.

The bullet struck my thigh, knocking me to the floor.

"What the hell is wrong with you?" I screamed, clutching my leg then peeking for blood soaking my jeans. My jeans remained dry. My leg hurt so badly I could barely stand, but the bullet hadn't penetrated.

"Fun, huh?" He reveled in my pain. "You thought this was a joke. Thought we couldn't control you without keeping you in a cell. Now you've learned your lesson and it's time to pay up."

Chapter Sixty-eight

He ordered me out of the truck.

I slid on my backside until my feet dangled to the rear bumper. From there I hopped to the ground and stumbled to find my balance, fighting the fire in my right thigh.

Seven armed men lined the space between the truck and the picket fence, looking eager to blast me with another rubber bullet, knock me down, and leave me bruised for the next week. I'd been scared of the black bats and their clubs for a week, but as I hobbled along the back of the building, I would have been more at ease surrounded by a bunch of guys with batons.

The building provided a perfect backstop for the bullets and the men from the truck aligned themselves in a moving firing squad. Twenty men emerged from the cars and trees at the far end of the lot to prevent me from running. Overkill, just like everything in reeducation. After one shot I couldn't run. The threat of more bullets kept me walking along the bricks, steadying myself with my hand when I wobbled too far that way.

The circle tightened until the men crowded in shoulder to shoulder at the back corner of the building. They funneled me through the open control room door, and I slipped into the light to find Wendell Cummings standing in front of the opaque window with a curious look on his face.

The little guy did a double take when he saw me, even straining to be sure it was me who'd walked in. He checked the doors at both ends of the hall, expecting his team to join him. When they didn't, he composed himself and walked out from between the partitions and pretended to inspect the jury room door.

The old man ordered me forward, but I wasn't about to step inside the partitions and leave him free on the outside. If he was going to lock me in front of the viewing window, he was going to be trapped in there, too. We took turns inching closer to the hidden partitions. Me with my hands empty after dropping the tracker and surrendering the gun. Him with the remote buried in his hand where he thought I couldn't see it. That little black bit of plastic with the red button gave him an illusion of power.

Wendell asked me what was wrong. Asked me if I was afraid. Challenging me directly now that he had me on his turf. Now that he believed he'd won.

I told him I wasn't afraid and he scoffed. "That's your biggest mistake. And it will be your undoing."

We both had the illusion of control. I wondered if Wendell had known about my trip to kill Chad Bergeron. He couldn't have been tracking me once I stripped off my clothes, unless there was a homing device in the tracking screen or the gun Winchester had given me. I wouldn't put it past these guys to go that far. Not after the night I had. But I was pretty sure Wendell Cummings was completely unprepared for this meeting. That he knew as little as I did about the armed men covering the exits and even less about what would happen when I finished my story.

He pretended not to look down when he stepped over the partition buried in the floor, but I knew it was there and I wasn't going to step into the fishbowl voluntarily. He tried to convince me, he tried pleading, if he was bigger he might have tried dragging me inside. When he finally realized he couldn't force me inside, he resorted to the only leverage he had. He clicked the red button, the nuclear warhead of reeducation.

I dropped to the floor and lay still, my arms and legs askew where they'd fallen. The red button triggered an implant woven into a relearner's spine to release a jolt of electricity that caused complete paralysis for a few minutes.

Wendell grabbed my calf and dragged me between the partitions and left me dead ahead of the window. When he moved to leave, I hooked his leg with my foot and he did the only thing he could. He pressed a second button to send the partitions shooting up out of the floor, locking us both in. Being trapped with me made him nervous, but he still didn't understand what he'd done to himself.

I pulled myself to my feet long before I should have been able to move, and the poor guy still didn't realize the button didn't work on me. The counselors had never tried the button. They had their feeling of security even though they had no control over me whatsoever. I guess my one acting job was good enough.

Wendell was exhausted after a solid week of my antics. He knew we were being watched by the people behind the window and after all the trouble he had in his program, he desperately wanted to appear to be in control of the situation. Meaning me.

We squared off in the little cube. Him nervous about my judgment. Nervous about his assessment by the people behind the window. Not really worried about the one thing that was coming straight for him.

I nodded toward the jury room, and he collected himself, facing the window and preparing a speech to tell me that I'd reached the end of my program, and it was time for me to be judged. He took a breath. Looked at me. When he turned to the window, I made my move.

My palm smacked the back of his hand, and the remote bobbed in the air between our faces. The poor old man's expression flashed shock, betrayal, a change of circumstances he couldn't imagine. There between us floated the only control he held over me. When I snatched it out of the air, Wendell was powerless.

I tossed the remote to the floor, and it rattled in the corner. Then I told him there'd be no more zapping. He tried to tell me there were others who could control me, but I wasn't worried.

"You're making a mess of this for both of us," he said.

I felt for the old guy then. He was completely unprepared for me, the way most relearners were when reeducation first began. They had no idea what they were up against and no idea how to react.

We argued back and forth about what he'd taught me. He wanted me to play nice and say that I'd learned my lesson. That being in his program had changed me, even though we both knew it hadn't changed anything. The poor old guy was completely flustered.

He never got beyond the idea that he couldn't teach me anything. That teaching me was not what this was all about. Rigid thinking traps lots of older people. Wendell for one couldn't escape his mental models of the world, even after they'd proven they didn't serve the situation. He clung to his beliefs even after I'd forced him into a corner. Locked him in a box. Strange considering this is exactly what he expected of every relearner who came into his care.

He sat on the floor while I told my story these last few hours and now that the story is done, he's on his feet again expecting someone to help him zap me, so he can poison me and have me thrown in acid.

"Thirty seconds," the voice overhead said.

I'd heard that voice hundreds of times, but I never expected it here. I'd been played by Forty-three, and I wasn't happy.

It wasn't the voice Wendell usually heard when he came here to pass judgment. He didn't show whether he recognized the voice or not, but his hands began fidgeting. He'd made a mess of my case and finally he began to understand there would be consequences.

I turned toward the door and waited for the voice's prediction to come true. Of course it did. The man knew everything that happened inside these walls and out.

Chapter Sixty-nine

The outer door squeaked open. Wendell turned away from the window and watched Charlotte come into the hall. She was confused by the two of us being in the box together. She moved up to the Plexiglass, hesitantly as if she didn't belong, but was being forced to come in anyway.

"What are you doing here?" Wendell asked. In his mind she should have been behind the window with the rest of the team, but he had no idea where the rest of the team was.

"Sixteen asked me to come."

Wendell turned his eyes to the ceiling and spoke as if he were talking to a deity. "I can't run my program effectively if you're interfering with my staff. If the Agency is going to go around me and manipulate my team, I can't be responsible for the outcome." Wendell thought the voice behind the glass was Sixteen.

"You can't manage the outcome anyway," I said.

"No one is talking to you."

"I'm the one who interfered," I said.

"You made a mess."

"And you let it happen. You let things spin out of control. You closed your eyes and put your team in danger. You let me kill—"

"Shut up!" the little man screamed. "Let's finish one thing at a time."

I stepped away from the corner and left the key fob unguarded. "It is time we get down to business," I said, taking a step forward right in front of the window with my back to Wendell and Charlotte, my face almost pressed up against the glass as though I were trying to see inside. I knew everyone behind the glass before coming into the room save one. Now that I'd heard the voice of judgment, I knew them all. Forty-three had chosen the referee for this case. It could have been anyone who'd been watching events unfold, and as usual, Forty-three had chosen well.

The little nerd hesitated, calculating how fast he could dive for the corner and retrieve his keys. I decided to spur him on.

"When a murder is committed, members of the Agency, even members of the public, have a duty to report to the authorities. When someone is kidnapped, especially someone who works for us, it is our obligation to help that person."

Wendell couldn't stand my indictment. He scrambled across the floor and came up with his finger on the red button.

I turned and smiled at him.

The tiny tracking device strapped to my leg hissed. Wendell's middle-aged ears didn't hear the sound. Even if he did, he couldn't have understood why pressing the red button didn't knock me flat.

Forty-three was infuriated he hadn't done it sooner. Through all the times I threatened him and Charlotte, he refused to discipline me in any meaningful way. Now that his rage was unleashed, he furiously pressed the button and wondered why I didn't fall.

I unzipped my jeans and lowered my pants until I could unsnap the strap on my inner thigh. Then I held the tiny glass container in my palm and showed it to him.

Even then Wendell didn't understand what he was seeing.

"Most relearners get this implanted in their spine. This is why I could leave my room without being tracked. That is until Forty-three put a new tracker in my sneakers."

Charlotte gasped and backed away toward the door.

"You can't leave, dear," I said, zipping my pants back up.

"Who do you think you are?" Wendell asked. "You have no say here. You're on trial, and when this is over, you'll be lucky to be alive." Wendell stuck his finger in my face. "Shut up and let us finish."

"I'm sorry, Wendell. It's you that's confused. I know you think my being in this box means that I've failed and I'm going to die. You're wrong about that. If you stop and think for a second about what's happening here, I think you'll agree. You didn't assemble this gathering and you don't know who's behind the window."

Wendell held his ground, but Charlotte seemed to understand all at once that my odd behavior had been planned from the beginning. She took two hurried steps back.

"Charlotte dear, I suggest you stay away from that door. The nice men outside aren't going to let you leave. Better not get them all excited." I rubbed my thigh remembering the bullet I'd taken for Forty-three's amusement.

She looked at the door then back at me. We had both seen the swarm of men out back. Charlotte saw them as a safety net when she was in trouble and an annoyance when they went too far with one of her pupils. She hadn't imagined they'd be ordered to keep her inside, but she didn't try the door. She stepped back into the hall and looked at me through the glass.

"I'm sorry," I said. "I tried to give you every chance."

"You're him," she said.

Charlotte had a connection with both my personas and in that moment of stress, with her career on the line, I saw tears welling and felt I'd lost her. I'd been flirting with her over text since I first discovered her file at the Agency. I wasn't allowed to meet reeducation counselors because my job was so secretive, but Charlotte was a special combination of talent and compassion that demanded respect. After a while I became hooked on videos of her work. She always kept professional distance while getting just close enough to make her pupils willing to do anything to impress her. And it all came from somewhere personal, a need for her to find meaning in the lie that was her childhood.

Actress, psychologist, guidance counselor, Charlotte was the kind of woman the Agency couldn't hire enough of. Unfortunately, she was blindly loyal to a guy who fell down hard and took her with him.

I had no idea what would become of Charlotte when the team was dismantled, but I'd been the one to take her down and in a few seconds, she was going to understand exactly the role I'd played. Ironically, she'd done the same thing to hundreds of men, but that didn't mean she'd ever forgive me.

"What are you two talking about?" Wendell asked, irritation squawking in his voice. He looked us over, finally seeing the connection between us.

"I'm Sixteen," I said.

Charlotte's eyes dropped to the floor. The connection to my identity made, the connection between us irrevocably changed.

"You can't be from the Agency, you're in my program."

"Wow! Can you really be this slow? This isn't your program, Wendell. This is a test. You are being judged today."

Chapter Seventy

"You're out of your mind," Wendell yelled.

I smiled back at him, and he jammed the red button down with his thumb, pointing the fob at me when the button failed him, in the hope that getting closer might make it work.

I rattled the implant in its tiny plastic ball.

Wendell looked up to the ceiling. "I've done everything I can with this punk computer hacker. It's time for a decision. I can't do any more."

"Wendell, I told you, I'm not a hacker. My name is Sixteen."

He looked up again. Still not understanding.

I shook the implant again. "If I was a computer hacker, this would be in my head. I'm a programmer for the Agency."

"*The* programmer," the voice said.

Charlotte stepped over for a better look at my face. "You hacked the DNA database."

"Not exactly. I created the DNA database. Well, my team did. Part of running the Agency is an identity that can't be traced. Forty-three and I, and a few others have fingerprints and DNA that don't come up in any search. Our family records have been wiped clean to keep our relatives safe in case we're kidnapped."

"You *are* Sixteen," Charlotte said almost to herself.

Wendell looked from me to Charlotte. He couldn't understand what was happening, and finally I understood why. I'd done so many outrageous things that concocting this story wouldn't have surprised him at all. It took the voice overhead to convince him that he was the one being judged.

Exasperation finally showed on Wendell's face when he understood what was happening. The poor guy didn't have any energy left to fight. "What do you want from me?"

"Your rebuttal," the voice said.

"Now? It's five A.M."

The voice told him this was his chance, and I chuckled to myself. Wendell always brought relearners in to testify well after midnight. He said it wore away their ability to lie. When it was him defending his actions, he considered it cruel, but he'd done this to every relearner he'd condemned to the Plexiglass box since the very beginning.

"You have no right to judge me. I haven't committed a crime."

Charlotte covered her mouth as the implications sunk in. Their crimes were numerous and, as she finally understood, everything she'd done had been recorded on video the way any relearner was monitored. Wendell was stuck in the Plexiglass box. That meant he'd already been judged to fail. It would take an ingenious argument to free her boss and he was in no condition to make one.

Wendell hadn't known the man behind the window outside this single week. He may not have had the power to sentence Wendell without going through the criminal courts, but he certainly had the power to make Wendell Cummings disappear. It happened here in this room on a regular basis. His remains would dissolve like any other set of bones.

At the very least, the program would undergo big changes. Maybe even be shuttered for good if he was convicted.

"I've done my best under very stressful circumstances," Wendell said to the window. "It's unfair of me to be judged while I'm trying to help someone."

"Isn't that what you do to every relearner?" I asked.

"My credit was ruined. My reputation destroyed."

"Pressure," the voice from above said. "We apply pressure to every relearner to see how they will respond when things become difficult on the outside. Life is difficult, Wendell."

"Still, what have I done wrong?" Even as he said the words, his expression slackened. He must have been recounting the events of the last week and trying to differentiate fiction from reality. His lies and crimes were many.

I wondered if he sensed the irony as I began recounting the story of the night in the park. "Charlotte, Joel, and Nathan were all stationed around the park, watching me. They saw me shoot. They saw Mandla fall. And when they went back to the control room, they reported what they'd seen and pushed Wendell to report my actions to Forty-three."

"Why didn't you report this?" the voice asked.

The old man looked up at the overhead speaker and bit his lip.

"Nathan found the bloody clothes and Mandla's tracking device dumped near the park. Still nothing was done. Wendell even lied to city officials about his team's involvement in the park that night."

"Is this true, Wendell?"

The old man hung his head.

"Soon after, I kidnapped Charlotte and kept her in my room for two days. She contacted him for help, and he did nothing to free her. He saw her cuffed to the wall and still did nothing."

I waited for the voice to prompt Wendell and continued when the silence suggested I was on my own. "Instead of reporting her abduction, Wendell traded Agency files to me. Files on relearners he knew I was planning to kill."

This wasn't new information to the man behind the glass, but I took a long pause to let the gravity of the charges sink in. I had a lot riding on Wendell's conviction, and I wasn't about to give the old man an easy time, even if the referee wasn't helping me break him. Handing over those files should have been evidence enough to convict him, but Wendell was a legend at the Agency and he wasn't going to be an easy man to bring down.

"Wendell went so far as to erase data collected by Agency systems. And when his reporting deadline came due, he falsified simulation data to make it look like I was in compliance, when in reality I was playing the simulation like a computer game, doing my best to kill the other children on the playground. I did everything I could to exhibit behaviors that indicated I was unsafe to release and Wendell covered for me time and again."

I stood back. Signaling that I was done. Forcing Wendell to say something.

"I know these things are true," the voice said. "I've seen what happened. What I don't understand is why you would disregard such dangerous behavior. This case was clear cut from the beginning."

Wendell hunched down with his face buried in his hands. The poor old guy was done. I'd slowly turned the heat up on him and erased any doubt he was capable of running a reeducation program. The only question in my mind was the penalty. What would become of Wendell Cummings now that he'd lost his grip?

We all waited. The voice silent. Charlotte pressed up against the glass, unmoving. And me, unsure whether the old guy would spin and attack or fall to the floor in a puddle of sobs.

The old man's voice finally came through the cover of his hands. Soft, sad, but clear on the silent judgment stage. "He killed my friend."

I didn't understand why he didn't lash out in that moment. When Mandla was shot, he should have terminated the program. It was a huge risk on my part, a gamble I'd taken and won.

"I didn't kill Mandla," I said.

Charlotte and Wendell jolted at once.

I pointed toward the door at the end of the hall. The one connected to Charlotte's half of the hallway. It opened a moment later and Mandla stepped out.

Tears of relief streamed down Charlotte's face as she ran and embraced him. He apologized profusely for the deception. She cried harder, and they fell to their knees together. Maybe with the realization of the pain the team caused relearners on a daily basis. She hadn't ever expected the kind of

The Cat Bagger's Apprentice

deception they routinely meted out, and for once she understood how completely their fiction could change someone's world. She clutched the frail little man, amazed that her friend had been brought back from the dead.

I was proud and disturbed by my performance all at once.

Wendell's body went rigid. He had betrayed his friend by not reporting his murder, damning himself in the process, and hampering any chance he had of successfully handling my case. He must have stayed awake many nights cursing himself for his weakness. Seeing that it was all a lie, that his agony was of my creation, angered him to his boiling point.

"What about the others?" Charlotte asked. She realized much of what she had seen in the last week had been acted out for her benefit.

The door on the other side of the box opened, and the twelve black bats who had been in the firefight on the front lawn stepped into the hall. The short space between the Plexiglass barrier and the front door cramped with the throng, and I knew it was time to end the proceedings.

"What about Eli, Greg, and Chad?" Charlotte asked hopefully.

"Eli and Greg were killed," I said. "I was sent here because you failed in their cases. Neither man should have been allowed free. They were a danger to the public and had to be removed."

"Who are you to say that," Wendell asked.

I slipped off my ankle bracelet and showed it to him. "I created these," I said. "And the systems you use to track them. And the cameras you use to monitor criminals in their rooms."

"They're relearners."

"People who break the law need to be punished. Your problem is that you lost your nerve and couldn't stop coddling them."

Chapter Seventy-one

"You killed them," Charlotte said absently. Her feelings for me must have taken an upswing when she realized Mandla was alive. Had she been there when I shot Eli and Greg, she would have known those scenes couldn't have been faked. The bloody mess in Stoughton had reinforced the tragedy of Mandla's killing for Wendell, erasing all doubt that his friend was dead until that moment the thin Indian walked out into the hall.

"I'm not standing for this," Wendell yelled and pressed the button that sent the partitions back into the floor with a scraping thunk.

I stood squarely in front of the window while Wendell measured the distance to each of the doors.

Charlotte and Mandla stood and backed away to the far wall, anticipating a dash through the control room and out to the parking lot. The other end of the hall was clogged with reincarnated cops and it only took an instant for Wendell to make his decision.

"Don't run," I said. "It's not going to help."

Wendell ignored me and raced for the control room, awkwardly scrambling in dress shoes on the slippery tile floor. A drawer scraped open somewhere around the corner. My body registered the danger before my mind identified it. Adrenaline surged through me as the cops hustled in my direction. The men around us were unarmed, a requirement for those observing judgment day.

The outer door whipped open on command from behind the glass, but the gunshots I expected didn't sound.

The Cat Bagger's Apprentice

None of us expected Wendell to reappear in the hall.

When he did, Charlotte's terrified eyes locked on mine. I knew what was coming before I turned. I put both hands up to stop Charlotte from moving into harm's way. She wanted to intercede. To run between her crazed boss and me. My eyes begged her to stop. I held my arms out, pushing violently across a distance too far to reach. She took one single step and turned toward the little man in the doorway as I swung around.

The gun came up. I remembered using it against Eli and delivering it to Wendell here. The cops ducked low, but the mass of bodies hemmed me into the hall. I couldn't run closer to Charlotte and put her in jeopardy. My only choice was to stand in front of the window and hope the cops from the parking lot took him down before he fired.

Four reports sounded, momentarily deafening everyone in the hall.

The gun had been leveled on my chest from ten feet away, but I didn't feel the smack and sting of the bullets. My legs went weak, but I didn't drop. My heart beat hard in my chest. Could he have missed four times from such close range? Had one of the cops dropped him dead on the control room floor? He stood firm, gun pointed, confused why for the second time I didn't fall as expected.

"Holy God, man." The voice above was stunned Wendell would try and kill me knowing who I was. Hearing the harsh tone, Wendell finally recognized Winchester's voice and lowered the gun.

I hadn't known Winchester was the referee until I heard his voice over the speaker. Clever of him and Koch to choose their aliases after gun manufacturers. It should have been obvious when Smith and Colt were introduced, but the men played their roles to perfection.

I patted myself for bullet holes as I stood up.

"Relax, Sixteen," Winchester said. "Koch loaded that gun with blanks. We knew Wendell was unstable. We never figured he'd shoot you in front of so many cops, but we were worried about Joel."

The cops closed in and wrestled the pistol away from Wendell then stood him up in front of us.

"Wendell Cummings," Winchester said over the speaker. "You've committed several serious crimes in the last week."

Wendell yanked at his arms to get free. The two cops restraining him rocked back and forth, but their hold on him was never in doubt. The old guy's eyes went crazy, expecting a drop of poison on his skin and a quick end to his life.

The rest of us stood in awe, wondering what sentence Winchester would impose.

"You're no longer fit to run a reeducation program for the Agency. You will be held for two days then reassigned to a reeducation program designed to help you adjust to your new life."

The old man calmed upon hearing his life would be spared, then riled up again, "You can't put me in one of my competitor's programs. They'll terminate me for sure."

"Of course we won't do that. We'll create a new program especially designed for you."

Winchester pointed toward the jury room and the cops twisted Wendell's arms behind him and clamped down the cuffs.

Charlotte threw her arms around his neck and hugged him fiercely. Though, the cops refused to stop for the reunion. "I'm sorry. I'll do anything I can to help," she said as he disappeared through the door.

Winchester stepped out into the hall and the cops parted to let him through. He patted me on the shoulder as he passed, then squared off with Charlotte.

"Charlotte, I'm very disappointed with your performance."

"I'm sorry, Sir. I'll do better—"

"You don't understand. You helped cover up what you thought was a murder. You passed on sensitive Agency information. And you carried on a romantic relationship with one of your clients."

Two cops bracketed Charlotte.

"No. You can't."

The cops cuffed Charlotte and walked her down the hall. Her last look at me was a murderous scowl, blaming me for what happened.

Chapter Seventy-two

"There is one final matter to be settled," Winchester said, when the cops and counselors filtered out and it was just Forty-three and me with him in the jury room. "The wager is complete."

A young guy in a suit walked in with a fancy set of keys and handed them to Winchester. He took a step toward Forty-three.

"Wait a minute," I said. "You can't be the referee. You were supposed to be helping me."

"I helped you, didn't I?"

"You were helping him," I said, pointing to Forty-three. "How could you be impartial?"

"You liked that bit about the cat baggers, huh? We had you reeling, didn't we?" Winchester was proud.

"If you'd had the naked guy there, I would have bought it."

"I'm sure you would have," Winchester said, not buying that his helping Forty-three amounted to favoritism.

He'd been living in my apartment for days. He saw every move I made. Most of it he facilitated. I had been careful to solicit help through discreet channels. I'd never know how he captured my request and took it himself and that was a lesson for later. Winchester was playing this game four levels above the rest of us. That's why he ran the firm.

"What about Joel," I asked. "No way he was pressing that hard to flush me unless Forty-three was bribing him."

Forty-three started sputtering an explanation, but Winchester cut him off. "He was. But you both stepped outside the box."

Winchester took a step forward toward me.

"You can't be serious?" Forty-three said. "He can't win because he didn't complete either objective."

"You didn't fire Wendell, but only because of this wager. Any other man who looked the other way from a murder would have been fired on the spot. That objective was impossible from the start."

"That doesn't mean he should win."

"True. But you have to admit he pushed Wendell farther than either of us imagined he could."

"If I didn't fire Wendell and he didn't kill Chad Bergeron, I win," Forty-three sounded strong, but he didn't really believe his own line.

"Really?"

Seeing Winchester's face, I knew the bastard had set me up. Sent me after two hardcore drug dealers to win an unattainable prize. "You prick," I said. "Chad Bergeron doesn't exist, does he?"

"Oh, he exists." Winchester explained that Chad Bergeron was an Agency man. That he'd been the first to come in as a relearner and test Wendell, but he hadn't taken it far enough. Wendell let him off, but Chad's exploits weren't enough to indict Wendell and his team. That's why they got me involved. They knew I'd take it to the extreme and prove whether Wendell could handle his responsibilities or not.

"What about Lindsay Francis?" I asked.

"Fiction. To let Wendell know we were serious and to get you fired up enough to take the job." Winchester tossed me the keys. "Nice going, Sixteen. You've earned this."

"Come on!" Forty-three yelled.

I shook Winchester's hand, gave Forty-three a shove, and rushed out to the parking lot. The black Lamborghini Diablo the Agency had confiscated from a tax cheat waited twenty feet from the building with the driver's door folded toward the sky and a ring of admiring cops gawking at its gleaming body.

"Contrary to all that crap I said while I was in reeducation, I love the new tax laws."

"You would," Forty-three said and circled to the front of my new car.

Winchester stopped me before I got in. "I've got a new project for you two if you're interested."

"Running this rat trap? No thanks," I said.

"That job's going to Nathan Farnsworth. I think he's earned it."

I couldn't think of a better person for the job. Forty-three and I had no idea what he wanted from us and we'd learned that speculation only gave our bosses big ideas.

"I can't assign Wendell and Charlotte here. And I can't put them in one of their competitor's programs."

My thumb shot up before he finished. I couldn't refuse the opportunity to be with Charlotte. The details didn't matter.

Winchester paused a second for Forty-three to nod.

"Sixteen will run the day-to-day ops. Forty-three, you'll supervise."

I couldn't believe he'd assign Charlotte to my custody after what I'd done. I took it as his blessing to follow my heart.

"I'll be watching," Winchester said.

"Meow."

Please Stay in Touch

Find out what's next from CJ in his free newsletter.
Sign up at www.22wb.com/nl.htm

Your story is important, too.
How did you find this book?
What did you think of Wendell, Charlotte and Jordan?
Write CJ an email at cj@22wb.com.

And please consider telling the world what you thought of this book by leaving a review on Amazon.com or wherever you purchase books.

Books by CJ West

<u>Marking Time Series</u>
The End of Marking Time
The Cat Bagger's Apprentice

<u>Randy Black Series</u>
The Winemaker's Son
Black Heart
Gretchen Greene

<u>Standalone</u>
Dinner At Deadman's
Addicted To Love
Taking Stock